I0567261

Hired by a
DEMON

Gypsy Madden

Dedicated to Lune, Michael, and Jill, the best betas ever! And to Amber for being an inspiration! And to Alison, my fabulously wonderful editor! And to Mom for being always supportive!

Myrddin Publishing Group

Credits:
Editor: Alison DeLuca
Cover: Gypsy Madden

Check out some of the other wonderful Myrddin Publishing books at: http://www.myrddinpublishinggroup.com/

Copyright © 2012 Gypsy Madden
All rights reserved.

ISBN: 1939296129
ISBN-13: 978-1-939296-12-2

Chapter 1

It wasn't a dog that stalked them but a creature born from the moonlit night. Austen glimpsed white fur, a long dark muzzle, and demonic glowing red eyes that were anything but canine as it paused in a pool of light. It licked its chops hungrily.

The creature slipped back into the shadows as he stared at it. What was it doing here? Wolves never ventured this far into the city. And where there was one, there were often more. Still, it was just a wolf, and definitely nothing remotely as vicious and powerful as the nightmares that lurked in the mountains of his home. And with the girl of his dreams next to him, he felt like he could take on the world and come out unscathed. Not a bad idea, he thought to himself. He could score points with her in the name of protecting her from the beast. But maybe he should wait until Laris's muscular bodyguard was back from beating the stuffing out of a reporter who had pestered them earlier.

"So, what happened to this place anyway, Mr. Harpsichord?" Austen asked, picking his way carefully over a pile of charred wooden beams and sawdust. All he knew was that Laris's father had asked her to meet with the architect in his stead to see about rebuilding the place. And Austen had tagged along, as usual, as her personal assistant. But in his opinion, it didn't look salvageable. His nose wrinkled at the musty, raw wood smell that lingered in the air, drilling its way up his nostrils and coating the back of his tongue with the gritty taste of charcoal.

"It's Harper," the architect enunciated with a note of annoyance. "Not Harpsichord. How hard is it to remember? Darrington Harper of Harper Designs. And to answer your question, one of the students accidentally burned the place down." The architect ran a hand through his black curly hair and scowled at one of the charred doorways. He looked amazingly like Austen's father, though Austen's father had died before he had acquired Mr. Harper's grey patches around the temples and there was no way he would have worn Mr. Harper's geeky silver-rimmed glasses.

"One of the students did this? You're kidding!" Austen laughed.

"Some students just have more of a talent for trouble than others, I suppose," the architect said with his back to Austen. That comment sounded suspiciously like it had been directed at him. How dare a complete stranger judge him? The man didn't know him and certainly didn't know what his childhood had been like—the stigma of inheriting all of his father's humanity while his older brother and sisters all took after their mother and the constant teasing and tormenting he endured while growing up in a world where he didn't fit. But all that was in the past. He didn't need to be like them now that he had Laris.

The architect stopped in front of a large support beam that was charred from top to bottom. A huge crack ran down the length of it, nearly splitting it in two. "Now, as you can see, Miss Stadler, the supports are all rotted and the building needs to be demolished and completely rebuilt, so we will need your father's approval. . . ." The architect searched the space behind Austen and then fixed on the young man with a confused look. "Wasn't she right behind you?"

Austen spun around, searching the dimly lit hallway behind him. He realized they were completely alone—the wolf-creature had vanished as well.

A high-pitched ringing sound echoed down the hallway and wrapped itself around the two of them. Time stood still. All he heard was his ragged breaths, the pounding of his heart, and the scream. And not just any scream, but the terrified agonized scream of the young lady he was supposed to be watching over. His blood froze in his veins as he locked eyes with the architect.

A roaring in his ears drowned out everything around him. He realized it was his own voice frantically shouting her name. He hit the doors at a run and threw them open with all the strength he had.

She lay still on the pavement with her arm bent at an awkward angle. A dark red pool spread around her and stained her long blonde curls. He could see exposed skin through rips in her blue silk dress. The wolf sat on top of her chest. It lifted its white head and gave him a penetrating stare with its inhuman red eyes. He looked at its mouth, where razor-sharp fangs the size of his hand dripped blood. It snorted once in his direction and dropped its head back to its meal. There was an ugly sound as it ripped more flesh from her body and exposed the soft internal organs.

The acidic taste of anger and bile bubbled up inside of him. His hand lifted of its own volition and a warmth of magic raced up his arm, pooled in his open palm. It grew and twisted in a ball of red-orange fire, dancing in the evening air. The anger inside of him exploded, and propelled the ball of fire in the direction of the beast. The fireball smashed against the white fur in a burst of sparks.

The creature yelped and whipped in his direction. Its mouth widened in a guttural snarl exposing hundreds of sharp, gleaming white teeth and gums the color of blood. He could smell singed fur, but it looked like the only thing he had accomplished was to make it mad. It took one slow step toward him, followed by another, and then launched itself at him, going airborne, with all the power of its hind legs.

Austen cursed as the beast flew toward him, but he was ready for it. His knees quaked, but he was determined to stand his ground. He pulled up a larger mass of magic from beneath his feet and transformed it into another fireball, without even thinking, and pushed it out. It hit the wolf in the split second before the animal made contact with his chest. But it wasn't enough to stop the wolf's forward momentum.

The beast slammed into him, knocking him to the pavement. Austen smelled the sharp tang of wet dog hair and charred flesh. The wolf's eyes brightened in fury and pain. It filled the air with an anguished howl. The wolf struggled to its feet. There was a large black streak running from just under its chin down to its stomach. It snapped at him in a last attempt to be threatening, but stopped and snarled at the sound of oncoming footsteps. It turned tail and launched itself into the shadows of the evening. Someone large and muscular flew past him, racing into the darkness after the blur of white fur. Laris's hulking bodyguard was in pursuit. Austen felt all of his remaining energy drain out of him in a sickening realization. He had failed.

His eyes traced her lifeless body and he tried to ignore the nausea crawling up his throat. If only he had been a few minutes faster. If only he had noticed she had left his side. If only he hadn't just shrugged off the fact that they were being followed.

Blood continued to gush out of the gory remains of her chest. There was a slight twitch of her hand. It was just his imagination. She couldn't still be alive, could she? His heart attempted to jerk out of his chest as her body shook and a gurgle of blood erupted from her lips as she exhaled. Oh spirits and gods above, she wasn't dead!

He crawled over to her and let his hand slide over the front of her tattered and bloodied dress, hovering over the gaping hole in the center. A sick taste roiled in his stomach. There were lumpy things in the wound that he figured were internal organs. He pressed down, trying to ignore her dark blood oozing around his fingers.

"I won't allow you to die like this," he whispered.

One of her blue eyes flickered open and fixed on him. Her chest rumbled and blood spurted out from between her lips, still luscious pink with lipstick, and he thought he detected a hint of a smile. He cursed. He hadn't meant to make her laugh.

"I'm sorry. Just don't try to talk again. You've got internal bleeding."

The footsteps of someone running at full speed drew nearer. He felt an arm on his shoulder and the huff and puff of the architect trying to catch his breath.

"I tried to follow it," he wheezed, "but I couldn't keep up. Her guard is still chasing after it. How bad is she hurt?"

Austen turned to look at the man. His glasses were askew and his hair was flattened with sweat. Austen shook his own head of curly black hair. "She's losing too much blood. It took a large chunk out of her." He released his blood-coated hands for a second to show the man the damage. The girl gave a spluttering gasp.

The man sucked in his breath and took several steps back, as if repulsed by the sight. Outrage burned through Austen. She was beautiful. Even torn and bloodied, she shouldn't be treated as anything less than perfection.

"She's going to have the curse if she survives," the man noted. "Maybe you should just let her die. It would be merciful."

"No!" A drop of wetness trickled down his cheek and grew cold at the edge of his chin. "Stadler, just ignore him." Being her companion had become more than just a job to him. "I know it hurts, but I need you to live." He needed her more than he cared to admit, even to himself. There was no choice to be made—he couldn't let her die.

"This is going to feel hot, but hopefully it'll keep you from dying." He removed one of his hands from her wound. She gasped and her eyes rolled for a moment before they closed. He let his hand find a patch of grass next to the pavement. The green blades prickled at the soft flesh of his open palm, and he closed his eyes, letting his mind open to the microscopic life underneath it. He sucked in a lungful of air, trying to follow the earthy scent of the ground and the plants, blocking out the rusty stench of her blood. For the millionth time, he cursed his human side for diluting his Nature Child magic, and called with his mind to everything growing to lend him their will to live and felt the raw power run through his toes and up his legs.

"What are you doing? Stop!" A strong hand yanked his arm that was connected to the ground and twisted it around until he came face to face with the architect, and for a brief moment, hollow black eye sockets with a fire burning deep within stared back at him. It had to be the power coursing through him, skewing his vision. Austen blinked. The man's eyes were a normal dark brown, although they bored into him with a demanding intensity.

"If you save her, you are bringing this down on all of us," said the architect, his voice almost a hiss. "And I don't mean just the two of us, but everyone around her. Just stop and think this through. Her father will never let her near you again. It will be obvious that you touched her, even if it is only to save her."

"I don't care!" Austen said, the words catching uncomfortably in his throat. "Anything is better than just letting her die." Austen dropped to his knees next to her, replacing his hand over the wound in her chest. His head swam from the magic that raced through his body. He funneled it down through the hand that rested over the hole in her chest, feeling the searing power flow through her blood and knit together the damaged skin. Her chest jerked and there was the miraculous sound of an intake of breath.

"If you save her, she's going to turn. She'll become just like that wolf that bit her. She'll never be a normal human again. Do you really want that? Would she want that?"

Chapter 2

"Are all your characters that ugly? It's so thin and puny," said a deep voice, in breath that stank of dead fish and decaying corpses. A languid, ghostly white face leaned down next to Vara and stared at the computer screen with hollow black eye sockets. It was true that the elves in the game were a lot prettier than most of the other species, but they certainly weren't as fragile as they looked.

The demon's transparent hand rested over her hand on the computer mouse and guided it back to the main menu of the game where he proceeded to go through her list of customized characters. There was the willowy air spirit that she liked to use to sneak into dungeons with, and the nimble flame-haired fire elf who could slice and dice with a sword faster than the blades of the kitchen garbage disposal, and the painfully thin human healer with long curly blonde hair who was always welcome on dungeon raiding teams since everyone else in the game preferred fighting over healing. "Ah. All just as frail," the demon complained. He was still just as annoying as ever.

"Sam." Vara vented her irritation at her former temp agency supervisor. "I'm really not in the mood. I just spent most of the day at a job fair in a place where jobs obviously don't exist for losers like me. I just want to be left in peace to kill as many monsters in this game as I can. Besides, don't you have something better to do than harass me about my choice of characters? You know you're not supposed to be here. My mom would pitch a fit if she knew you were here in my room. She thinks I swore off all magic."

"And have you?" He sounded genuinely curious as his breath stirred the air next to her ear with a rancid gust. Maybe he had just dropped in for an innocent chat. Yeah, right. His familiar presence, as it pulsed against her back, made her tingle with the memory of magic pouring through her veins. She had forgotten the warmth and the feeling of belonging. No, she had made a promise, and she didn't need this reminder of what she had given up.

"Sam, magic can't survive in Salvation City and mine is gone. It drained out of me, bit by bit, during those first two years after I moved back here," she said, trying not to remember the agony of being a leaky faucet of magic that couldn't be turned off and not able to save even a precious drop of it.

"But what if you could return and set foot back on magical soil? Then is there no chance you would consider using magic again if it was perhaps for a good cause?"

She imagined the electric warmth race through her hands and up her arms. It would welcome her like the hug of a long lost friend. Her chest ached with the thought. She struggled to take a breath, felt it catch in her throat with the sob trying to force its way out. Samanith was temptation.

Her feet against the tile floor in the morning. . . . A shower with the water on cold. . . . She could resist him!

"I would give anything to, Sam, but I promised Mom." And a promise was a promise.

"She won't have to know," he said with a sly smile. "It can be our secret."

"Sam. . . ." He cut her off with one long finger on her lips. He reached into the pocket of his black jacket and withdrew a golden orb the size of a tennis ball and dropped it with a metallic thud onto the desk.

"Miss Vara Harper, I have come on behalf of the Kendrick & Clarke Temporary Placement Agency to formally offer you a job." His bony finger glided around the golden orb, spinning it slightly. The reflection of her thin pale face framed by straight chin-length black hair danced and distorted as she watched it, mesmerized. The feverish magic encased inside it was singing her name. "The job will require minimal magic, enough to work transit spells. And if you do this, the Agency said it would put in a good word for you with some of the businesses around here."

"Why me?" she asked. "I haven't worked for the Agency in three years. And I thought they wouldn't want me after the fire."

"Ah yes, the fire," Sam smiled, the skin crinkling at the edges of his black eye sockets. Even then he seemed amused that it had been a human that had triggered it. It shouldn't have been any surprise, considering it was her after all. Only at that time, she had magic at her disposal to make everything astronomically worse. "The Agency feels that you owe them substantially after that incident. And they are calling in that marker."

"But it was all Lulu's fault," she protested.

"That's not how the Agency sees it," he reminded her. "The imps had been summoned by you and they were supposed to be under your control."

"But Lulu was the one who screwed up on the locator spell to find her book and they just showed up along with everything else we had lost," she said, remembering Luannalu, her roommate at the Stadler Conservatory for four years who adored animals. Lulu even managed to hide a pet snake in their tiny room for an entire year until it escaped and surprised resident advisor in the shower.

The demon shrugged in an all-too-human expression. "But it wasn't her fault they had been lost in the first place," he reminded her with a gleeful smile. "She wasn't the one who had summoned them originally. You were."

Vara scowled at him. He was right, of course.

"Even human children can control imps," he chided her, obviously having fun pointing out her faults. "They're the first demons your kind is taught to summon."

She gritted her teeth. It was true that it was an elementary spell, but each time she summoned one, it grinned at her with sharp teeth and evil in its eyes and she could see it was just itching to do something painful to her—she saw it in the eyes of the very first one she had summoned and she had seen it in the eyes of all of the others since.

"Mine just won't stay put," she said as she pulled out the only other excuse she had rather than admit to her former supervisor that demons terrified her. "They wander off without being banished and no matter how hard I look, I just can't find them. I figured the spell just wasn't taking and they were vanishing on their own."

"So you conjured more to replace them," he supplied with a laugh.

Heat flooded Vara's face. "Twenty of them appeared with Lulu's spell, all looking at me," she said. A shudder ran through her body as she thought of them with their squat green bodies, yellowed curling horns, and arms that stretched down to the floor.

"I don't even remember losing that many," she continued quietly. "But the one in the middle was Varandarath, my first summon." There had been no mistaking the red fire of pure hate in his eyes. All of the other imps she had encountered were playfully vicious, but there had been something different about Varandarath making him entirely evil.

"He smiled at me with those sharp white teeth," she said, as she cringed at the thought of him, "and he ordered the others from the room and conjured a handful of fire." She snapped her fingers together in demonstration and held out her empty palm toward Sam.

"But imps can't think for themselves," said Sam thoughtfully, spinning the gold orb between his long white fingers.

Vara looked at him sharply. Being a demon himself, he would know. But he was almost playing at the thoughtfulness.

"Varandarath could," she said simply. "I certainly didn't tell him to burn down the school."

"Maybe you thought it at some point," suggested Sam, still on his thoughtful look. "Just to get out of classes for a day, or remove a teacher you didn't like."

Vara scowled at him again.

"In either case, it was your fault," the sharp-dressed demon reminded her.

"I know and that's why I left and I'm here now where magic is just something created with wires and trick photography in a TV show." She slumped back in her chair and tried not to remember what she had given up to move to Salvation City—the island in the middle of nowhere—with her mother who had needed a break from magic, too.

"Was it worth it?" the demon asked. He cocked his ghostly white head to the side, bird-like.

Was he reading her mind? She looked at him through suspiciously narrowed eyes. After three boring years, it felt like Salvation City didn't want her in it any more than the rest of the world.

"So, what exactly is this job you have for me?" Vara asked, feeling her resolve crumble around her.

"Consider it a high-paid babysitting position. The baby in this case is a young woman about sixteen of your years. You just need to be a friend to her and make certain she doesn't get into any trouble."

"And if I say no?"

Sam picked up the golden ball and held it up to the desk lamp. It glittered and sparkled, throwing rainbows in every direction, painted her room with a palette of forgotten colors.

"If you don't want it, I will give the position to someone else." His hand closed around the ball and the glittering rainbows brightening her room vanished, returning it to its usual bleak grey.

"No!" She hadn't meant for it to come out. But could someone die from a missed opportunity? In that moment she felt like she could.

Sam's eyes glinted with amusement. Damn it. He obviously knew he had her hooked.

"When does the client want me to start?" she asked.

Samanith smiled and withdrew a legal-size envelope from a pocket inside his jacket. He dramatically laid it on the keyboard of her computer. It was white and had a gold metallic seal in the center embossed with a silhouette of a man wearing an old-fashioned top hat and evening cloak, the Agency logo.

"All of your instructions are in here, as well as your timesheet. The orb has enough power for the one transit. It has already been spell-locked with where you are to report to."

"How long will this job be anyway?"

He shrugged in an all too human expression. "It should be just a few days, until the client can make better arrangements. I shall tell my employer that you have accepted then?"

Three years and she had stuck by her promise not to practice magic ever again. And now she was about to break that promise with a single word. "Yes."

"Very good. Now, I need you to sign the timesheet." He pressed a pen into her hand.

She broke open the Agency seal and pulled out the timesheet. It had a grid for her to fill out her hours and blanks at the bottom for her signature and the client's signature. She felt a sharp pain in her thumb and a small red blob pooled at the base of the pen. Sam snatched the pen from her and smiled, showing off his sharpened teeth.

"You are now under contract to finish the position, unless the client decides to release you. And one more thing, you shall tell no one." His black eye sockets glowed with twin points of fire deep inside them as the spell twisted its way around her. He couldn't have worked magic over a human without an order from his master. "I am sorry, but it is to protect the client."

"But my mom. . . ."

"It shall be taken care of," he said as he faded away. The putrid odor from his breath still lingered in the air.

"It shall be taken care of," Vara muttered, not liking the sound of that one bit. Her mother liked to know where she was at all times, since her parents' separation.

She pulled out a black bag from her closet and set it down on the floor next to her bed. She glanced through her closet, wondered how much fashion had changed in three years, not that she was ever in fashion to begin with. She preferred wearing black. Black dresses, black shirts with jeans, she wasn't picky. It made her feel mysterious and more in tune with the dark realm. Every little bit helped, considering her luck with imps.

She jumped at the sound of the phone. She could hear

her mother pick up the extension in the kitchen. Vara listened, trying to catch any words out of the sharp whispers, but it was all gibberish, followed by the eventual click as her mother hung up.

"Vara?"

"Yes, Mom?" She prayed she didn't sound guilty and then caught the look on her mother's face as she spun around to see her mother standing in the doorway of her room, still dressed in her formal work clothes. It sent a cold chill racing up Vara's spine. The corners of her mother's mouth were jerked up in an overly happy smile, but her eyes were dark with worry.

"Mom, what's wrong?"

"Nothing."

"But, Mom. . . ."

"Your father's . . . run into some trouble and I need to check on things." There was too much hesitation. She was lying. "Vara, stop looking at me like that. Your father is fine. Since it's the beginning of the week, the refrigerator is stocked with food and I'll leave you a list of ideas for dinners." There was still that odd note in her voice. Obviously, she planned to be gone for a while. That wasn't a good sign. "I need you to stay here."

"Why?" Vara asked. Had her mother noticed the half-packed bag?

"Are you arguing with me?" The imperious tone suddenly flared into her voice.

"Mom. . . ." But as soon as the word was out, Sam's spell against telling anyone about the job bound her mouth as if her jaw had been wired shut.

"Is it too hard for you to just obey me and stay here out of trouble? I don't want anything to happen to you."

Vara glared at her mother as the words registered. "Obey you? What am I, one of your subjects? You actually expect me to get into trouble! Hasn't it been enough years since the fire? But, no, you won't ever see me as anything other than a screw-up!"

Vara slammed her bedroom door shut and collapsed behind it. She was glad she had taken Sam up on the job. She needed to prove to herself that she could do something right

Gypsy Madden

for once in her life.

Chapter 3

Laris's sticky blood was everywhere. It covered Austen's palms and tainted the air with its metallic smell. He could even feel it inside his eyes and in his ears, coloring his sight red and muffling everything around him. He longed to be clean again and to rid himself of the nightmare image of his failure to protect her. And though he couldn't hear it, he knew the cause of his failure was in the darkness with him, the creature too large to be a mere dog.

The animal musk choked the air and even drowned out the smell of her blood. Rage burned through him. It had ravaged such a beautiful angel and had gotten away with no more than a black streak in its fur and now it was back to devour what was left of her. Laris!

Austen reached down low into the darkness. He didn't want to find the gooey, wet mess of what was left of her corpse, but he couldn't let it have her. But instead something warm brushed under his hands. He felt fine and glossy strands of hair and for a moment he felt a flood of relief as the memory of her smiled back at him. But the strands were too short, and close together, and . . . . They weren't strands of hair at all, but fur.

A sandpaper tongue licked the blood on his palms. His skin roiled with the heat of his volcanic temper that itched to explode as the beast sniffed at his hair and clothes. It would only take a bit of magic. He scooped up the warm power under his feet ready to shoot it through his hands.

The wolf gave his face a lover's lick as it lapped a trickle of blood just below his ear. And in that instant the rage vanished and he could feel his gathered magic slip from his grasp. He knew this wasn't the wolf he had hunted every night for nearly the entire month. This wasn't the wolf he sought to kill. He could kill her no more than he could kill himself. This was his beloved, the wolf she had become. He held his breath and welcomed her to take what she wanted of him and to let the two of them become one.

"I don't care if you're telling me you are the center of the galaxy and everything revolves around you!" shouted a dusty cragged voice through the darkness of his dream. "It would make just as much sense and the math would probably be more accurate! I want you and your snoring friend to remove yourselves from my class!"

Austen cracked his eyes open. Had it really been just a dream?

He stared toward the illuminated podium where two figures stood arguing face to face. One was the wizened astronomy professor and the other was a ghostly demon. And not just any demon, but Samaninth, the supervisor of his recently terminated position at the Agency.

Sam was here because Austen was here.

"On whose authority?" Sam's deep gravelly voice asked.

"Don't do it," Austen begged from the back row of the darkened lecture hall. He didn't want to be permanently booted from the class and have to find a new place to sleep. He only needed one more week on campus to find the wolf and kill it and save Laris.

The demon glanced in his direction with a malicious smirk. And then something hit Austen in the back of the head. A crumpled up ball of paper rolled around on the floor next to his feet. With a sinking feeling, he looked up and saw that in addition to the colored planetary orbs swirling about the lecture hall ceiling, there were wads of paper flying around the room in circular orbits. He counted about ten as they whizzed past his head. He spotted a textbook with a section of pages ripped out just to his right.

"This is a public institution and my subordinate has

every right to be here!" Sam fixed the professor with a devilish smile.

"This is my class, and if you two don't remove yourselves, I will send for campus security to eject you."

"It's okay." Austen raised his voice so he could be heard all the way from the back row of the auditorium. "We'll go." He scooped up his backpack and left, hoping Sam would follow his lead.

The old stone campus was quiet in the drowsy mid-afternoon. No one lounged on the grass to study. Even all of the benches scattered nearby were empty. He saw a couple of students walking quickly between classes or the dorms, and they were all in groups of two or more, huddled together as if for warmth. But he knew it was because of the recent attacks. The two who had been attacked after Laris hadn't been so lucky, or unlucky if you considered what she was going to have to live with.

Time was running out and he needed to change his tactics. He sat down on one of the empty benches. He opened his bag and checked to make certain the silver knife was still where he could get to it easily. According to everything he had read, silver was the only way to permanently kill the wolf. All he needed was for campus security to come and find that on him. Then he would spend the rest of the week in a cell. He closed his bag and picked up the newspaper that stirred in the chilled autumn air next to him.

What caught his eye was a small blurb near the top announcing "Exclusive Update on Stadler Heiress Tomorrow" with a black and white picture of a rat-like man in a tweed suit next to it. The man had a lecherous look on his face and clenched a cigar between his teeth. It was the same reporter who had been following them the night Laris got bitten.

"Yes, talk to him," said Sam's sarcastic raspy voice from behind him. "He'll point you in the right direction and have Miss Stadler's best interests at heart. How you humans like to think the best of everyone."

"Like you even care," Austen retorted. "You did that deliberately to get me kicked out! Why?"

"Because it was fun," the demon answered, "and because the Agency has another job lined up for you."

"I don't need another job! I just need a week to kill the wolf that bit Laris. And then they'll beg me to take my old job back."

"But you've been replaced," Sam said with a grin, exposing a row of sharpened white teeth. "The contract was signed yesterday."

"Was he her choice?"

"She has a female companion this time," said Sam. "And she was the Agency's choice and approved by the girl's father."

"What's her name?"

"Vara Harper," answered the demon with a smile.

Austen laughed. "She won't last long. Laris goes through personal assistants like she goes through designer dresses." But it hurt that they felt he was so easy to replace. He doubted the new girl would stand in his way when he would be ready to reclaim his job. He smiled at the thought. He would show Laris that he was still important to her, her father would forgive him for using nature magic to save her, and then everything would be as it was before.

"Just give me the week and I'll do whatever you want me to do."

The demon smiled, showing off his sharp teeth. "Do I have your word on that?" He held out a long bony hand to Austen.

"Yes." He grasped Sam's hand and gave it a firm shake. There was a stab of pain as the demon's bony hand bit into the flesh of his palm. A simple agreement that bound him back under the Agency with a drop of blood that dribbled down his wrist.

Chapter 4

Vara didn't know what she had expected of the place where she was to work, but this certainly wasn't it. She had activated the transit orb, per Sam's instruction, and let the warm magic flow through her in an intoxicating embrace. But when the magic vanished, she realized she stood in the middle of nowhere with nothing around her but trees and a lonely stretch of road. Gloomy clouds drifted in the sky overhead and she could smell rain in the air. Maybe whoever had put the spell together had gotten the location wrong.

Covington was supposed to be a community crammed full of sumptuous mansions—only the wildly rich could afford to live there. The travel guide had made it sound like it was wall-to-wall concrete, and highly expensive concrete at that.

She felt around in the pocket of her jacket for the envelope Sam had given her yesterday and pulled it out. There were only two things inside the envelope: her timesheet and a short letter of instruction listing the time she needed to report to the position and the address.

"Why couldn't it have at least mentioned which direction I should walk in? Or even a note on how far away the spell dropped me?" she grumbled. Frustrated, she stuffed both items back into the envelope and shoved it back into her pocket.

In one direction the small dirt road connected to a two-lane paved road. She decided to try her luck in the other direction. Loose stones crunched like cubes of ice under her feet. And then she caught sight of the monster of a building that loomed on the horizon in front of her, like a massive gothic mausoleum. Her jaw fell open in awe. They certainly didn't have buildings like that in Sanctuary City. Even the houses in her dad's residential neighborhood of Summerville looked like they had been built in a different century from this monument of architecture.

There was an expanse of thick spruce trees framing both sides of the gigantic mansion and a line of sleeping gargoyles placed artfully by the edge of the road, perhaps as a warning to people to turn back before it was too late.

And then the first one in the line lifted his heavy stone head and stared directly at her. A chill stole over her as if her blood had drained out of her body.

The gargoyle stretched his granite wings, shook his horned head, and stood up. She heard something soft and large drop onto the gravel road next to her and the recesses of her brain told her that she had just dropped her bag, which was news to her since she hadn't even felt her hand stop gripping it. Two of the other gargoyles stretched their forepaws and stood up as well. They left their positions in line and crept over to her. They snuffled at her clothes, their stone noses bumping painfully into her legs.

The one on the end, still silently looking at her, sat back on its haunches and howled. It was a low rumbling mournful foghorn sound. The two that were sniffing at her stopped and hung their heads. They shuffled back to their original places in line and lay back down.

Her eyes were glued on the one that had howled. It watched her with intelligent black eyes. It had a beak nose and long talons that jutted out of the fingers of its paws. It cocked its head to the side, and she did the same, probably because her mind had forgotten everything but the shape of its horns and how long its talons were.

And then it moved toward her. She took a step backwards and suddenly found herself falling through the air as the back of her heels caught on something. She landed in a musty grey cloud of loose gravel. Her bag that she had dropped earlier now sat between her and the gargoyle.

Now it could chew its way through her entirely, starting

with her chest rather than be satisfied with just a leg. She watched it, frozen, not able to take her eyes off it. Any second it would pounce and her life would be over.

The gargoyle stopped, crouched, looked up at her, and whined. Maybe it just didn't like her being on its driveway.

It took a couple of steps closer, but instead of pouncing on her and ripping her to shreds as a proper guard dog would have, it circled around behind her, and finally bumped its head against her back. It gently pushed her a little harder.

It seemed like it was urging her to move to the front of the mansion. There was a cold nudge to the back of her legs as she stood up. She looked over her shoulder to make certain that the gargoyle was still in its crouched position and didn't have its mouth open ready to take a chunk out of her leg.

She dusted gravel off her plain black skirt, heaved her bag onto her shoulder, and trudged up to the front of the building. As soon as she left the driveway, the nudges stopped. She turned around in time to see her gargoyle companion rock back on its haunches, lift one leg and give the back of one of its ears a thorough scratch before it sprinted back to its place at the head of the line.

She turned back to the front of the mansion and was greeted by a malevolent brass gargoyle door knocker that grinned at her with a mouth full of vicious sharpened teeth and clutched a heavy ring with its feet. It had to be just as real as the gargoyle statues. Was its toothy smile growing broader? Her heart hammered in her chest. She wasn't ready for this.

She had spent too many years hiding in non-magical Sanctuary City, where a statue was just that, an inanimate statue. Even at her dad's house, things didn't come alive of their own volition unless his imps were playing tricks on her.

She needed to pull herself together and get this over with. If she went home now, the Agency would make future employment impossible. Besides, Sam had said it was just a simple babysitting companion-type job. She was being silly and making herself late. She willed her hand to grasp the metal ring of the door knocker.

Just as she lifted it, the door swung open on its own. It dragged her several paces along with it, and nearly wrenched her arm out of its socket in the process.

A young boy about ten years old dressed in a black suit with a white apron over it stood in the doorway. He regarded her with wide bright ice blue eyes. He had frizzy white hair that looked like a glowing white aura around his head and the sharp pointed ears of the Nature Children. A smile instantly blossomed on his tiny face.

"Hello!" he piped. "Who are you? Are you expected? Did you come from very far away? You dress oddly. You know that look on your face makes you look like a fish opening and closing your mouth like that. Is there something wrong with you?"

Was there something wrong with her? She tried to focus on him and not on the nightmare image of the army of imps that danced before her eyes. He had the same mischievous grin as the imps, and the same fiery malevolence burning in the depths of his blue eyes.

"My name is Vara Harper," she belatedly responded. She gave the boy a forced bright smile. "I was instructed to come here for a position by the Kendrick & Clarke Placement Agency."

"Yes, yes, you are expected!" The tight ashen skin around his eyes crinkled as he beamed at her. "Come in, come in!" he urged. He grabbed her wrist with one hand and dragged her the rest of the way into the foyer. He closed the door behind her with a dull boom that echoed through the entire building.

He tugged the bag off her shoulder and slung it onto his own shoulder as if it weighed no more than a couple of feathers and not the sack of bricks that it felt like to her. "Come right this way!" He swiftly turned on his heel with the ease of a professional dancer and skipped down the dimly lit hallway in front of her.

She realized then her mouth had been gaping open and that her feet were still stuck to the foyer floor as if they had been glued in place. She belatedly followed, surprised at his energy.

The hallway emptied into a large parlor with a grand staircase at the back of the room that climbed up into darkness. Several velvet couches and random sofa chairs decorated the corners. A window that spread the length and height of the wall let the setting sunlight flood the right side of the room, reminding her strongly of the inside of the gothic manors from the low-budget horror movies that she'd spent midnight hours watching curled up in front of the TV long after her mother had gone to bed.

Sitting in a chair illuminated by the window, a man gracefully lounged. He looked somewhere in his early forties, with silver strands sparkling in his long blond hair that cascaded down the sides of his face and pooled around his shoulders. He was dressed in brown slacks, a ruffled white shirt, and a burgundy smoking jacket, like some sort of rich cheesy vampire. He was only missing the cape and cheap plastic fangs. He held his head high as he surveyed the landscape outside the window, lost in thought. A thrill shot through her. This had to be the client!

"Yes, what is it?" the man asked with an impatient note in his deep velvet voice. He had to be some sort of public speaker.

"A Miss Vara Harper here for you, sir," the servant chirped. "She said she is with the Kendrick & Clarke Agency. She looks really, really nervous."

A smile crept across his lips. "Yes, thank you, Ren."
The boy bent his head in a quick bow and skipped out of the room still carrying her bag.

"Take a seat, Miss Harper," the man commanded.
She sat down, feeling his eyes follow her every movement as if she were a bird and he a hungry cat. Maybe he really was a vampire. What sort of trouble had Sam gotten her into now? "Yes, you'll do nicely," he commented. "Do you know who I am?"

"No, sir. Sam only referred to you as the Agency's client," she answered.

His lips swept up in a slight smile. "It's rare to find someone who doesn't recognize me. Did they tell you what I'm hiring you to do?"

"Sam said babysitting a sixteen-year-old."

"I'm surprised they told you that much. My name is Lord Teryll Stadler and I'm hiring you to watch over my daughter Laris."

She could feel all the color drain out of her face and the room grow hot and stuffy around her. She took a slow breath, feeling it catch in her throat. "You're Lord Stadler?" she stammered. "You're the owner of the Conservatory?"

"Of the Conservatory that you burned down, yes," he said with a smile.

Sam was lucky he didn't have much in the way of substance to him. She itched to wring his neck.

"She just needs someone near her own age that she can trust and confide in," he continued. "I need you to watch over her and keep her from getting into trouble. The person you are replacing wasn't able to keep things professional and I was forced to dismiss him. I'm certain that won't be a problem this time around. And I need someone I can trust not to go running to the media with this." He paused to look her directly in the eyes. "I will consider your debt repaid in full if you do this for me."

"Watching over a teenager for a few days seems too easy to repay the millions of dollars of damages," she said. "What's the catch?"

His face brightened as he caught sight of something behind Vara. "My daughter! Come and meet your new companion!"

Laris's loose red silk blouse rustled as she approached her father's chair. She was gorgeous. She had the exquisite fashion model beauty Vara had only ever seen in magazines and movies, and had been convinced didn't exist in real life. Here was proof otherwise, and it made her feel plain and insignificant in comparison.

Vara's jealous eyes swallowed up every curl and wave of Laris's long sunflower yellow hair. She had it tied into a ponytail with a red ribbon, though several strands had come loose and curled elegantly against the side of her face. Her blue eyes glittered as the setting sunlight danced and rippled over them.

Vara jumped when she realized the girl's face was just a few inches from hers, and a smile was stealing across Laris's red lips.

"Magic," Laris breathed. "I can smell it on her." But just

as soon as the smile had appeared, it vanished, replaced by a scowl.

The room had grown dark around them. The girl's father was looking at Vara with a relieved smile creeping across his elegant face. Vara blinked. His daughter no longer stood in front of her. The girl was now behind her father's chair. Her eyes had changed from blue to black, having lost the light of the setting sun, but they lingered wistfully on Vara's face.

Vara felt her face flush uncomfortably.

"But is it tolerable, my dear?" he asked quietly.

"So you can have me watched over like a rat in a cage? Yes," Laris spat. She glared at her father and stalked out of the room. He watched her leave with an agonized expression on his face.

"I had to find someone with enough magic to be able to take care of situations, but not too much to truly tempt her," he said with a desperate note in his voice, turning back to Vara with watery eyes. "You do understand, don't you?"

"No, I don't understand. What was that all about?" There was clearly something not right with the girl. Vara should not have been that drawn to her. She couldn't think straight in that moment and she hadn't seen Laris move until she was right next to her. And then sniffing at her like that, as if savoring Vara's scent. "It's like she wanted to eat me!"

Chapter 5

"She's been bitten by a werewolf, Miss Harper. They feed on meat and magic. The stronger the use of magic, the more she will have trouble controlling her condition, so do try to keep your use of magic to a minimum while you are around my daughter. With the time you've spent away from magic, you should be able to get close to her without being too delicious a snack to her."

"Without being a delicious snack to her? Are you nuts?" Vara bit down on her tongue. It wasn't good to call the client names to his face. She regretted it immediately seeing the long suffering look in his tired eyes.

"I'm sorry, but you're planning for me to be around her on a daily basis and hoping that my abstinence from magic will keep me from getting ripped apart by her?" He was insane. Was risking her life really worth the fate of her future?

"Miss Harper, my daughter needs a friend through this who can support her and keep her safe. I will not stoop to begging, but my daughter needs you. You only have to watch over her until Saturday."

"What happens then?" she asked.

"The full moon will rise and the transformation will be complete." His tired, nervous gaze slid from her face back to the window.

"And if it becomes complete?" she prompted.

"That is none of your business," he snapped. His eyes searched her face. "Let's just say that your services will no longer be needed and arrangements have been made."

She'd seen enough horror movies not to have to rely on her imagination for the possibilities of what would happen at that point. Either he'd have to kill his daughter, keep her, or let her go, which led to the possibility of her being killed by other people.

This world wasn't a stranger to the existence of werewolves, and there were killers who worked professionally to rid the world of monsters. Or maybe he was working on a cure, which meant killing off the person who had infected her.

"No one knows yet, do they?" Vara asked.

"It would be disastrous to our family image if it were to get out that my daughter is afflicted by such a vulgar disease. Our name must not be dragged through the mud in that way. Now, you shall be paid for your services at the end of the position. I'm also including an allowance for expenses since I'm certain you'll have need of it while looking after my daughter. She can have rather expensive tastes. Ren will show you to your room. Dinner will be in an hour."

As if he had been listening for his name, the servant was standing behind Vara's chair, bouncing on the balls of his tiny feet.

"Thank you again for the position," she said, grasping Lord Stadler's hand in a quick shake. Though it sounded genuine in her ears, she wondered just how thankful she was for this position.

"It's a very beautiful room," commented the tiny servant as he led her all the way upstairs and down several hallways, "though the last companion for the mistress didn't like it much. Don't know why, other than not liking the color. But I didn't like him much either. I'm very glad he's gone and you're here."

He paused for a moment to drop her bag in the middle of the hallway. He leaned over the lock of the door. She hadn't seen him pull out any keys, but after a moment, it clicked, and he pushed the door open.

Red seemed to be the overall theme for the room. The walls and carpet and even the ceiling were all in shades of red, as well as all of all the furnishings. There was a large canopy

Gypsy Madden

bed with red draperies and a red bedspread and a small red sofa and a red lounge chair in the opposite corner of the room with a small window with red curtains, as if someone had exploded a family there and the blood had gotten everywhere.

Even her skin was drenched red in the glow from one of the red shaded lamps. How soon would that red glow be replaced by her red blood? With a werewolf under the same roof as her, she was inviting her own death.

"Dinner is in an hour in the dining room. Master dislikes people being late. I hope you're not planning to wear that to dinner. Master expects his staff to be better dressed." He bobbed a quick bow and left.

She was bound to a job she probably wouldn't live through, and she was getting complaints about her clothes from the staff.

She pulled out her cell phone and dialed her mother's number. "Hi Mom!" She hated talking to machines. "About yesterday, I'm sorry. I shouldn't have snapped at you. I just really would like someone to talk to. So, please, call me back. Let me know what's going on, what the news is about Dad, and if you two are just hanging out at a restaurant catching up on old times." Vara laughed uneasily. Her mother was probably perfectly fine and just too busy to call. "I just need someone to talk to." She ended the message and set the phone aside.

Light chatter and clinking of glasses drew her down the staircase when it grew nearer to the dinner hour. She followed the sounds down the hallway and into a large room with a long table in its center. About half of the seats around it were filled, but her eyes skidded to a stop when she caught sight of an agonizingly familiar shock of blood red hair attached to a glorious golden-skinned man seated at the middle of the table.

Derek. Why was he here?

She needed to leave fast, before he noticed her, but her feet wouldn't respond. They felt like they had stubbornly merged with the solid tile beneath them. Besides, her eyes didn't want to give up looking at him. He looked just as devastatingly gorgeous as the last time she had seen him, though he had filled out and now looked like he had muscles to spare, barely fitting in his formal black suit. His dark red hair was radically different. Instead of being short like she remembered it, it had grown out in straight waves down to the base of his chin. She imagined running her fingers through his hair like she used to, trying to remember the silken feel of it.

They had dated for several months before the fire after meeting at the Agency Winter party. He was the one thing she truly regretted leaving behind when she had chosen to join her mom. During those three years, his attractive boyish good looks had been replaced with a smoldering masculine maturity.

Her heart skipped a beat as his eyes stopped scanning the room and locked with hers. His golden slanted eyes almost popped out of their sockets with the shock of recognition. And in the space of two thunderous heartbeats, a myriad of expressions shifted through his eyes. She could feel the blush of surprise radiate out from him, changing quickly to a warm curiosity of what brought her there, and then her stomach churned as his eyes clouded with suspicion.

She closed her eyes, knowing what emotion it would eventually all be replaced with and hating herself for it. Maybe, possibly, three years had been enough time and the last emotion had been forgotten. She prayed with all her might that when she met his eyes again the suspicion would still be there. Suspicion, she could work with.

She tentatively looked up and felt her heart constrict painfully. His jaw was clenched and his long red brows were knitted together in a dark look of contempt. He deliberately turned his head away and focused his attention on the other side of the room.

She knew that look well. It cut just as deep now as it did then. Three years and he still hadn't forgiven her.

Chapter 6

"Miss Harper, rather than just standing there, I suggest you take a seat." Lord Stadler motioned for Vara to take the chair across from his daughter. Laris sat on her father's right-hand side, dressed in an expensive burgundy dress, her hair elaborately braided and piled with curls that spilled out on top.

Next to Laris sat a middle-aged woman in a garish sea-green gown with a long feather that bobbed over a mess of white-blonde curls. She favored Vara with a good-natured smile, which just made her overly painted face look even more clownish.

"You must be the new companion." Her voice was as warm as her smile. "It's nice to see Teri bring in young people to amuse his daughter with. And you are a vast improvement on the last one. I didn't like the look of him at all. I apologize for what a poor host my friend is for not making proper introductions. I am Lynnis Carter. I'm Teri's closest neighbor."

"Vara Harper," she automatically responded.

"Well, Miss Harper, it's very nice to meet you. This is my husband, Harrison," she said, as she clapped the rat-faced man next to her on the shoulder. The man's head snapped away from staring at Laris with an open leer to look at Vara. He was possibly a decade older than Vara with sandy brown hair and a mustache that twitched up every so often as he licked his lips. His expression shifted from irritated to calculating as he stared back at Vara.

"You wanted something, my dear," his voice dripped with false affection.

"I was just making introductions for our new friend here," Lynnis said, giving him a smile.

His mustache twitched as he returned her smile, his eyes never wavering from Vara. "Friend is she? If you say so, dear." He flipped the page of his paper, and let his eyes drop back to it.

Vara watched him for another moment as he sneaked another odious look at Laris.

"Next to you are Morlan Stadler, younger brother to our gracious host, and his son Zavian," continued Lynnis.

Morlan looked identical to Lord Stadler in face, though instead of Lord Stadler's long silver-blond tresses, he had hair that was the color of the blackest of nights. He wore a white suit, with a green dinner jacket and a pair of spectacles perched on the edge of his nose. Every so often he would lean over to whisper something to his son, though his son looked less than interested and didn't bother to whisper back.

Zavian had his father's black hair and wore it fashionably long and tied back. The darkness of the room seemed to cling to him and he smoldered with an intensity that was breathtaking. He stopped pushing around the vegetables in his nearly empty bowl of soup and glanced up at the sound of his name. There was a glimmer of interest as his brown eyes raked Vara's face and his mouth quirked up in a smirk. His father said something sharp to him, and he broke eye contact to scowl at his father for a moment. The scowl remained on his features as he dropped his gaze back to the depths of his soup bowl.

"And on the end are Miss Stadler's bodyguards Richard and Derek." Richard was also one of the cat-people, like Derek.

It wasn't surprising they were employed as bodyguards since the feline race was inherently strong and had reflexes far exceeding human speed, which made them formidable in security positions.

They both had the same golden-tanned skin and both looked like bodybuilders with their black suits barely stretching over their taught muscles. The only difference between the two of them was their hair. Richard had neatly brushed slightly curled brown hair, while Derek's was dark red and reminded her of sparkling rubies.

Richard's eyes scanned the room with the watchfulness of a hungry hawk, while Derek still glared daggers in her direction.

The remains of their meal sat in front of them, waiting for the servant to return to clear the dishes and serve dessert. Laris still had one hand clenched so tightly her knuckles were white. Her other hand was curled around her glass, picking off some minute flakes with her thumbnail. Every time she made a loud chip, Vara braced for the sound of shattering glass. Laris abruptly pushed her chair back and got up from the table.

"I'm sorry, but I need some fresh air," she said, with undisguised disgust. She threw a lethal look at the mustached man on the other side of the table, who had ogled her through dinner. He now seemed to have given up his fascination with her and was writing in a small pocket-size notepad. With a swirl of red silk and perfume, she stalked out of the room in the direction of the parlor.

All of the eyes in the room were glued on the door as it slammed shut behind her. Richard and Derek stood up to follow her.

"Sit down, both of you!" barked Lord Stadler. "I'm certain Miss Harper would enjoy the opportunity to talk to my daughter. Are you going to do what I hired you for, or not?"

Both Derek and Richard slowly sat back down, but their muscles remained taught under their suits as if they both itched to follow the young heiress despite their orders. Derek leveled a dark look in Vara's direction.

It was like he wanted to do his job with every inch of his body and he resented her keeping him from his duty as a bodyguard. Was it more than that? Did he actually feel something toward the girl? His face was set in stiff lines. There was definitely another emotion there that seethed under the surface, barely under his control. There was no other explanation other than she was keeping him apart from a girl he loved. Vara's heart contracted painfully in her chest. She hated to admit it to herself, but why shouldn't he love Laris? The girl was rich and blonde and gorgeous.

"Miss Harper, I could have a word with your superiors if you'd like," Lord Stadler threatened.

"I'm sorry," Vara apologized automatically. A breath of cold twitched through her body at the mention of the mysterious Kendrick & Clarke superiors. There were whispers about them through the temp agency that they were beings conjured by nightmares.

Vara made a quick escape from the room and went in the direction she had seen Laris disappear.

The aroma of Laris's lilac-scented perfume led her through the parlor and out the front door. She stepped out into the frigid night air, regretting that she didn't have the luxury to go back to her room to grab her jacket. The gravel crunched underneath her feet as she gained some distance from the mansion.

She passed the sleeping gargoyle statues that guarded the front of the house. The one who had herded her to the front of the door earlier lifted his head and curiously watched her pass, though he didn't make any move to follow her.

Her feet carried her all the way to the transit circle. Could Laris have left? Vara didn't remember her wearing a handbag to dinner and she hadn't noticed her scent going in the direction of the bedrooms. If Laris had left, she had no idea where she would have gone, but she didn't catch any lingering whiffs of her perfume.

Vara continued to make a wide circle around the house, cursing herself for wearing dress shoes to dinner and not a decent pair of walking shoes. But then she had expected the first day on the job to be like a first day of classes where the teacher just does the introduction without getting into any proper lessons.

She entered a wall of spruce trees by the right side of the house, belatedly realizing just how dark it was now that she could no longer see the moon. She caught herself several times, before she slammed headfirst into trees.

"I don't need a babysitter," said Laris's sultry voice through the darkness.

Vara spun around trying to figure out which direction the voice came from, but it seemed to echo off all the trees surrounding her.

"Your father apparently thinks you do," Vara pointed out with her back to the mansion. Chances were Laris had put at least a little bit more distance from it.

"My father just wants to keep up appearances," said Laris's voice, again. "I wish you'd leave me alone. I just need to clear my head. That man in there. . . . I wanted him."

"I know." The voice definitely came from in front of her somewhere. Was that a silhouette of her a couple of paces away or an oddly bent tree?

"But you don't know how much I wanted him. And the hunger gets harder and harder to resist each day."

"You don't have to fight this alone," Vara reminded her and took a step closer to what looked like Laris's dark shape. "You have friends and family who want to help you."

"No, I don't," said Laris's voice sadly. There was a rustle of leaves and the dark shadowy shape in front of Vara vanished.

"All my father cares about is keeping up appearances," continued Laris's voice, though this time it seemed to come from somewhere behind Vara. "I don't have any real friends. People are friendly enough to me, but I can never be certain if they're trying to get close to me just because of my fame and money. The only friends I have are business contacts and employees, and they're all paid to be with me, just like you. If my father didn't pay you, would you be here, knowing what I'm becoming?"

Laris was right. If Vara wasn't blood contract bound and her future wasn't hanging in the balance, her sense of self-preservation would have kicked in and she would have laughed in Lord Stadler's face. Her stomach roiled at the thought of wanting to run from someone very much in need of a friend.

Her head swam and she needed her sight back. There was just the darkness, and Laris's soft caressing voice and the fragrance of her perfume so strong that she could nearly taste its sweetness. She saw a break in the trees ahead of her and stumbled toward it.

The trees opened out into a large clearing with a meadow and grass up to her knees that tickled her legs. The expanse of grass and occasional trees stretched out into the distance. On the very edge of the horizon she could see faint lights of a small village.

"They say when a person turns into a werewolf they can smell human flesh over a mile away," Laris whispered. Vara couldn't tell where her voice was coming from. "And it is the only thing that will satisfy the hunger. Will I want to eat even my father? Oh, imagine the headlines for that one!"

Vara shook her head, to clear it from the intoxicating scent of Laris's perfume, and looked at her carefully. Laris's face was heavily made up, covering sickly pale skin and heavy bags under the eyes as if she hadn't slept in weeks, but she still looked like a normal, average person. There weren't fuzzy tufts to her ears, or jutting canines, or even a feral cast to her luminous blue eyes. She looked like she was fighting just a bad case of the flu, if anything. "No, I can't imagine you would do something like that."

"Oh, wouldn't I?" Laris's teeth glint in the darkness as she smiled and the feral cast that had been absent crept into her eyes. "Is it because you think I'm too beautiful and refined to do something that uncivilized?" She brushed her hair back with her hand, regally, and then she vanished. Suddenly Vara could feel her vibrant presence behind her, and warm breath tickled the back of her neck. It sent a thrill of electricity up her spine.

"You've only just met me. You have no idea what I'm capable of. I used to be a vegetarian. I used to spend nights at nightclubs and parties. Each day I feel more and more of who I used to be slipping away. It might be fun just to prove you wrong. The only thing keeping me from tearing you apart right here and now is the feeling that I won't be able to regain control. The wolf inside me gets stronger by the day and devours more and more of who I am. Soon there won't be anything left other than the wolf."

Her breath felt hot against the back of Vara's throat. Laris was too close, and Vara felt every instinct inside her itch to get away. She fought the feeling and turned to face the blonde girl. They were so close they could have kissed. Vara fought the instinct that screamed at her to take a step back from the girl. Laris needed a friend—a friend who wasn't afraid to stand with her. "Maybe the wolf can be reasoned with."

Laris threw her head back and laughed, stirring a flock of birds into the night sky. Vara could hear their surprised honks to each other and rush of wings diminish into the distance.

Suddenly her eyes were blinded by a flash of light and the acrid smell of smoke hit her nostrils. It drove away all memory of Laris's lilac perfume. She coughed as the smoke hit her throat, as if someone had suddenly stuffed it with wads of cotton.

"Ah. Two lovers in a midnight tryst," said a maliciously-edged voice. "That's what I should call it."

As her eyes cleared, still dazzling with stars on the edges of her vision, she could see the lecherous man from the dinner table standing in front of them. In his hands he held an antiquated camera with a huge flashbulb attachment. The wiring inside the blub still glowed orange, as if there was any doubt to the source of the flash of light. She could hear a deep growl growing in the back of Laris's throat.

He pulled a notepad out of the inside of his tweed jacket and flipped through the pages with his thumb. "Lord Stadler's harlot daughter caught in the arms of yet another of the household staff," he crowed. "Is this a plea for her father's love or just another notch for her bedpost? And to think I had come to ask you if you wanted company for the evening."

Laris's growl was growing louder. Vara wondered why the reporter couldn't hear it. Probably too excited by his good fortune at finding a headline. Muscles tightened in Laris's arms and her fingers slowly curled into fists.

"Laris, don't do it," Vara whispered under her breath. She put a hand on Laris's arm, though she didn't think she would be able to restrain Laris if the heiress was determined enough. "He's not worth it."

"There's no story here," Vara said as she turned to the reporter. "We were only talking. If you bothered to actually look at us rather than just blindly snap pictures, you would have noticed we weren't even touching."

"No matter. People can connect the dots with my article anyway. But I can see she would much rather take pleasure in your company than mine, so I shall watch."

Laris wrenched her arm from Vara's restraining hand and took another step toward him. There was another flash of light from the camera that dazzled the both of them and a rustle of branches as he disappeared back into the darkness, no doubt to rejoin his wife. Vara wondered just how happy that marriage could be.

Chapter 7

An open-topped green car sat in front of the house, and the chauffeur in the driver's seat glanced at Vara with distaste as she stumbled out of the thicket of trees. The end of his cigar glowed red as he took a drag from it and blew the smoke in a ring.

The front door of the mansion stood open and she heard the sound of laughter. Morlan Stadler, the younger brother of Lord Stadler and his bored-looking son, Zavian, stood in the doorway, along with Lord Stadler himself.

Morlan exuberantly shook his hand and gave him a quick hug. Zavian turned his back on the mansion and ran to open the door of the car, pointedly avoiding looking in Vara's direction. Then again, she figured she shouldn't be surprised. She had been center of quite a scene at dinner. He shouted something to his father.

Morlan turned his head in his son's direction. He looked a bit annoyed at his son, but turned back to Lord Stadler again and smiled. He gave his brother's hand a squeeze before he let go and walked toward the car. Vara watched as they sped off into the distance.

Lord Stadler gave her an anxious look as she passed him in the open doorway but didn't say anything because another couple entered the foyer just then.

The reporter smirked when he saw her, with a malicious glint in his eyes. She didn't like that smile one bit. She itched to remove it from his face, preferably violently. The couple left and Lord Stadler turned his attention to her.

"I trust you took care of everything out there?"

"You could have warned me that you had invited a reporter hungry for turning your family into a gossip column headline," she grumbled.

"I shouldn't have to," he said with an aggravated sigh. "It's to be expected with our level of fame. I take it I shall have to make some calls to get his story pulled in the morning then. This had better not become a habit."

"So, what am I supposed to do anyway? Just watch her? Or are we searching for a cure for her? Or do you have people working on that? Or is it just none of my business and I'm supposed to guard her while the madness takes her? I saw how she was with that reporter. She's not going to be able to control it for much longer."

"Then you shall have to prevent her from doing others any harm," he said. "I know you have the power to. I just want to keep everything looking normal, so try to be discrete. She starts her day early, so I would consider calling it a night. Ren can show you to your room."

That was a dismissal. The servant was waiting behind her as she turned to leave as if he had materialized there at the sound of his name.

"The master is only harsh at first," he chattered away as he led her back to her room. "And he wasn't happy at all with his daughter's previous companion. But not knowing that man was a reporter certainly wasn't good. I could have told you, had you asked. But it will take more than that to get fired around here, unless you actually want to be sent away already. I wouldn't. The master doesn't handle disappointment well and will make certain it goes against your future employment. He has shares in most of the major companies, after all. Still, you will need a good night's sleep for tomorrow's outing."

"What outing?" she asked.

"Miss Laris has a full day planned for you tomorrow," said a deep voice behind her.

Ren bowed and disappeared down the hallway.

Vara whirled around to face the black wall that was Derek. His face was devoid of emotion except for his golden eyes, which boiled with unrestrained fury, like a pot of water on an oven. She half expected the heat from his glare to scald her skin red. She could already feel the room grow stuffy hot around her. But the heat just reminded her of what it felt like being close to him in the past. Her traitorous hands itched to reach out and touch him and feel his warmth again.

"Vara, why are you here?" he growled through gritted teeth, as if he had to talk through a mouth full of sewing needles to say her name.

She looked away. It was like the Derek she remembered, who loved everything about her, had died and been replaced by a complete stranger. "Sam sent me," she finally forced out.

"Why you?" he spat, punctuating each word.

"I get it." She felt her throat tighten painfully. "You don't want me here. Why don't you take it up with him and leave me alone."

"Fine, I will." He turned his brick wall of a back to her and stomped off down the hallway.

Her lower lip trembled and her face grew hot as tears spilled over. It had been stupid to think he would have forgiven her for leaving. Her mom was right. She was a screw-up. The sooner she put an end to the evening the better.

She checked her cell phone before she climbed into bed. It was blinking. She dialed the voicemail and felt the tears threatening to return at the sound of her mom's voice.

"Vara, this is your mother. I can't talk right now, but both of us are fine. Don't worry. I still have to take care of a couple of things here and I'll be home at the end of the week. Love you lots, and don't burn the house down."

Her voice was still too cheery and it sounded like she didn't want Vara to call her back. What was the problem? Her mother had the power to solve any situation, but yet something still sounded wrong. Vara grumbled to herself. It burned in her gut that there was no one she could talk to.

She switched off the red shaded lamp next to her bed and let her mind jabber away to itself over all the problems of the day. Nightfall on Saturday would be the first time Laris would be fully transformed, but just how long did she have before Laris's bloodlust would take over? What would her werewolf canines feel like when they ripped through her flesh? And just how badly would her mom kill her once she found out that she skipped town without her? Would being smote by her mom's wrath be more instantaneous than being ripped to shreds by a werewolf? And were either of those two fates worth it for this job?

Though in all honesty, Vara needed the money. And Laris did seem rather lost and like she needed a friend through all of this. But was the money and feeling good about herself worth it? There was a good chance that she wouldn't survive to Saturday if Laris ended up losing her battle with the hunger before then. And what was that smell? Had her mind conjured up what her desiccated remains might smell like once either Laris or her mom had decided to end her existence?

"Does your mouth always hang open when you sleep?" asked a gravelly voice, invading her dream.

Vara awoke, certain that it hadn't come from within her head. She groped around in the darkness for the lamp and switched it on. Her bleary eyes focused on a blurry ghostly white human shape wrapped in a black suit. It lounged length-wise on the small red sofa in the far corner of her room. It watched her with its lanky legs crossed and an amused smile played about its mouth.

"Sam, any chance you could knock next time you feel like dropping in on me?"

"You mean like this?" He knocked his fist against the back of the sofa.

"Never mind. So, why are you here and couldn't this have waited until morning?"

"I am here to review your first day's work," he said with a note of glee in his rumbling voice. "You know the client wasn't happy with your performance."

She pulled her pillow over her head. She really didn't need this. "What does he expect when he had a reporter hungry for a front page story at his dinner table? And did you know about his daughter's condition?"

"Yes, the specifics were known by the Agency."

"So, when were you planning on telling me?" she asked suspiciously.

"It was on a need-to-know basis, according to the client."

"Well, I needed to know."

"Why?"

Though her mind was still half asleep, his voice sounded a little too innocent. "It might have made a difference on my accepting the position."

"Your not accepting the position was not an option."

"What?" She turned to look at him. She knew demons didn't have normal human emotions, but she could swear his smile turned rather smug.

"I had specific orders to recruit you for the position. And your compliance was mandatory. If you had said no, I had orders to command you to come."

Wow. That sent a chill down her spine. Summoned demons couldn't control humans on their own unless they had been ordered to by the humans that controlled them, and they had to have justifiable reasons or they could be brought to trial. So it must have been for a very important reason to actually risk legal proceedings.

"Do you know why they wanted me so badly? I mean, I understand that I owe the client, but surely there were others in the Agency database who would have taken the chance on a soon-to-be-werewolf?"

Sam looked at her through his hollow black eye sockets and laughed, exposing his sharp white teeth. "It was the will of the Agency Heads."

That was largely unhelpful. "What about my father? Did you arrange for something to happen to him?"

"No, didn't your mother just tell you he was fine?"

"Yes, but. . . . Were you listening in on my phone call?"

Sam grinned. There was no such thing as privacy when there were demons around. She certainly wasn't going to tell him she thought her mom might be hiding something and probably lying about her dad being fine.

"So, what exactly is it I'm supposed to do here? Just watch her and wait for her to turn into a werewolf and then go home? Or should I be helping her find a cure? Or hunt down the guy who bit her or something?"

"So curious for a mortal."

"More like so frustrated for a mortal," she grumbled.

"I wasn't given any specific orders other than the client

wanted you to watch over her and not to let her get into any trouble."

"And what happened to the guy before me? Why exactly was he fired?"

"Let's just say that the client thought that your predecessor wasn't acting with propriety. Now if you don't have any more questions for me, I need to make my report to my superiors." He started to rise from her sofa, stirring the rancid air around him, so that the reek of dead fish and onions amplified for a moment.

"Are you going to be dropping in on me each night?"

"You don't have anything to hide from me, do you?" There was a rush of air, as he rushed at her like the smoke from an out of control fire, and swirled around her. His dead corpse smell drove its way up her nostrils. She choked, coughed, and her stomach threatened to heave. She felt the brimstone heat radiating off him, as he wrapped around her and slid over her skin. He paused in front of her and opened his mouth, full of sharp white teeth. An eerie laugh filled the room and with a twirl of his black suit, he vanished with a devilish smile on his lips.

Damn demons.

Chapter 8

Austen crouched in the bushes with his silver knife flat on the ground so that the light from the security guard's flashlight wouldn't reflect off the bright metal as he searched in Austen's direction, again.

He held his breath, letting the sounds of the night blanket him. His joints welcomed the end of the week to come since it would mean an end to sleeping in deserted lecture halls.

He dreaded returning home since Kalen was certain to give him an earful on his failings. No matter how much he tried to prove himself, his older brother still found fault with just about everything he did. He had stopped by only long enough to borrow the ritual knives from his mother. She had quietly given them to him with her only response being a sad smile. She was the one person he could trust to never judge or mock him.

The security guard's boots crunched against the winding sidewalk as he continued his patrol. Austen's eyes scanned the darkened campus buildings. It had been three days since he had last glimpsed the wolf and he was starting to wonder if maybe it had decided to seek out the country, where it could run and hunt without having to worry about hunters.

A branch snapped behind him. A bird probably just dislodged it from a nearby tree. He held his breath with his knife raised and searched the area. There didn't seem to be any extra bulky outlines lurking in the shadows.

Austen glided across the grass lawn. He relished the

freshness of the teeming life underneath his feet. He breathed in the electric energy and let it fill him. Two more steps and he disappeared into the shadow cast by the administration building.

He edged himself further into the darkness until his back was against the side of the building. He felt reassured to have solid brick at his back. He looked across the courtyard to the ruined building. He needed to check it one last time since it was where he had first spotted the wolf the night Laris had been attacked. He would be exposed, for there was nothing to camouflage his approach. It was a three-story building with charred stains in a flowing wave design that covered the outside. Most of the windows were broken and some were missing their glass entirely.

Austen looked around. There didn't seem to be any dancing lights of the security guards' flashlights. He pulled his backpack closer to his body, kept his knife in front of him, and ran across the courtyard.

He heard the crunch of his footsteps in the grass and the pounding of his heartbeat in his ears. He didn't stop running until he had his back pressed against the charred brick of the ruined building.

His eyes drifted to the blackened mark on the pavement where Laris's blood had pooled just under a month ago. Most of it had been cleaned up, but he could still see the dark ring where it had stained.

He tore his eyes away before they could conjure the image of her ravaged body sprawled on the pavement. He looked away and focused on the night sky, the stars, the nearly full moon, anything other than the pain of how he had failed to keep her safe that night.

The full moon was like a slap in the face. It reminded him of what he was here to do. He wouldn't fail her again.

He snuck around the side of the building and eased open the main door. He could still see their footprints in the debris, though lightly coated with dust. He heard creaks and splintering of rotted beams all around him. And then he saw two glowing red eyes staring back at him through the darkness.

It was sitting back on its haunches, with its head raised,

watching him. He tightened his grip on the silver knife. The designs on the ornate handle bit into his flesh.

A sliver of moonlight arched through the fallen supports from a hole in the insulation above him and glinted off the blade of the knife.

Austen could see the reflection dance in the wolf's red eyes. It exposed its red gums and finely sharpened fangs in a snarl. His ears were deafened to everything other than the wolf's feral growl. It crouched, taking a step toward him, and another step.

Austen stood his ground and made certain his feet were planted firmly. He took a deep breath and let his magic run along his arm and into his hand with the silver blade. With another breath, he let the blade fly. It whispered her name as it soared through the air straight and true toward the wolf's heart.

And then the wolf jumped. It twisted and darted its head toward the blade and then the knife was gone from the air. Austen couldn't breathe. Where had the knife vanished to? Silver glinted from the wolf's mouth and he smelled the sizzling sweetness of meat cooking. The wolf had caught the knife between its teeth. It dropped the knife at its feet and lifted its head in a howl.

Austen tried to keep his footing through the debris as he backed toward the door. His foot caught on something, nearly pitching him forward into the dust. He regained his balance and felt wildly around in his bag for his spare knife with a mixture of panic and outrage.

With his magic guiding the knife, the throw should have been perfect. He hadn't expected to need a second knife. At least he had the satisfaction of wounding the beast.

A mixture of thick clear drool and bright red blood dripped from the side of the wolf's mouth. It took another step toward him. The growl grew in intensity and ferociousness.

It was a surprised relief when his back hit the door behind him. He felt behind him for the door handle and pushed it down. He threw his weight against the door to ease it open. The cool night air and the moonlight washed his face. The door slammed closed in front of him with a clang.

HIRED BY A DEMON

Where was that knife? He opened his bag wide enough that the contents were illuminated by the moonlight. He pushed aside some half-eaten food and his spare change of clothes. There it was! It had fallen all the way to the bottom and was wedged under a small canteen of water. As his finger brushed the handle, a growl filled his ears.

A heavy furry weight bowled him over and knocked the bag out of his grasp. He rolled to his feet and crouched. The wolf snarled and leapt at him again. It moved faster than any dog he had ever seen before.

Austen didn't even have time to build up a magic burst to defend himself. He felt a sharp pain in his chest as the wolf's claws raked through his thin black shirt. Teeth snapped, just missing the skin of his cheek. The stench of its breath made his stomach roil as the warm air assaulted his face.

He pushed the beast off him and scooped up his bag. The creature yelped and rolled. Its red eyes flashed angrily. He thrust his hand into the bag, determined to pull out the extra knife. His hand closed around the hilt and he pulled with all the strength he had.

With his hand still in the bag, he turned and ran. He let all of his remaining energy carry him as fast as he could go.

A heavy weight from behind crashed into him. It sent him sprawling onto the paved sidewalk. He heard a snap and a sharp pain in his chest. Another pain shot straight up his left arm from the elbow to his hand.

The wolf howled.

He yanked his hand, still clutching the handle of the knife with a death grip and ripped it out of the bag. He twisted underneath the wolf and sank the blade deep into the monster's side.

It yelped and turned its head to snap at the blade. As the beast shifted on top of him, it released him from the ground. Its teeth closed on the blade with a pained whine and the blade inched out of its side. He didn't wait around to see the creature free itself from the silver blade.

He just had to make it to the transit circle in the center of campus. Pain ripped through his chest as his feet pounded against the pavement. He heard an angry howl spike the air—the wolf was on the move. He gave another burst of speed. He could see the transit circle now, illuminated under a lone street lamp, just in front of the glass-fronted student union building.

A growl echoed against the concrete buildings around him. He turned his head enough to see glowing red eyes closing in on him.

He frantically pulled energy from the ground around him. As he did a homerun slide, he threw his magic into the transit circle. The command ripped from his lungs, "Ashwood Informer Home Office."

The hazy red light drowned him as the frustrated howl filled his ears.

Chapter 9

"Would you like me to call a doctor for you, Mr. Hadley?"

The lady at the front desk of the Ashwood Informer tabloid paper stared at him with wide open eyes. Austen shook his head and self-consciously tried to pull the shreds of his black shirt together.

His chest itched and ached where the wolf had clawed him. His left arm hurt so much it had started to go numb with pins and needles. But as far as he could tell, it wasn't broken, which meant he couldn't just use the mending spell on it. And he didn't have time for a doctor. Laris only had a couple of days left.

"I could get the first-aid kit in the break room," she suggested.

"I'd rather just wait for Mr. Carter."

"It wouldn't be any trouble," she tried again. "That cut on your chest needs to be cleaned or it's going to get infected."

He almost smiled at the thought. An infected wound was the least of his worries. "Thanks, but no. I'll clean it later," he reassured her.

"Mr. Carter called to say he would be in shortly. You can wait for him in his office." She gave him a bright smile.

Austen claimed a cushioned chair in the reporter's office and sunk gratefully into it. He hadn't realized before just how much he missed normal furniture after spending a month in nothing but wooden and plastic chairs and sleeping on tiled classroom floors.

He was almost on the verge of drifting off when the glass door flew open and threatened to break as it slammed against the wall.

A waft of cigar smoke swirled around the room. A middle-aged man stood in the doorway with a cigar protruding underneath a mustache that dominated his rat-like face.

His sandy brown hair was mussed and his tweed suit was rumpled as if he had slept in it. Harrison Carter hadn't changed any since the last time Austen had seen him, though at least he could see his face clearly this time since it wasn't obscured by a hulking bodyguard throttling him into next year.

"Mr. Hadley, you look like you've fallen on bad times," said the reporter as he took a seat behind his desk. He pulled out some paper from one of the drawers and put a sheet into the typewriter that dominated the surface.

"If you don't mind, I need to get this done for the morning issue. It won't take more than a minute." He stared intently at the page in front of him, and as if it had read his mind, the typewriter sprang to life and started to fill up the page.

Pink morning light was starting to color the sky outside and chase away the darkness of the previous evening. Austen assessed his injuries while he waited. Maybe the secretary was right. Perhaps he should consider letting a doctor look at him.

He fingered the front of his shirt where it had been slashed into ribbons. There were four deep lines sliced into his chest with blood oozing from them. Most of the blood had crusted over, but the top line seemed to be deeper and was taking longer to mend. His left arm felt immobile. Most likely it was just sprained since the bone seemed to be whole.

The reporter pulled the sheet of paper out of the typewriter with a flourish. "Now, before you ask, yes, I do remember you. You were in the employ of Miss Stadler."

He opened the door and motioned to someone outside. The sheet of paper disappeared from his hand and he closed the door. He turned his attention to Austen. "You know, I was just with them last night. They were showing off your new replacement at dinner. She looked rather out of place and a bit shell-shocked. Though Miss Stadler seemed quite attached to her already."

The reporter's eyes raked his face, searching for any hint of a reaction. Austen schooled his face into a neutral expression, determined not to give the reporter the satisfaction.

"I caught a rather compromising picture of Miss Stadler and your replacement enjoying the evening air together," the reporter continued. His mustache quirked up in a lecherous smile. "Your Miss Stadler certainly never disappoints me when I need a good story."

Austen's fingers dug into the arms of the plush chair.

Harrison smiled knowingly. "Yes, that wasn't just a job to you, was it?"

"It's none of your business," Austen snapped.

"Ah, but it is. Miss Stadler is a favorite of my readers. And we should know if her new assistant is going to lead her astray, unless there are other reasons for her showing her wilder nature?"

Austen averted his eyes. When he looked back up, he didn't like what he saw in the reporter's eyes. There was a new degree of watchfulness and suspicion. Just how much did the man know?

"Now then, why are you here, Mr. Hadley, and not in a doctor's office? Should I be worried that some muscle-bound goon is going to break down my door looking for you to finish the job he started?"

"You were there that night Laris got attacked."

The reporter smiled. "I thought it might come back to that. I hadn't been following your precious Miss Stadler, you know. It was just luck that I happened to run into the three of you."

He massaged the back of his neck, as if remembering the pressure Laris's bodyguard had exerted on him. "It was interesting that her father paid for an entire media blackout on the incident. My paper has threatened more than once to fire me if I lift a finger to look into anything connected to it. But then, I'm hoping that if I keep close to the source, Miss

Stadler will give me an exclusive."

Austen's eyes burned with rage. He felt so impotent that he couldn't be there to protect her from leeches like this.

"Not to worry, dear boy, I'm certain that new replacement of yours won't last long. She seems rather inexperienced. I'll have to look into her background and see if there are any good stories there." The reporter whipped out his notepad from a pocket and scribbled in it. "I suppose you want her discredited. It shouldn't be too hard to do."

"About that night. There was a wolf. . . ."

"Yes, I know, dear boy," he said with a sly smile. "I was doing a story on it. It's odd for one of them to be this far into the city. I take it that's what you tangled with this evening? Didn't get bitten, did you?"

Austen shook his head.

"I suppose you want me to put you in touch with some hunters who might be able to help you?"

Austen nodded.

The reporter smiled and flipped through his rolodex. He pulled out a card and handed it to Austen. "I did a story on her a couple of weeks ago. Just mention my name. And I speak for everyone when I say that we'd all like to see you succeed so that Miss Stadler might continue to grace the pages of my tabloid."

The door of the reporter's office flew open. The glass quivered and threatened to break. Lord Stadler stood in the doorway, his furious eyes fixed on Mr. Carter.

"Ah, the illustrious Lord Stadler. Do you have any further comments you'd like to add to my story?"

"I am ordering you to silence your story immediately!"

"But it's too late, my good sir. It's already being printed and distributed. Now, is there anything further I can help you with?"

Lord Stadler's face flushed scarlet and his eyes roved around the reporter's office. They fixed on Austen and looked as if they might pop out of their sockets. "You!"

Austen pushed himself out of the chair and took a step away from Lord Stadler.

"This is all your fault!" Lord Stadler quivered with rage.

"She wouldn't have been in this mess if you had done your job properly and kept her safe from harm! I should never have put my daughter's life in the hands of someone with Nature blood! And it wasn't enough that you let her get hurt, but you couldn't keep your filthy hands off her afterward! Don't even imagine you could ever be on the same social level as she is. It's charity to give your kind servant positions."

Austen took several steps backwards until he bumped into the wall behind him.

Lord Stadler let the red flush fade from his face, and he focused on Austen. His blue eyes blazed with an inner fire and his deep velvety voice weaved around the room with a calm mesmerizing authority. "Do you understand me? You aren't worthy of my daughter. You never will be. It was a mistake to have put someone like you in that position. You are dirty, unclean, and not fit to grace the presence of the pure humans. You should just go back to where you came from."

With every word, Austen slid farther onto the floor. He wished he could hide from Lord Stadler's words. They whirled around in his head; they shoved everything else out. It couldn't be anything other than the truth. He was nothing but a dirty half-breed. He could feel it in his bones. Laris was royalty and he was nothing more than a beggar, not fit to clean her shoes.

"As for you," Lord Stadler said, turning back to the reporter, "we shall see what your boss has to say." He turned from the room and let the glass door slam behind him.

"Seventh time this month he's been in here shouting like that," the reporter muttered to the closed door. "He's full of nothing but hot air."

Austen picked at his shirt distractedly. "I'm dirty," he muttered. "Unclean. He's right." Lord Stadler's words pumped through his body like blood, echoing in his head. Laris could never be in love with someone who wasn't pure. He itched to remove the foreign part of himself.

"Nonsense. Just because the man has some powers of suggestion doesn't mean you should just accept what he says at face value. Just because he thinks all non-humans are a plague on the world doesn't make it true. Besides, I can't have you just sit here quivering all day in my office. I'd never get any work done."

The reporter pulled Austen to his feet and clapped him on the shoulder. "Now, go save your lady love and tell me all about it after you succeed. Remember, I expect an exclusive!"

Chapter 10

"I was wondering when you would make an appearance," a rich voice said behind Vara as soon as she closed the door to her room that morning. "I saw you at dinner last night and thought you might like the chance to get to know me better."

She turned around and came face to face with the young dark-haired man who stared at her during dinner the previous night. He leaned against the wall and let his green shirt hang open, suggestively displaying defined chest muscles. A long thin black robe richly embroidered with silver stars about the edges covered his arms—though still thin enough to show off traces of developed muscles as he moved one arm. He obviously knew he was good-looking and was well-accustomed to girls throwing themselves at him. An arrogant smile played at the corner of his lips.

His smile grew larger as he noticed that her glance lingered. She turned away and made for the stairs. "Don't flatter yourself," she muttered. She hated that type and it was definitely too early in the morning to deal with that sort of personality.

"Wait a minute!" said his indignant voice behind her. "Where do you think you're going? No one turns their back on me."

Correction: arrogant *and* bossy. There was nothing in the world that would get her to turn around now. "I'm getting breakfast."

"Do you know who *I* am?"

"No, and I don't really care." She continued down the hallway, determined not to give him the satisfaction of a look back.

"I command you to stop."

Now he was getting truly annoying. "You're not my boss." She pushed the door open to the dining room. Ren had just finished setting out several plates loaded with food as if he had expected her to walk in at just that very minute.

Laris was seated at the head of the dining table. "Took you long enough! I've been ordered to bring you along on my shopping trip, so you can carry my bags. My bodyguards are waiting for us in the foyer. Zavian, you're not invited."

"*Fine*," said the snooty black-haired young man as he sat down next to Vara. "I didn't want to tag along on your stupid outing anyway. Just tell your servant here to at least give me some proper respect when she speaks."

"Why?" Laris batted her eyes at him innocently.

"Because, *dear cousin*, she's your paid employee. Now, what's your name, girl?"

"Vara," Vara answered between mouthfuls of delicious French toast.

"I am Master Zavian Stadler, nephew of your employer." He dipped a finger into the sticky maple syrup that her French toast swam in, pulled up a glob of the syrup, and sucked on his finger suggestively watching her.

"Miss Laris, there—" Derek's rich, deep voice said behind Vara, making her jump. How long had he been standing there? She turned around in time to see a look of shock frozen on his face. In an instant, his eyes clouded back over. "I'm sorry to disturb you," he said to Laris, though Vara had the distinct impression he was talking to her instead. "There is someone here to see you." He turned and left the room as rigid as a wind-up soldier. *Great*, one more thing for him to hate her for.

"Zavian, don't do anything that would make her unable to carry my bags today," Laris said. She frowned, but she also wore a trace of a smile on her lips.

As Laris left, the smile on Zavian's lips turned

calculating. He brushed aside a strand of Vara's chin-length black hair that had escaped from the headband she had trapped it in and ran a finger down the side of her cheek. "What is that bodyguard to you?"

She shook her head as she turned away from him. "No one."

"Don't deny it. I saw the way he looked at you. No one can be that mad without something between them." He laughed. It was a warm, rich sound that made her knees tremble. He looked like a dark hero out of an old romance novel, with his shoulder length black hair tied back in a ponytail. But there was still the arrogance in his eyes.

"You're used to girls throwing themselves at you, aren't you?" she asked.

He leaned closer to her. She could feel his warmth and the silken brush of his robe. "And what if I am?"

"Zavian!" Laris shouted from the parlor.

He smiled and leaned back. "Some other time then." He swept out of the room. Vara finished the last couple of bites of her breakfast, opened the door to the parlor, and was immediately assaulted by raised voices.

"How dare you show your face here, you foul slimy toad!" Zavian shouted at a young man with curly black hair who stood an entire head shorter than him. "You violated my cousin, embarrassed my family, and have the nerve to talk to her like she's your equal! Cousin, say the word and I'll throw him out!"

The young man was angelic with thin bones, a rounded face, and bright blue eyes that looked like they were on the verge of tears. His black shirt was in tatters and he had several ugly oozing slashes over his stomach. He looked like the lone survivor of a slasher movie, who had gotten raked over by the killer, and barely lived to tell the tale.

"Laris, please, I'm doing this for you. Just tell me you'll take me back once I get rid of the wolf." His tear-filled blue eyes flickered in Vara's direction and immediately darkened with an intense glare. She looked behind her, but she was the only one he could be looking at. Why was he looking at her with such intense hate? He didn't look like anyone she knew. But she could just about taste the hate that emanated from him.

"I'm sorry, but I can't," Laris said quietly. "Father has forbidden me to have contact with you."

"Then we'll find a way," the young man said adamantly. "I love you."

Zavian snorted. "Your kind isn't capable of love. Besides, you've already defiled her. Isn't that enough for you?"

"I just healed her! I just wanted her to live!"

Tears brimmed in Laris's eyes. "You call this living?" She turned her back on the young man and marched out of the room. The door slammed behind her.

"Go back to where you came from and leave my cousin alone," said Zavian. "Or better yet, let that wolf have you."

The young man opened and closed his mouth a couple of times, but nothing came out. "I'm sorry. It's all my fault," he muttered. He turned and left.

"You bet it is," agreed Zavian.

Vara hated the thought of acknowledging him, but he obviously knew the black-haired young man. "So, who was that?" she asked Zavian. She tried to make her voice sound as neutral as possible.

"Austen Hadley. That was the creep you replaced."

Laris was already waiting for Vara in the foyer, with her two bodyguards behind her resembling rigid black columns in their identical black suits. She had dried her tears and reapplied her makeup.

Derek still leveled the same look of pure hatred at Vara as soon as she entered the room. Her heart felt like it wanted to curl up and die inside of her. His brows were knitted together and it looked as though he was trying to wish her away with every ounce of power he had in him.

She couldn't blame him. She was the one who had left him. She was the one who had rejected him and everything that he loved in order to renounce magic and move to a place where she could never be touched by it again. She was a traitor and not worthy to be anywhere near him, though her arms longed to encircle him, hold him close, lean her head against his warm skin, and breathe in his strong essence.

She opened her mouth, but she couldn't think of anything that would even remotely come close to apologizing for how much she had hurt him.

Laris smiled as she noticed Vara's hesitation. "Vara, these are my bodyguards. This is Derek." She turned toward Vara's former boyfriend. He nodded in deference to her as he kept his glowering eyes fixed on Vara. "And this is Richard." Laris turned toward the second bodyguard. It was a blessed relief to look away from Derek's malevolent hate.

Richard looked several inches shorter than Derek and had short brown hair that curled. Vara noticed a trace of a smile as he looked at Laris, and as quickly as she had noticed it, it had vanished and his face looked impassive, as if it had been carved out of stone.

Laris took in Vara's appearance with displeasure. "You'll never pass for one of my friends dressed like that. It's so obvious you're staff." She wore a long-sleeved dark pink coat on with what looked like mink lining and a red pleated skirt with matching red shoes. Her hair was done up in entwined braids, circled into a loose bun, with a small red hat cocked to the right side.

She pulled open the front door and walked out onto the gravel driveway. Vara followed her, passing the gargoyles as they frolicked on the edge.

She could hear the simultaneous crunch of gravel several steps behind us as Laris's bodyguards kept pace with them. They finally reached the stone with the transit circle engraved into it. She traced the runic glyphs with her eyes. It was just a basic sending and receiving circle. Most residences and businesses owned by magic users had them. She would just have to tell it where they were going.

"We're going to Titania's House of Fashion at the Ashwood Shopping Plaza," Laris supplied. "My bodyguards have to go first and secure the area. We wait two minutes before following them through. It's more than enough time for them to come back if it isn't safe."

The two guards stepped onto the transit circle. They faced each other and placed their palms together between them. They looked almost like they were trying to mirror-image each other.

Vara sighed as she heard Derek's baritone whisper the location name and felt her face flush as it brought to mind all the times he had held her close.

In a surge of magic that enveloped them in a red glow, they vanished out of existence as if they had been nothing more than a soap bubble popped with a breath of air.

The after-image burned into Vara's retina was still vanishing from her vision when Laris stepped into the center of the circle and held her hand out impatiently.

Vara stepped next to Laris and took her hand. She could feel the magic inside her that had been slowly building since she had arrived there, sponging itself from the energy that flowed through the air around her. She drew a minuscule amount of that energy out with her mind and let it flow into the circle beneath their feet. The symbols pulsed with red light.

"Titania's House of Fashion at the Ashwood Shopping Plaza," Vara commanded. The circle underneath them pulsed brighter for a moment and then grew upward. It engulfed the both of them in the red glow.

Laris looked exultant with the energy flowing through her. As the glow vanished, they were immediately assaulted by the blaring honks and screeches of traffic. The pungent smell of burnt rubber and asphalt writhed around them as if a dragon had suddenly breathed in their faces.

Laris held her free hand to her mouth. She looked at Vara for a moment as she noticed the worried expression on Vara's face. Laris shook her head and said, "I'm fine. It was just the exhaust from the cars." She took a deep breath, smiled, and released Vara's hand. She nodded to her two guards who stood on either side of them gazing vacantly into the pedestrian traffic.

Richard nodded and started at a brisk pace toward the nearest of the stores with Laris following him. Vara ran to keep up and Derek took the rear. He scanned every so often all around them.

She glanced a couple of times back at Derek and held her breath each time his gaze swept in her direction as she waited for the scowl to darken his face.

The Ashwood Shopping Plaza was a small high-class open-air fashion mall with the stores all painted the same white on the outside with neat ornate hanging signs over the entrances. She followed Laris and Richard inside Titania's House of Fashion, which proved to be an expensive boutique. Just one dress alone was the average amount of her paycheck.

Richard and Derek positioned themselves near the doorway. Vara decided to park herself on a chair near the dressing room. She fixed her gaze on Derek's back as Laris sifted through a rack of frilly blouses.

After going through pretty much everything in Titania's, they moved on to a jewelry store and several more stores after that. The morning passed by in a blur of colored silks, sparkling diamonds, and more high heels than Vara had seen in a lifetime. Along the way she had acquired about five bags and a hat box.

With Derek just behind her, she had to run to keep up with Laris and Richard as they strode quickly past the stores and finally stopped outside a large building with glass windows that spanned the entire length of it. Above the doorway a sign announced it as being "Morelli's Fine Italian Pasta." There was a line of people standing outside waiting to be seated.

She heard a shriek from one of the young girls in line, and Richard and Derek suddenly went rigid. Their muscles tightened as they braced for whatever was coming. Both of them stepped quickly around Laris. Vara's eyes darted to where she heard the girl's voice. The girl was whispering something to her trio of friends.

After a couple more moments, the four of them rushed over and hunted through their bags for paper and pens. Derek nodded to Richard. Richard left Laris's side and walked over to the uniformed head waiter who stood in front of the front door of the restaurant.

Laris smiled at the small group of girls with Derek still standing between her and them. She took their proffered pieces of paper and scribbled her autograph on them and waited for them to finish snapping pictures of her. Vara wondered just how much of Laris's beaming smile was forced as she fought the hunger. Still, she admired Laris for not just turning them away.

Vara darted a glance at Richard. He was deep in conversation with the waiter. He gestured toward Laris and the eyes of the waiter bulged and his pale face seemed to lose what little color it had.

The waiter quickly scratched something out on a seating chart in front and beckoned to the nearest waiter inside. They talked rapidly as they both darted looks of awe mixed with curiosity at Laris. The second waiter dashed back into the restaurant.

The group around Laris had grown from four young girls to about eight with a couple of boys as well. She animatedly talked with the nearest boy, and every so often the group would laugh. After a couple more minutes, Richard motioned back to Vara and the others. The man at the front door gave them a bright smile.

"I'm so sorry about the wait. My staff has finished clearing out the section nearest to the window so that Miss Stadler can have a quiet undisturbed dining experience with us. I shall personally show you to your seats."

He motioned for them to follow him and led them to a large booth against a glass window that looked out into the green garden behind the building. It was also far enough away from the kitchen that they couldn't hear the crash and clatter of dishes.

Laris slid in one side of the booth. Vara slid into the seat across from her and set the packages on the floor next to her. Derek and Richard took up a position several paces away from their table, stood at attention, and stared vacantly into the dark recesses of the dining room. The entire area had been emptied and the nearest occupied table was all the way on the other side of the room.

The waiter set menus down in front of them, made a quick bow, and retreated to the kitchen. He returned shortly with two glasses and a pitcher of water. He poured the water into both of their glasses without dropping anything and set them down in front of each of them.

"We will need a third glass of water," Laris announced.

The waiter nodded and vanished back into the kitchen for another glass.

She met Vara's questioning gaze with a wicked smile and a bright sparkle in her eyes. "Richard, you can join us."

Where the two bodyguards stood, the smaller one relaxed and turned around to face them. A smile brighten up his face and for the first time he looked playfully handsome instead of the rigid impersonal statue that he imitated.

"Hello, Kitten," he said. He slid into the booth next to Laris and gave her a kiss on the cheek. Laris laughed with a carefree blissful tone. She threw her arms around his neck and gave him an affectionate squeeze. Then she turned back to face Vara. "Just don't tell my father."

No wonder Laris wasn't giving that young man, Austen, the time of day. Vara wondered if he knew about Laris and Richard. Did Laris make it a habit of getting involved with the staff? Vara recovered enough from her surprise to ask, "Are you sure he doesn't already know?"

Richard shook his head. "We've been careful to be discrete. We've been nothing but professional at the mansion. She doesn't even talk to me directly there."

Laris's eyes sparkled in the dim light. "Father wouldn't understand. It isn't that he'd have a fit if he found out I was dating staff. I've already done that stunt before. It's that Richard isn't human." She ran a hand through his short brown hair as she showed off one of his furry pointed feline ears. She touched the tip of it and smiled, almost seeming to forget herself for a moment. "He doesn't approve of humans stooping to socialize with the lower species."

Vara glanced at Derek's immobile form. The Derek she used to know would have taken offense at being called a 'lower species,' but the set of his shoulders didn't shift in the slightest. Another surge of guilt washed over her. Because of what she had done, had he lost the pride that she used to find so endearing? If Laris had been involved with Austen and now Richard, what about Derek? The set of his immobile shoulders looked as though he was bracing himself against their fraternizing. She felt her heart sink into her stomach.

Richard looked at Vara imploringly. "We hope we can trust you. We get so little time when we're not being monitored by her father. Though we will deny it if you go to a reporter with this."

"Yes, of course," Vara answered automatically. Was that a smirk she noticed on Laris's lips?

The waiter returned at that point with the other glass of water and a plate of bread. He quickly jotted down their orders and vanished back into the kitchen.

Why would Laris know about her and Derek? Derek had made it abundantly clear he hated her guts. She'd show him. It was time to move on and play the part of a dutiful companion. "How long have you two been together?" Vara asked.

"Since a little under a month ago, when I started the position, though it feels like it's been a lot longer than that, right, Kitty-Kat?"

Laris kissed him again in agreement. They did look happy together.

"Apparently after the incident her father decided that she needed more security," Richard confided. "A little too late, if you ask me. So, why did you agree to work for her father anyway? He didn't even give you the lengthy interview process like he did me, which suggests he knew you prior to this."

"I owed him," Vara admitted. "And he said he'd call us even if I did this."

"All the more interesting! What did you do to make yourself indebted?" She could see why Laris had gotten involved with him. He had a loveable eagerness about him.

"I burned down the school he owned." She stole a quick glance at Derek and was disappointed when he didn't twitch in the slightest. Though Laris choked on the water she had been drinking and tried to stifle a laugh.

"Now that certainly must be a story!" Richard said. Vara caught a brief glimpse of his pointed feline teeth as he laughed.

"Not really," she answered. "What are you, the press?"

"Speaking of which, you should see the paper this morning," he said as he pulled out a folded square of newspaper from his back pocket. He unfolded it and smoothed it out on a clear space in the middle of the table. It had a black and white picture of Laris and Vara with the headline STADLER HEIRESS IN WHIRLWIND AFFAIR in bold print above it.

"Should I be jealous?" he asked as he looked at Vara with exaggerated suspicion. "Are you going to steal her away from me?"

Laris grumbled something under her breath and grabbed the article. She crumpled it into a ball and dropped the wad back onto the table.

"You know that was a test, right?" said Richard with an amused smile.

Vara sighed and looked down at the small plate of bread that she had absently picked to pieces. "One that I miserably failed."

"There will be other tests," he cautioned. "Her father doesn't take failure lightly."

The waiter appeared by their table and quickly slid the meals onto the table. "If you need anything else, just let me know."

They ate in silence, though Laris and Richard looked happy to be with each other.

After the plates were emptied, and the check was paid, Laris gave Richard one last long kiss as he rose from the booth. "Duty calls," he reminded her and resumed his place next to Derek.

Vara's feet ached and she had trouble balancing all Laris's purchases. She breathed a sigh of relief when they finally approached the large transit circle in the center of the mall.

"Vara, this time you're going first with Derek," Laris said with a smile. "There shouldn't be any problems at home, but I shouldn't travel first. Richard will travel with me."

Derek stepped into the center of the circle and held a hand out toward Vara with the glower back on his face. Laris had her arms folded in impatience as she waited.

Vara stared at the ground, determined that she wouldn't give him the satisfaction of seeing how much being near him was tearing her up inside. She made certain she had a firm grip on all the packages and then gave Derek her free hand. She let him pull her into the circle as if she was nothing more than a rag doll.

As his large hand encased hers, she tried to remember his warm smile and his rich golden eyes and not the fact that he could potentially crush all the bones in her hand with his brutal strength. But in place of the warmth he used to look at her with, his eyes were frigid and icy. She could feel his strong muscles barely restrained by the fabric of his suit as he steadied her in the circle. At that moment, she yearned to free herself from him and curl up in a corner and cry.

"Stadler Estate," she heard him whisper in a low growl. She could feel the magic pulse through him. His species had magic inherently running through their bodies so he didn't even need to draw power from the outside.

As soon as the magic hit the circle, a red glow blossomed from their feet and radiated out to the edges of the circle. It made her realize just how infatuated Laris must be with Richard with all the magical energy permeating him.

She glanced over at Laris and noticed a wicked glint in her eyes. Laris raised her hand in a brief wave, and Vara could hear her laugh as the red glow surged and grew around them. It blinded her vision to nothing but red. When the light subsided, Vara was standing with Derek on the transit circle in front of the Stadler mansion. She felt so gullible.

She yanked her hand out of Derek's grasp and turned on him accusingly. "Did you know they were planning to ditch us?"

His silence spoke volumes.

"Think her father won't fire me if I return without his daughter?" Her eyes traced the dark expression still plastered across his face. "You'd like that, wouldn't you?" she accused.

He shot her a look of frustration and let his steely eyes rake her face. "They only did it so they could have some time alone. And you could have some time alone with Master Zavian." His deep rich voice had a resentful edge to it.

Vara itched to slap him. It wasn't his fault, she reminded herself. And not losing her job on the first full day needed to come first. She decided to take advantage of the fact that he was in a mood to talk to her. "How much time alone? Do you think they're planning a hotel stay somewhere? Do you think her father will make it so that I won't be able to get a job anywhere on this planet after this?" There was a note of hysteria and desperation in her voice as she saw what was left of her future going up in smoke.

The bags and box had started to slip out of her grasp. She tightened her grip on them. She couldn't just leave them behind since they would give it away that they had come back to the Estate. "You don't have to come with me if you don't want to. I don't want you along if you're going to purposely lead me in the wrong direction."

"Miss Laris won't be happy if we find them this soon."

"Take us back to the mall," she barked at Derek. "I'd rather face her wrath than her father's." The little resolve she had left quivered the longer she looked up at him. "I don't have time for this. If you won't, I'll do it myself."

He put his massive hand around her hand that was holding the shopping bags and whispered, "Ashwood Shopping Plaza."

She felt the warm magic spread out from him, blanket her, and drip into the circle under their feet. Pins and needles prickled under her feet for a moment and then surged up. It washed her vision with nothing but red light. As her vision cleared and she could see the swirling script of the sign hanging over the entrance to the boutique.

Shoppers passed by them, carrying armloads of brightly colored bags. But there was no sign of Laris or Richard.

Chapter 11

Austen stood outside a small building painted an eyesore red with "Sally's Sizzling Sandwiches" in large neon yellow letters dominating the front. He checked the address on the card the reporter had given him for the fourth time. Maybe the reporter was having a laugh at his expense. Then again, maybe it was just a disguise to keep out the curious.

The inside didn't look any more like a hunter training headquarters than the outside had. Yellow plastic chairs and tables crowded the front of the room with a center aisle that led to the front counter where several young people in bright red uniforms stood at attention behind cash registers. An extensive menu was displayed on the wall behind them.

"Sally's Sizzling Sandwiches, may I take your order?" asked an enthusiastic young lady who stood behind the front counter. Her bright red hair was tied up in a ponytail and she flashed him a wide smile.

"I was told I could find Veronika Greylight here."

The girl's eyes immediately darted to the wounds on his chest and gave them a very long look. The smile faded from her face. "Niki, there's some guy here to see you," she said as she turned her head to shout in the direction of the kitchen in the back.

An equally young woman shuffled out from the kitchen. She had on the same red uniform, but with an apron over the front decorated with several yellow-brown grease stains. Her frizzy blonde hair was also tied back into a ponytail, and she peered at him with rather tired brown eyes through a pair of red-rimmed glasses.

She turned back to the girl behind the register. "Trish, you mind if I take a short break?"

"Yeah, sure," the red-haired girl answered.

"Follow me," the blonde said to Austen and led him to a room marked "employees only." She held the door open for him and let him stumble into the dark room.

Instead of the snap of a light switch, he heard a click of the door lock behind him. Something solid cracked against the back of his knees and his legs buckled underneath him. He threw a hand behind him to brace himself before he hit the floor. He rolled for a moment in the darkness and hoped maybe he could get to a wall or the door.

His momentum was suddenly stopped by a foot. A second foot came down against his other side that pinned him in place. Two muscular legs joined the feet and he felt a heavy weight on top of his chest. Rough fabric rubbed painfully over his recent wounds. He wriggled to get free, but the legs squeezed tighter against his sides.

"Who sent you?" demanded a frosty voice somewhere above him.

Austen felt a sharp pain slice through his throat.

"I said who sent you?" the voice demanded again.

The pain in his throat increased and he could feel the icy coldness of a metal blade pressed against his skin. He swallowed, painfully choking around the edge of the blade.

"You've been following me and I want to know why! Rant, get the lights."

Blue stars danced in his vision as the room suddenly dazzled in brilliance. There was nothing tired about her eyes now as the girl with the red-rimmed glasses glared down at him. "Now, who sent you and why are you following me?" The knife bit deeper into his skin. "I don't want to have to repeat myself again."

"I would answer her questions if I were you," said a deep rumbling voice from somewhere off to the side. "She has very limited patience."

"Rant, no one asked you," the girl retorted.

Austen bit back a cry as her legs constricted against his

sides and pain flooded through his ribcage. "The reporter Carter sent me," he gasped.

The pressure of her legs lessened and he heard her give a rather aggravated sigh. "I knew I should never have given him that interview. He promised he wouldn't tell anyone where I was. Rant, have a word with the reporter in the morning, okay?"

"Gotcha, Boss," the deep voice rumbled.

"That answers the question of how you found me here, but why have you been getting in my way of killing that wolf on the campus? I'm not even going to say how many of my traps you've bungled into."

"I didn't know you were there."

"A good hunter is the one who can't be seen," she said as though reciting a lesson she had learned the hard way. "It's a wonder you're still alive."

He felt her trail a hand over his chest and pull apart the shreds of his shirt that were stuck to his wound. "She got you good." He felt one of her fingers trace the edges of the wound. She brought a bloody finger to her lips and licked at it thoughtfully. "We've been on the trail of that one for a while now. Though she's smart and stays hidden. So, why are you playing vigilante killer and hunting her?"

"Because it scratched me and I need it dead."

The girl leaned in close and gave him a long sniff. "You haven't been bitten. And you're not the killer type, so who is she to you that you need her dead?"

He tried to turn his head away, which was rather difficult since she still had the knife pressed to his throat.

"She bit someone or killed someone close to you," she reasoned. "Who?"

"None of your business," he retorted.

"It's my business if she passed the curse on."

"Fine then. I don't need any help."

"Yes, he does," said a deep gravelly voice.

Austen slammed his eyes shut and wished away the new voice with all the power he had. But already the sour rotting smell circled the room.

"Keep out of this, Sam," ordered Austen.

HIRED BY A DEMON

"I'm not yours to command," the ghostly demon reminded him with an indignant tone in his gravelly voice. He passed Austen without glancing at him and glided over to Veronika. "I am his supervisor at the Kendrick & Clarke Placement Agency." Samanith straightened his posture and held the lapels of his black suit proudly. "The sooner he takes care of this, the sooner he can start his new position." He threw Austen a malicious grin over his shoulder.

Austen felt his stomach churn and panic course through his body. Sam was going to tell! "No, don't do it!"

Sam laughed devilishly. "To answer your question, it was a girl our young man here had his eye on. She's living at the Stadler mansion. I'm certain you'll be able to put the rest of the pieces together since they don't have too many females living at the estate. And if my charge here needs to pay for your services, you can send the bill to the Agency. We would like you to consider using our services should you need any temporary staffing."

The demon smiled at Veronika, showing off his needle-fine white teeth. "Could I persuade you to dispatch the young lady in question? Her first change will come in less than a week, after all."

"No! Sam, I forbid. . . ." Austen didn't finish his sentence as Samanith blew a noxious cloud in his direction. Austen felt his eyes roll back into his head and his legs give way underneath him.

"Sleep," commanded the demon.

Chapter 12

Vara scanned the crowd around her. She really didn't know Laris well enough to attempt to divine where she might have gone. Vara gave up and faced Derek's resigned scowl that was unbelievably growing even darker. Miraculously it didn't look like he blamed her. His mood seemed inner directed as his gaze swept the crowd.

"Did they tell you where they were going?" she asked.

His gaze dropped to the ground for a moment and his jaw shifted as if he had made up his mind about something. "We could try going back to the restaurant."

She hoped he was right. "Okay then, to the restaurant."

They hit the doors of Morelli's at a run, ignoring the line of people waiting to be seated, all giving them dirty looks for cutting ahead of them. Her eyes took a moment to adjust to the dimly lit room, while her feet automatically took her in the direction of where they had sat for lunch.

"Ma'am, if you could wait to be seated," said a waiter as he jumped in front of her.

"We were here earlier with Miss Stadler. We got separated and we were hoping she might've come back here. I just need a minute to check," Vara said as she pushed past him. She wasn't used to being rude, but she was tired of being polite.

"Miss Stadler hasn't come back here since her meal," he insisted as he followed behind her. She ignored him and continued on to where they had sat. The booth was empty and looked like it had been freshly cleaned and cleared.

Derek gave the place a quick search with his feline eyes, which were better trained at seeing in the dim light than hers. He shook his head.

She turned back to the waiter. "Have you seen her pass by at all within the last fifteen minutes?"

"No, Miss. The last time we saw her, you and your friend here were with her."

"It's quite all right," she reassured him. "Thank you for your help."

She left the restaurant, and searched the air with a long sniff as she tried to catch even a vague whiff of Laris's overpowering lilac perfume. But all she could smell at that moment was the reek of the garbage from behind the restaurant.

"I'm sorry they lied to you," she said to Derek.

He shrugged. "I'm used to it," he said, his voice barely a whisper. "You should try a locator spell to find them, provided you remember how to."

Vara bit back the retort that bubbled to the surface. "I'm sorry. I needed. . . ."

He cut her off. "I don't want to hear it. Just do the spell, if you can."

He was baiting her. She wasn't going to give him the satisfaction of an argument. She shot him a dirty look and dug around inside her purse for the piece of chalk that she kept for emergencies and her small pair of cuticle scissors. With the chalk, she drew a small version of the transit circle and hoped that she got all the surrounding runes right. She had to modify the spell in several places since it wouldn't have a set destination. With the cuticle scissors, she sliced a short line down her thumb on her right hand. The sharp stab of pain only lasted for a minute. Blood welled up and dripped from her hand into the middle of the circle.

Transit circles all had blood ingrained in them by the people who had originally carved them. Anyone with enough magic flowing through them could work an already existing transit circle, but to actually create a spell, one needed to have studied the craft.

She finished the last couple of symbols and made a silent prayer that she had gotten everything correct.

"Are you sure you have all the right marks?" he asked as he dubiously looked at the complicated design.

"Look, it's either going to work or it's not. We're wasting time." She extended her bleeding hand in his direction, since her other arm was still laden down by shopping bags.

He joined her in the circle with a look of determination, his gaze fixed somewhere above her head. He grasped her hand and let his fingers entwine with hers. She could feel her traitorous fingers tighten their grip, determined not to let him go. She didn't know if she could release her grip when the spell was over. A cold tear slid down her cheek.

"Find Laris Stadler," she whispered and tried not to hear the sob choking the words. She let the magic flow through her into the circle beneath her feet.

The surge of magic enveloped them like a warm electric-charged cloud and dissipated. It left them standing in a darkened parking structure. Cars with huge headlights ravenously stared at them. And for a nightmarish moment she saw sharp teeth beneath the shiny headlight eyes, as the world pitched dizzyingly.

The shopping bags and hatbox toppled onto the ground and her feet vanished out from under her, but surprisingly she didn't hit the pavement. Her disoriented gaze swung from the pavement that remained at a distance to Derek who held her in a rock-hard grip.

He stared at her with an agonized expression. And in that stolen moment she had a glimpse of how close their relationship would have been had she stayed. How she would have known what every crease in his face meant and every flicker of emotion in his eyes. And then his face turned back to the same worried scowl as before and he let go, and she was alone again.

It was embarrassing how much just casting a simple locator spell had drained her. It would take a while before she would have enough energy for any large spells. She was weak, and useless, and even if he hated her, she didn't want him to

HIRED BY A DEMON

see her this way. She turned her back firmly toward him and pulled out a band-aid from her purse and put it on the cut. She retrieved the bags and box from the ground and took a couple of deep breaths to clear her head. She could faintly smell Laris's heady lilac perfume.

"Come on, I think she's near," she said to Derek, not bothering to look at him.

Vara followed the aroma like a fairytale character following breadcrumbs. The scent led her past the polished cards and down a short flight of stairs to a darkened hallway, where she saw a body lying on the ground. Blonde hair draped over its face.

Derek pushed past her and stooped down next to the figure on the ground.

"Vara, I'm going to get a security guard. Stay here with her," he ordered. He ran down the hallway and she could hear the loud clang of a door as he continued outside.

The colors of the scene muddled and blurred in her still woozy mind. The blonde hair shifted and jerked up. Laris's glorious hair was in disarray and her face was covered with splotches of glistening red blood. She stared at Vara with a look of horror and anguish.

"Help me," Laris pleaded, her voice barely above a whisper. "I couldn't stop him," she sobbed. With each breath, the sobs slowed, and underneath the sobs, Vara heard a low hungry growl coming from the back of Laris's throat.

Vara could now see Richard lying on the ground with his face contorted in a look of pain and surprise. His right hand clutched at his chest, where a dark red stain radiated out like a flower blooming. His burnished gold skin was now a corpse-like waxy white, and he didn't move, not even to breathe.

Vara grabbed Laris's arm and pulled her away from Richard.

"Laris, stop it!" Vara's heart hammered painfully inside her chest. Could Laris have killed him? He had to have been killed within the last five minutes and there wasn't anyone else around. But she hadn't shown any sign that she was losing her battle against the hunger before she had escaped with Richard.

Guilt washed over Vara. Laris was an innocent and in

trouble, and she was condemning her for a crime that there was no solid proof that she had committed only because Vara was prejudiced against the beast growing within her.

The hungry glint in Laris's eyes diminished once she had enough breathing space from the body. A look of pure horror and revulsion crossed her face, and her hand, still covered with Richard's blood, flew to her mouth. She pushed Vara away and staggered several steps toward one of the walls. She dropped to her knees, and her body heaved with the force of her stomach emptying itself. She collapsed the rest of the way on the ground and curled up in a fetal position. Her body shook with sobs.

"It's all my fault! He wouldn't be dead if it wasn't for me!" she wailed.

Vara winced. Laris was blaming herself just as she had blamed her moments before. It made her wish she could cast a spell to play back the scene, rather than have Laris relive the pain while relating it to others.

Vara knelt down next to Laris and put a hand on her shoulder. "Derek has gone to get security. We just need to hold it together until they get here."

In the distance she heard the door of the parking lot swing open and the voices of Derek and someone else. Their footsteps echoed as they drew closer. She looked up just as Derek's flaming red hair turned the corner and came into view.

He ran over to them and knelt down on Laris's other side. His eyes flickered over her worriedly, his scowl from earlier completely gone.

The other man with him wore a black uniform with "Security" printed in neon orange on the back of his jacket.

Instead of coming over to them, he approached the body and pulled out a flashlight from where it was fastened on his belt. He let the light play over Richard's bloody corpse. "Body of a male cat-person in his late teens with multiple lacerations to his chest." He was talking telepathically to the other security guards.

Vara hadn't seen a system like that in place before, but with magic being inherent in everything in this world, she wasn't surprised that the police had used it to their advantage. It was certainly a lot more reliable than walkie-talkies. Actual telepathic abilities were rare, but people could learn a simple telepathic system with certain spells.

The heavy door behind them opened and three more security guards entered and passed by them to where Richard lay. One of the guards came over to where they stood.

"We're sealing off the scene of the crime. You three are going to have to come with me to the station to make statements. Do you understand?" He was young and his voice trembled when he talked.

Vara nodded. She could feel Laris beside her do the same.

The police station was a squat three-story building painted a deep cobalt blue, with a short flight of stairs that led up to the front door.

The security guard led them to a line of chairs off to the side while he went to find someone in charge. It was a large room with desks scattered around and people in navy blue uniforms sitting at them. Some were dictating their reports to old-fashioned looking typewriters. The typewriters were actually typing away, manually shifting at the end of each line by themselves.

Vara glanced up in time to see a group of officers walking toward them. "We're going to take your statements, so we'd like you to come with us into the back," said the tallest of the officers. He had a long grey beard and was built broad in the chest and shoulders without looking overweight. He led them to a hallway of offices in the back.

"We're questioning you separately. So, please, have a seat inside, Miss. And your friends can follow me." He opened the door for her.

It was a small room with black and white tiles on the floor. The walls were completely empty and in the middle of the room sat a table with chairs on both sides of it.

Vara obediently went inside and sat down. One of the officers from further back in the group entered behind her and closed the door. He sat down on the chair facing her and set a sheet of paper down onto the table in front of him. His pen flew across the page, making some preliminary notes.

After a minute, his pen stopped and he looked up at her with a reassuring smile. "My name is Lieutenant Harish Lawrence. If you need anything like a glass of water or tissues, just let me know. We're just taking this statement to find out what happened. Full name?"

"Vara Lynnette Harper."

"Residence?"

"I live with my mother in Salvation City. But I'm currently staying at the Stadler Estate while I watch over Laris, the girl who was with me."

"What's your relationship to her?"

"I was hired by her father as a companion through the Kendrick & Clarke Agency."

"When did you start working for them?"

"Yesterday."

The lieutenant's pen stopped in mid-scribble and he looked at her through narrowed blue-grey eyes, as if reading her face for some sign. He ran a hand through his thinning reddish-grey hair and made some more notes on the pad. "If you're from Salvation, you would be working here illegally?"

"No, I moved there three years ago. I'm originally from Summerville."

"Do you still have immediate family there?"

"Yes, my father, Darrington Harper." He paused in his notes to look up at her again for a minute. His grey eyes searched her face.

"What?" she asked. That nagging feeling that her mother was lying returned triple-fold. Why had he paused on her dad's name? Just what could he have done to get noticed by the cops? Maybe it was something illegal that her mother was trying to hide from her. Or was he seriously in trouble?

The officer shook his head dismissively. "You're a magic user?"

"Demon Summoner, though I wasn't able to do any magic while I was in Salvation City."

"What level is your magic at?"

"I had finished my final year at the Conservatory and was about to start training for an apprenticeship when I left.

Does this have any bearing on the investigation?"

"It might. Our investigation team will check for residual magic in the area. Was the deceased man anyone you knew?"

"Yes, he's the bodyguard of Laris, the girl I was with."

"Did you see him die?"

"No. Derek and I got separated from Laris while at the mall. I did a spell to find her, and that's when I found the two of them. He was on the ground, already dead, and she was kneeling over him, crying."

"Did you see anyone else nearby?"

"No."

"Did you see anything that could have been used as a weapon nearby?"

"No."

"When was the last time you saw him alive?"

"We ate lunch at Morelli's and then they went with us to the mall's central transit circle."

"And how were relations between the four of you?"

"I just met Laris and Richard last night, but they seemed friendly enough. Derek and I knew each other before I moved to Salvation City."

The lieutenant scribbled some more notes. "And between the deceased and the other girl?"

"They seemed happy together. It didn't sound like she would kill him."

"Can you really make an assumption like that when you've known her and the deceased for less than a day?"

She looked down. He was right. She really didn't know anything about Laris, like how she normally reacted to things, or even if she had other dealings with the law in the past.

"Did you notice anyone suspicious watching your group when you were at lunch? Or did anyone suspicious follow you to the transit circle?"

"Aside from the waiters, and the people we cut in line in front of outside, no."

"Did the deceased mention anyone else who might have a grudge against him?"

"No."

"Is there anything else you'd like to add to your statement?"

"There was a reporter hanging around Laris last night looking for a story," Vara suggested.

"Did you see him at the scene of the crime or any sign that he might have been there?"

"No," she admitted.

He made a couple more notes on the page and then spun the form around in her direction and pushed it toward her. "Please read it over and tell me if I made any mistakes or if you don't agree with anything in it. Or if you have anything further to add."

She read it over. It was a word-for-word transcription of what she just said. "It looks okay."

"Then sign and date at the bottom."

She signed it and returned it to him. He escorted her to the seats where the three of them had been sitting earlier. Derek was already waiting in one of them. The worried look was back on his face and his eyes nervously darted around the office. His gaze rested on Vara for a fraction of a moment before they skimmed the room one more time and hovered on the doorway behind her.

"I'll just get you that cup of water now," said the lieutenant and left the two of them alone.

"I shouldn't have left them!" Derek muttered despairingly. "This wasn't supposed to happen!"

"Derek. . . ."

"I don't want to hear it, Vara!" he thundered at her like a storm cloud about to burst. "This job was going fine until you got here! Why are you here anyway? And don't give me that lie about Sam. We both know that wouldn't have been enough to bring you back here. Was it not enough to turn your back on everything that mattered to me, but now you're back to rub my face in it?"

"I didn't know you were working for the Stadlers," she said lamely.

She heard a deep cough and turned to see the lieutenant watching the two of them with a bemused expression on his face and a paper cup full of water in one hand. "Once your friend finishes with her statement, the three of you are free to go."

"And that's it?" Vara asked.

"To the investigation, you mean? Heavens, no. There's the investigation of the crime scene, which they're currently performing, and the autopsy of the corpse. Not to mention the necromancy session."

"Necro . . . mancy? You mean you're going to talk to the dead body?" she asked incredulously. "But I thought that wasn't allowed. When I left three years ago, necromancers were shunned and treated like outcasts."

"For the most part they still are. But it's now common practice for police stations to employ one in-house. Has been for the last two years."

There seemed to be a lot of new magic practices being employed by the police now. But she wasn't surprised they had made use of that since being able to have the victim name the person who had killed them was revolutionary. Of course, there would still be problems of the dead person covering up for someone they still loved, or trying to exact revenge beyond the grave.

It was a job that was frowned on mainly because people didn't like the thought of their friends and relatives being disturbed from whatever peace they had moved on to. Better just to let the dead remain dead.

Laris stepped out of the hallway in the back, flanked by several officers. She looked several shades whiter, and one of the younger officers supported her. Her face had been cleaned and her makeup looked freshly applied. She gave the officer who held her arm a luminous smile. His face lit up and his cheeks turned a rosy pink.

The bright smile on her lips worried Vara. Had Richard's death meant nothing to her? Had any of the warmth between the two of them been real or had it all been just a show for her benefit? Laris had a distant, vacant expression on her face as if she wasn't fully registering things around her.

Lieutenant Lawrence cleared his throat and narrowed his eyes. "Philips, you shouldn't be harassing the witness like that."

The officer holding Laris's arm jerked his head in the direction of the lieutenant who stood beside Vara. The color drained just as quickly from his face as it had blossomed there.

"Sir, but she. . . . Sorry, sir." He dropped her arm and looked more than a little sad.

"Now, can you three get home on your own, or do you need one of us to give you a ride home?"

Vara noticed the several young officers who flanked Lieutenant Lawrence all had hopeful looks on their faces. She grimaced. "Well, if it wouldn't be too much trouble. . . ."

"Oh, not at all. It isn't often that people as famous as Miss Stadler visit us. It's the least we can do, especially when she's been through so much today."

Vara wondered how Lord Stadler would take seeing them come home with a police escort home from their shopping trip. The lieutenant nodded to one of his junior officers, who smiled happily and ran off with a spring in his step.

"Conroy will bring the car around front."

It was a long drive in silence out of the city through quiet suburbs and past long expanses of countryside to the Stadler Estate. They finally turned off the main road and into a small lane framed by a scattering of trees. The gargoyles were lazily basking in the light of the setting sun and didn't even bother to lift their heads when they rumbled past them.

Officer Conroy brought the cruiser to a halt in front of the main door of the mansion and turned off the engine. He got out and opened Laris's door. He had a bright smile on his face, though it seemed to falter a bit when Laris only gave him the barest of smiles. It ate at Vara wondering what Laris was thinking. She watched Laris robotically walk to the front door of her house and enter with Derek following close behind. Vara turned back to the young police officer.

"Thank you again for the lift. She's been through a lot today."

"It's okay, Miss. Just hope she'll be all right. Some people get pretty screwed up when someone close to them dies. If either of you need anything just let me know."

Vara smiled. He nodded and jumped back into the cruiser. He revved the engine and drove off in a puff of exhaust.

HIRED BY A DEMON

The sun had set and darkness had settled in as she walked into the foyer. The door slammed behind her. She whirled around to face the cherubic Ren.

"The master wants to see you in the parlor," he said with an ominous threat in his ethereal voice. He leaned close to her as if to confide a secret and stretched to reach her height. His lips swept upwards in a crooked smile and with a mischievous laugh he whispered, "You're in trouble now."

Chapter 13

It had been a long time since Austen had felt soft cushions underneath him. How long had it been exactly? Just under a month. A month! Laris! Austen jolted upright. How could he have forgotten her?

And where was he, for that matter? It certainly wasn't the campus. The room itself was painted in shades of brown. Sofas and chairs were clustered around a large table in the center of the room with several stacks of books piled on top.

How many hours had he lost and just how had he ended up here? He threw off the red blanket someone had thoughtfully covered him with and felt the chilled air against his skin. He looked down, but instead of his black shirt, a large stiff white bandage encircled his waist.

"If you're wondering, your jacket and bag are in the chair next to you," offered a whispery male voice from somewhere off to the side. "Your shirt was too ruined to bother keeping. I'm sorry if you were particularly attached to it."

Austen searched the room for the source of the voice and finally spotted an odd cloud of smoke condensed against a chair in a corner of the room.

As he stared at it, the face of a young man formed in the mist. The transparent face glanced at him for a moment before it rose from the chair. The mist glided along with it mimicking the shape of a person walking. He could almost see the ruffles and trimmings on the antiquated outfit the specter wore.

The ghost waved a hand toward the bookcase against one of the walls and a book pulled itself out from it and sailed through the air toward him. It hovered in front of him for a moment as he considered it. The book spun around in mid-air, then sailed back to the bookcase, and pushed itself into an empty space in the shelf. His gaze searched the rows of books before he waved a hand and another book eased itself out from the shelf and floated over to him. The ghost turned his attention from the book back to Austen.

"You know, I don't like being stared at," the ghost said with a note of disdain. "Is there anything I can do for you while you wait for Niki?"

"Niki?"

"Veronika," the ghost clarified. "She dumped you here, dressed your wounds, and ordered me to watch over you. Those wounds aren't because of her, are they? She can be rather careless when she's on the hunt."

With his book hovering next to him, the ghost drifted back to his chair and transformed back into a hazy cloud. The pages of the book flipped absently and stopped about halfway through.

"Where am I?" asked Austen.

"This is the bustling social area of our base of operations, if you can call it that," the ghost answered. "And Niki will be back just as soon as she finishes her hunt for the night."

"Hunt?"

The ghost looked at him as if he was particularly dense.

"Laris!" The name sprang from Austen's lips before he could stop it. He remembered Samanith making a deal with the were-hunter. He needed to stop her somehow.

Austin scooped up his bag and jacket in a fluid movement. He tried to ignore the way world spun for a dizzying moment.

"You can just stop that," the ghost said from his chair. His gaze drifted from the book in front of him to follow Austin's movements suspiciously. "I have specific orders not to let you leave."

"But I can't just sit here and let your hunter kill Laris!"

"And if she doesn't, it'll eventually spread to the rest of the human populace. Fur everywhere. . . ." The ghost's transparent nose wrinkled as if he was about to sneeze just thinking about it.

Austen strode to the nearest doorway. "I don't care," he muttered. Every minute he spent arguing with the specter was another minute that Laris's life could be slipping away with silver in her body.

The air stirred around Austen and then grew dense as a thick fog surrounded him. He felt as if he couldn't draw a full breath of air. The cloud twirled around him, as if he was the center of a mini-cyclone.

"I said I have orders not to let you leave," the ghostly voice whispered all around him. "If I have to cage you, then so be it. It would disappoint Niki if you left, and I can't allow that."

Austen took a last long shuddering gasp of air as his knees buckled and he fell to the floor. He forced his head to lift and blew out every ounce of breath that remained in his body. He hoped he still had enough control over his body to do what he wanted.

He smiled as he felt the air around him drop in temperature to a wintry chill. The freezing breath of wind hit the wall of his ghostly prison and turned it into a curtain of ice. The lids of his eyes slammed shut as unconsciousness threatened to overtake him. He balled his hand into a fist and wildly threw a punch in front of him with his last bit of strength. He hoped beyond hope that it was enough.

The bones of his knuckles screamed in pain as his fist impacted the solid wall. Everywhere around him he could hear the sharp splintering of glass, and suddenly hundreds of shards of ice rained down on him. Intoxicating, wonderful air rushed at him and he let his aching lungs take several frantic gasps.

He struggled to his feet and staggered out into the hallway. It was just a short dash to the large set of double doors. Before he could reach it, the latch clicked and it started to swing open. It was most likely the hunter girl, and there was no chance he would be able to take on a professional hunter, not with his head swimming and his legs just barely holding him upright.

He turned right and yanked open a small door. He really

didn't want to have to do this, but he didn't have any other means of escape. He wedged himself among the jackets and boots stuffed haphazardly inside, and pulled the door shut behind him.

Veronika caught the knob before the latch could click and threw the door to the coat closet open. The door banged against the empty wall.

She eyed the closet carefully and pushed aside the jackets and boots until she could put her hand against the solid plaster of the back of the closet. Then she slammed the door shut and stomped her way to the living room.

"Geoffrey, was what I asked too complicated for you?" Veronika kicked lightly at the melting shards of ice on the carpeted floor. "What part of 'keep him here' did you not understand?"

"I tried, but he was insistent." Geoffrey's normally whispery voice tinkled as shards of ice shifted. Already there was a dark puddle spreading in the center of the brown carpeting and ghostly mist rising slowly above it.

"You know there are ways other than force to keep someone from leaving. I should never have trusted you with this." She turned her head in the direction of the hallway. "Rant, get a towel."

"Sure thing, Boss," said a deep rumbling voice somewhere behind her.

"I'm sorry, Niki. I know how much of a disappointment I am." Geoffrey's voice was barely a whisper.

It hurt Veronika to see him turn from a thick fog into almost a transparent nothing in depression. "No, it isn't your fault," she tried to reassure him. He always took it personally, especially lately.

He'd been with the team ever since her father first started training her eleven years ago. Geoffrey was good at research: hunting through the newspapers for possible sightings, mapping out the areas they needed to hunt, finding possible lair locations, and arranging all of their permits and legal work.

He even dealt with local politicians to help funnel money into their small fund, which kept their headquarters running at full capacity. There wasn't a chance her part-time job would have covered all of their expenses. He was a lifesaver in so many ways, but lately it seemed like if there was a way to screw something up, he'd find it.

"Had he been full-blooded human, that demon's sleep spell would've lasted longer and I would've made it back here before he woke up. Now he'll be able to get to his wolf girlfriend before us."

"But I know which one she is!" breathed Geoffrey as the mist condensed and his ghostly face peered at her with a smile on his thin lips. "He said her name was Laris."

Chapter 14

"Miss Harper, you disregarded curfew and you encouraged the police to interact with my daughter! Not to mention, you let my daughter be involved in a murder!" Lord Stadler took a deep breath in and let it out slowly.

Some of the fury vanished from his face, to be replaced by a steely calm. He had the lamp turned on next to him, bathing him in a yellow glow. He sat with his legs crossed in the chair nearest to the window, the same chair he had been sitting in when they first met.

"I'm sorry, sir," apologized Vara.

"Sorry doesn't precisely cover it. If you persist in disobeying me, I won't hesitate in making your future prospects for employment slim," he reminded her.

"What do you suggest we should have done?" Vara argued. "Run from the scene of the crime? The police would have found out eventually that we had been there, and then it would have looked like we were guilty or hiding something."

"You could have stopped it from happening! I've read your file. You are fully capable of keeping her contained. I hope that my trust isn't misplaced. I just spent all morning covering for your last scandal. May I remind you that I specifically instructed you that I want everything looking normal. Spending the afternoon at the police station is not what I would define as looking normal!"

"Don't you care about your daughter at all? She just witnessed someone get killed in front of her! And whatever you did to silence that story didn't work. Richard had a clipping of the article that ran in today's paper."

His eyes burned with a deep fire. "I love my daughter very much," he said through gritted teeth, his fury barely restrained. Vara felt the air grow hot around them from his temper. "I resent that you would suggest otherwise. But I still have need of your services so I shall overlook that for the time being. It is unfortunate that my daughter had to be exposed to that, but it wasn't unexpected in his line of work. Now, I'd better not have any further reason to have words with you."

"It won't happen again, sir," she responded.

"Ren has dinner waiting for you in the dining room."

Vara took that as a dismissal and scuttled out of the room. The whole conversation left her with a sick feeling in the depths of her stomach. It was as if he didn't even care that one of his staff had died.

Vara was in the middle of leaving yet another message on her mom's voice mail when the call waiting rudely beeped at her.

Her mother's voice crackled on the other end. "Vara, what's wrong?"

"I—" She could feel Sam's spell taking hold, gluing her mouth shut. There was nothing she could say that wouldn't involve telling her mother about the job. "Tell me you and Dad are both all right. I need to hear it from you and not a recording."

Thunder rumbled outside as if sensing her mother's emotions. Maybe it was. It had been a clear night when Vara had closed the window curtains.

"I need to know the truth. I need to know that Dad isn't lying in a ditch somewhere like—" The spell refused to let her say Richard's name. It probably wouldn't let her talk to her mom about Derek then either.

"Vara, you shouldn't worry about us. Your father is fine. And don't come here looking for us. I need you to stay home and away from any and all magic. Can you do that for me?"

She felt like her jaw was about to break holding in what she couldn't say.

"Good," her mother said without even waiting for Vara's response. "I'll be here for another couple of days." The dial tone clicked on as she hung up on her end.

Vara had been lying in bed for half an hour and sleep was remaining just out of reach. Richard's dead body appeared each time her eyes closed.

His eyes stared vacantly at the ceiling above him, his shirt drenched with blood. His chest rose and fell once, and his brown eyes swiveled in their sockets to rest on her. His mouth opened, but instead of words, an agonized scream escaped.

Laris bent over his body. "It's my fault he's dead," she whispered. She lifted her hand that pressed the wound on his chest and brought it to her face, painting a trail of blood from her hairline to her mouth. Richard's blood dripped down from her forehead past her eyes and over her nose. The corners of her mouth turned up in a smile as she gently tasted the blood in her hand with her tongue.

There was a pounding on the parking lot door behind Vara and the raised voices of security guards. Her eyes cracked open in the darkness, as the pounding continued. It dawned on her that the knocking sound was coming from her bedroom door. She felt around for the lamp beside her bed and turned it on.

Light illuminated the dark red room. She got out of bed, unlocked the door, and pulled it open.

Laris stood in the open doorway. Her slightly curled golden hair hung loose about her shoulders. She looked rather disheveled and she was still in the same pink blouse and red pleated skirt from earlier. There were several disturbing rust-colored splotches on her blouse as if an artist had attacked her while in the middle of painting a shaded fire engine.

Vara looked at her for a couple of minutes before it registered that Laris hadn't said anything and was just staring through her as if she was invisible.

"Did you want something?" Vara asked, still bleary with sleep.

Laris's eyes focused on Vara, and her body shuddered for a moment. Her eyes welled up and spilled over. Tears streamed down her face. Vara felt panic bubble to the surface.

She was way out of her league.

She awkwardly grabbed Laris's wrist and pulled her from the hallway and into the red room. She guided Laris over to the bed and made her sit down.

A sob forced its way out of Laris's throat, followed by another and yet another. Vara hugged Laris as the girl shook with sobs. Vara waited until the sobs subsided before she released her.

"Feel any better?" Vara asked.

"A little. I'm sorry. But there wasn't anyone else to talk to."

"How about your father?"

Laris shook her head. "He can't ever know about Richard and me. He'd disown me."

"I doubt it. He's your father."

"You don't know him. He thinks it tarnishes my reputation just talking to people of other species as if they were on my social level. But Richard. . . ." Laris closed her eyes and a sad smile pulled up the corners of her mouth. "He made me feel so safe."

"What happened anyway? You didn't . . . did you?"

"I don't. . . . I couldn't. . . ." she sobbed and covered her face with her hands.

Vara put a hand on her shoulder. "It's okay. I shouldn't have asked. I'm sorry."

Laris took a long breath and peeked through her fingers. Her eyes focused on the red-shaded bedside lamp. "There was a demon," she said barely above a whisper.

That wasn't good. Most demons loved to torment people, but they couldn't kill on their own. And to be able to control a demon enough to direct it to kill a specific person would take a lot of power.

Making her remember the scene of the crime wasn't helping. "Tell me about Richard," Vara said as she tried to change the topic. "What was he like?"

Laris closed her eyes and smiled weakly. "I had only known him for a month, but it felt like I hadn't really been happy before meeting him. Have you ever been with anyone like that?"

"There was someone for a while. But we had some differences." Vara felt her throat constrict painfully and her voice start to tremble. "At least you know he loved you right up till the end." She tried to smile. Laris didn't need to see her pain in addition to her own.

"How about we plan to spend tomorrow here?" Vara suggested. "Your father made it very clear that he doesn't want us involved in any more scandals or it will mean the end of my working anywhere."

Laris scrunched up her face in a pout. "But it's so boring around here."

"I wouldn't mind walking around that village down the road. Do they have any interesting shops there?"

"I don't know," she admitted. "I've only been to Father's nightclub there. There weren't any shopping malls, so I never bothered to check the rest of the village out."

"Well then, it'll be new to both of us. Now, let's get some sleep."

Laris paused in the open doorway and turned to face Vara. "Why do you lock your door? Is it because of me?"

She mentally kicked herself. The wolf inside Laris hadn't even crossed her mind. "I lock it because there are others in this house I don't trust," she admitted truthfully.

"My father?" Laris looked shocked.

"I don't trust your housekeeper, Ren." Vara shivered as she thought of Ren's tiny inhuman eyes boring into her soul.

Laris seemed to mull the information over. "I'm just glad it's not because of me." She gave Vara a slight smile and left the room. Vara locked the door and climbed back into bed. It was hard to think of Laris as a killer. She seemed so weak and defenseless and like she had given up the passion to fight that she had had just the previous evening. It was unnerving to see so much change in a person.

"And it's not because of me either."

Vara sat up with a jolt as she realized that she wasn't alone. Laris's lilac perfume had dissipated enough that she could smell the rank scent of onions building in power. Sam lounged on the small sofa in the corner of her room. He had his ghostly legs crossed and was leisurely swinging them over the end of the sofa. The translucent white skin at the corners of his hollow eyes crinkled as his grin grew broader.

"Let's hear it," she said with a yawn. "Go ahead and go through your list of how I screwed up the day. Just get it over with so I can go back to sleep."

His grin puckered into a playful pout. "But you are so much fun to watch over. Where to start . . . where to start. . . . The client was furious that you allowed your charge out of your eyesight. That is never to happen again while you are on this position."

"Hang on, who told him that I lost Laris?" She didn't want to admit to herself that it had most likely been Derek, trying to make her lose her job. She knew he didn't want her there, but would he have actually gone to that extreme? Could the day get any worse?

"Suffice to say, he knows," he continued. "And the Agency is furious that you went to the local police without checking with them first."

"They actually expect me to call them first when there is someone about to bleed to death? That's rich."

"The client isn't happy that you have brought his family into the papers with negative publicity, yet again. He is adamant that you should have been able to prevent it or at least have been able to keep his family from being mentioned or seen."

"He's famous. You'd think he'd welcome being the talk of the town."

Sam's empty eye sockets narrowed. "He doesn't appreciate his daughter being labeled a murderess," he said with a dangerous edge to his gravelly voice.

Vara winced. But it wasn't like she could have just covered it up. Reporters had been lying in wait, just outside of the parking lot, drawn by the blood of the crime scene like vultures. "Well then, he should be happy tomorrow since I have convinced Laris to spend the day around here."

"The Agency feels that it would be best if you come to the office in person tomorrow," Sam said with a grin. "They don't think you properly grasp just how important this position is. And bring your charge. They wish to know her emotional state after this incident."

HIRED BY A DEMON

"She's devastated, of course," Vara told him, exasperated. "It isn't every day a girl loses someone she was attached to."

"Are you attached to that red-haired guard of hers?" His empty eye sockets narrowed, as if watching her closely. His gravelly voice dropped another octave, as if imparting some vital secret. "I saw the way you were looking at him."

If she didn't know any better, she would have sworn he was jealous. But he was a demon, and demons weren't supposed to have emotions, other than a love of seeing others in pain. "It's all in the past."

He opened his mouth as he let the light glitter off his pointed teeth. His eerie booming laughter filled the room. "I don't believe you." His voice dropped dangerously low and flames flickered in his eye sockets.

She rolled onto her side, pulled up the covers, and hoped he didn't notice the faint shiver that ran through her body. "Whatever," she whispered as she tried to put enough volume into it for him to hear. Had she managed to keep the tremor out of her voice? Sam had been her supervisor for a little over a year, and he had played the part of being scary before. He seemed to like how she jumped at the sight of his teeth, but never had he been downright dangerous to her before, where she actually had to worry that he might do something to her.

She peeked out of the covers. It had gotten too quiet in her room.

The ghostly demon rose from the sofa. His green cloud of rotting onions and decay followed in his wake. "You have a 9:00 a.m. appointment with Mr. Kendrick and Ms. Clarke."

He glided over to where Vara lay in bed. She felt his sharp teeth against her ear as he leaned down next to her. His voice dropped to a nightmarish rumble as he pronounced each word distinctly. It echoed in the confines of her skull. "Don't be late."

"The Heads of the Agency?" she sputtered and clutched the blanket tighter about her. Her teeth chattered as a cold chill ran up her spine and spread through to her fingers and toes, and the nightmare image of Sam grinning at her with his pointed teeth ceased to be scary in relation to a meeting with the Agency Heads. She felt each breath in her chest and the pounding of her heart in her ears. She had thought they were just an urban legend to keep the employees in line.

No one had ever met with them. But there were rumors flying around about them. She heard that they weren't human, not even vaguely. They were actually the great forces of the universe, of good and evil, destiny and fate, light and darkness.

They had eyes that could see into the depths of your soul and know everything about you right down to the dreams that you keep hidden deep in your subconscious.

It was said no one had ever returned from a meeting with the Agency Heads.

Chapter 15

Time was running out and Austen could feel the frost of morning in the air. Another day had slipped by and he still hadn't made any progress toward saving Laris. If anything, he had just doomed her.

His heart labored in his chest as he pushed on. Just a little further and he would be home, he told his aching feet. And then he could ask his family for help. He hated having to admit defeat, especially to his older brother Kalen.

The forest finally gave way to the large grassy meadow that lay at the base of the mountain where their family grotto was built.

His momentum carried him right into a dense crowd of people. No, he corrected himself, not people. The crowd was entirely made up of Nature Children. Every single one of them looked underfed, with taut grey skin stretched over high cheek bones, long pointed ears, and most importantly, the bulk of the crowd stood a head or two shorter than him. He felt his spine unconsciously slouching since he had gotten used to looking up at people while being around the humans.

The gathering stretched all the way to the base of the mountain. Most of them had their hands raised to the sky and chanted in high trills. The air around him was alive with the angelic humming of hundreds of voices.

On the other side of the meadow, in front of the base of the mountain, a lady with long gleaming white hair stood on a large stone that towered over the crowd.

She wore an ice blue gossamer dress that rippled in the chill wind and a crystal crown that reflected the light of the rising sun. It sent splinters of prismatic color across the crowd in front of her. Her high shimmering voice carried on the wind above everyone else's. It was his mother.

He could almost catch the faint notes of the flute player accompanying her mournful chant. He knew the melody well. They played it each year to say a sad farewell to the warmth of summer and welcome in the bitter winter.

His blood suddenly shifted to ice water in his veins. This was the Winter Ceremony and he was supposed to be doing the flute accompaniment himself. With trying to solve Laris's problem, he had completely forgotten.

It couldn't be helped now. He would just have to hide until the ceremony was over. Then he could make a proper apology to his mother. He turned to duck back into the forest.

"Where have you been, and why aren't you dressed for the ceremony?" demanded a young woman in a short golden dress standing directly in front of him. She had her arms folded and a murderous look on her sharp face. Even with being a full head shorter than him, she was very intimidating. "You aren't even wearing a shirt! I can't believe you came dressed like this to the ceremony!"

She pushed herself up on the tips of her toes, bringing her face practically within kissing range of his lips. Her eyes narrowed as they flitted over every crease in his face. She took a step back as her face contorted into a mangled look of fury. "You forgot, didn't you!" her squeaky voice wailed in outrage. "Austen, Mother was counting on you to be here!"

"Tari, I'm sorry," he said more out of reflex than actual apology. He knew there was nothing he could do to appease her. He would always be a disappointment in his older sister's eyes. She had inherited their father's desire for perfection, same as Kalen.

Austen knew he was a far cry from perfect with his tangled black curls and the fact that formal clothes never hung right on him, not to mention that he just didn't have the ethereal grace of the rest of his family. He felt like a bumbling buffoon in comparison.

"How could you let Mother down like this?" Tari accused. "This is one of the most important ceremonies of the year! You know that! Nevi had to step in as her Second because you couldn't be bothered to be here on time."

"Nevi?" His mother must have been desperate. Nevi was a year younger than Tari, but they were as different as night and day. Where Tari was strong and outgoing, Nevi was frail and fragile. Even now he could hear the flute notes wavering. "Why isn't Kalen here?"

"The King sent for him," Tari answered simply.

"The King? Why?" Their mother was the King's favorite cousin and she was called to the Court frequently. Because she had to perform the Winter Ceremony, it was only natural for Kalen to be sent in her place. He was first in line to inherit the family position and responsibilities since their father had passed away several years ago. But what was so important for the King to actually drag one of their family members away from the ceremony?

"I don't know," said Tari. "You'll have to ask him when he gets back." She grabbed his wrist and painfully yanked him through the crowd. "I suppose we should be glad you showed up at all."

His wrist had turned an ugly shade of red by the time Tari had succeeded in pulling him the entire way across the crowded meadow to the door to their home. There were several circular carvings swirled together in the rugged stone of the mountain that looked something like an ancient ancestor of a musical note.

Tari grasped the edge of the stone carving and pulled it open just as easily as if it had been made out of wood. Behind it was a short flight of stairs that descended into the darkness.

She paused to light a couple of the floating orbs which made the interior dance with a soft glow, which was just a show of power since the Nature Children could see in the darkness just as easily as broad daylight.

She didn't lessen her grip on his wrist until they had reached his room. She pulled open the large trunk next to his bed and rifled through it. She pulled out his blue tunic and dress pants.

"Tari, just stop it! I didn't mean to miss the ceremony, but I don't have time for it. I only came back here to get help."

"You don't understand how important this ceremony is, do you?" The look on her face was exasperation warring with despair. "She needed all of us with her."

Austen seethed. He hated her reminding him just how much more important Nature matters were compared to his human life. She didn't have any concept of what was at stake here. And why was he the only one getting blamed for being absent? "If it's so important, why isn't Kalen here, too? He could have said no to the King and that the obligation to his family was more important."

"Because I had important matters to discuss with the King, Little Brother." Kalen's voice was pure magic to listen to. It was the rumbling of a summertime rain shower with the promise of warm sunlight. He stood in the empty doorway with the light from the orbs dancing over his long white hair, which fell past his shoulders and over his muscular biceps.

His elaborately embroidered silver court tunic stretched taut over muscles, honed from daily hunting after forest nymphs. And for all of his breadth, he still had the sinuous grace of everyone in their family, save Austen. "Now, what brings you back here, if not the Winter Ceremony?"

Austen sucked in his breath and braced himself for either Kalen's taunting laughter or an inevitable lecture. There was no chance his brother would pass up the opportunity to take pleasure in Austen's defeat. "I need help, Brother. The girl I was working for got bit by a wolf. I sought out a professional hunter to kill the wolf that bit her, so the curse would be removed. And now the hunter is after her, as well. She doesn't stand a chance against a professional killer."

A smile pulled at the edge of Kalen's thin lips. "I'll give you a piece of advice, Little Brother. Forget about her."

"No! Kalen, please, I need to save her." Desperation saturated Austen's voice.

"I'm sorry then."

"You won't help me?" He had counted too much on his family being obligated to help him. He felt his muscles tighten and itched to knock the smile off Kalen's face so much that it hurt.

"I mean, I can't help you," Kalen said as the smile on his lips faltered slightly. "And you won't be able to return to her either. I'm sorry, Brother."

Kalen had never stood in his way before. He usually took a perverse pleasure in watching Austen fail at things rather than lift a finger to stop him. He didn't know what Kalen was trying to accomplish, nor did he care. He wasn't tied up, and Kalen didn't look like he was tensing himself to physically or even magically restrain him. He would just have to figure out a way to take out the hunter on his own.

He leveled a glare at Kalen. "You don't have the power to keep me here."

"Go ahead and try to get back to the humans, if you don't believe me."

Slowly, letting each word bite the air as if they were poisonous, Austen asked, "Kalen, what did you do?"

Chapter 16

Before Vara knew it, morning light filtered through the mansion and her dreams were vanishing quickly, though she could still recall images of blood and razor-sharp white teeth.

She was not starting the day off on a good foot. She had wanted to call her mom. She needed some reassurance before facing the Agency Heads. But her cell phone was nowhere to be found. She searched her bag twice, and even crawled all the way under the bed, and came back out with no phone and her hair completely grey with dust.

Her mind immediately suspected Ren, but she couldn't just outright go to Lord Stadler when she was already in such poor favor. Most likely she had probably left it somewhere and it got knocked off and rolled out of sight. She would just have to hunt her room thoroughly later.

She found Laris eating breakfast in the dining room by herself. She was devouring her way through a small plate of sausages.

"Where's your father this morning?" Vara asked as she tried not to stare.

Laris's head whipped in Vara's direction, startled. Her eyes narrowed as she watched Vara, while one hand wrapped itself around the plate in front of her, as if she was waiting for Vara to try to grab it away from her. "He left before I woke up. He probably had a business meeting."

"I would've thought he would be here with you."

She gave Vara a long searching look, as if she had come

up with a completely foreign concept.

"I know you were looking forward to our exploration of the village, but would you mind a change in plans?" Vara asked.

The edge of Laris's mouth swept upwards as she attempted to smother a laugh. "By all means, change away."

"My supervisor mentioned that the superiors at my Placement Agency would like a word with me."

She smothered a laugh. "Not surprising."

"He also said I should bring you along with me."

"Why?" she asked suspiciously.

"He said they wish to know your emotional state. They probably just want to make certain that I haven't completely botched this job and turned you into an emotional wreck."

"I wouldn't mind being allowed to voice my own opinion on your performance," said the socialite. A malicious smile danced about her lips. "We shall go in twenty minutes then." She daintily dabbed at the edges of her mouth with her napkin and set it down next to her empty breakfast plate.

She swept out of the dining room and left Vara alone with just the lingering sticky scent of maple syrup.

Vara stared at the yellow stained napkin. There didn't seem to be anything left of the distraught girl crying last night in her doorway. Was this her superior façade taking control, or was the wolf now in charge?

In dark sunglasses, looking like a famous movie star, Laris pulled open the front door and strolled out into the warm morning light. It glittered and danced off her curly blonde hair. She wore a light blue dress in a similar style to Vara's, but with matching shoes and a wide brimmed hat that shaded her blue eyes.

Derek followed behind her like a storm cloud with a scowl plastered on his face, as if letting Laris leave the mansion went against his better judgment. He shot Vara a quick glare that seemed to blame her for whatever bad events he was imagining.

Even the scope of his hate didn't compare to the pain of her stomach eating itself from the inside out as she imagined the horrors of what the Agency Heads might look like or what they could do to her.

"The Kendrick & Clarke Temp Agency," she told Derek as she tried to force her voice above a whisper when they finally reached the transit circle.

She needed a friend. She wished she could talk to him the way she used to. She knew the tightened ball of electricity that crackled in her stomach would ease with just a glimpse of his warm smile. If only she could catch his eyes for a moment. He'd see how much having to go in to see the bosses was gnawing at her, but his eyes persistently remained glued somewhere above her head.

He stepped into the center of the circle and let his gaze sweep over to Laris. He gave her a curt nod. His lips quietly moved and then he was encased by the usual red glow and vanished, leaving the circle empty.

They waited the couple of minutes in silence. Vara actually wished that Derek would come back and tell them that there were tabloid reporters mobbing the place, or a pack of Laris's fans waiting to ambush her, anything that would delay them from seeing the Agency Heads. It felt like a betrayal when the circle remained empty. Maybe he thought she deserved to be thrown to the lions.

Laris and Vara stepped into the center of the circle, and Vara searched around inside herself for the usual minuscule wad of magic. She grasped Laris's hand. "The Kendrick & Clarke Placement Agency," she ordered and pushed the magic down through her feet. It danced along the carved rune markings, turning them red with electricity. It radiated out to the edges of the circle and then grew upward and engulfed them in the energy.

As soon as the red haze vanished, they were assaulted by the honks of the traffic around them. Skyscrapers loomed over them, shadowing them from the mid-morning sun.

Vara yelped in sudden pain, as Laris gripped her hand so hard her nails dug into her flesh. Laris's rosy cheeks were nearly scarlet and her eyes glowed with a fevered brightness.

"Derek!" Vara shouted.

He stopped scanning the street for any sign of recognition from any of the passersby, shot her a look of undisguised fury, and bolted to where they stood. He forced one of Laris's hands to release her excruciating grip on Vara and wrapped it around his shoulders.

He led them into the nearest building and guided them over to a small cushioned bench off to the side. The people who rushed to and from the elevators toward the back of the lobby paid them no attention.

After a couple of minutes, Laris's flushed face slowly returned to its normal shade. She took a shaky breath in and let it out. "I'm all right. It was just the magic."

"I shouldn't have brought you," said Vara. "You're going to be exposed to a lot of people with magic inside the Agency. Not to mention the demons and other spirits employed there. Do you think you will be able to keep yourself under control?"

"You said they want me here. And who am I to deny my adoring public?" Laris gave her a carefree smile, tossed a lock of her hair over one shoulder, and struck a pose as if for a publicity photograph.

Vara stood up to follow Laris to the elevators, when a muscular hand clamped onto her wrist.

Derek's eyes still refused to acknowledge her and were glued on Laris as she approached the elevators. "Vara, this is a bad idea."

"And what would you have me do?" she asked. "If the Agency Heads want to talk to her, they'll find a way, whether we want them to or not."

"They're not gods. There's no possible way they could be that powerful." Was he actually trying to alleviate her fears? His eyes were still glued on Laris as she hunted through the list of offices displayed next to the elevator doors. No, he was just trying to convince himself he could protect her from them.

"How do you know?" Vara asked. "Have you ever met with them?"

"Vara, it's just a job," he reminded her. "And they are just employers. We shouldn't be risking her life just because you're afraid of getting fired."

No wonder he was mad at her. "I have more on the line than just this job. Now, if you don't let me go, she's going to end up going to the office without us."

Derek let go of her wrist and they hurried to join Laris before she slipped inside the elevator.

They finally reached their floor and piled out with several young men and an elderly woman. The woman had a green imp with her carrying her briefcase under one arm as he waddled along next to her.

Laris had been pinching her nose delicately ever since they got into the elevator. She stared at the imp's back with a burning, unfocused look. They followed the lady with the imp all the way to the glass doors of the Agency's main office.

"May I help you?" asked one of the young ladies at the front desk. She had her dark hair up in a bun and wore a pair of gold-rimmed glasses. She smiled as Vara approached her.

"My name is Vara Harper and my supervisor Samanith said I should come in. He said that the company heads want to have a word with me."

The lady behind the desk cocked her head to the side and a vacant look crossed her eyes for a moment as she talked to someone telepathically. "Ah, yes, they are expecting you. And your charge is to wait for you in the meeting room next door to the senior office. You can follow me."

She came out from behind the desk and took the three of them to the door that led into the back of the office. They followed her down a long corridor lined with doors that led to smaller office rooms.

"Your charge and her guard are to wait here," she said as she pushed open a door to a small room with a table in the center with chairs around it.

A lady in a dark red dress with black hair that curled fashionably around her chin sat in one of the chairs and smiled at Laris.

Laris joined the lady at the table, with Derek following behind her. The receptionist closed the door and continued to the room next to it and knocked politely. She pushed the door open, let Vara enter, and closed it behind her.

The room was the size of a game field with the ceiling at least a mile above her. She heard the pounding of her heart echo off the walls around her as she crossed the room.

In front of her sat four people at a desk perched on a ledge high above her head. The angle forced her to look up at them. Three of them were men all dressed in black business suits, along with one lady dressed completely in white. Against the blue and green of the room, she was almost blinding to look at. The lady smiled down on Vara and reminded her of a snake looking at a fat mouse.

"I am Hallcine Clarke and this is my associate Crane Kendrick," the woman in white said as she turned slightly to the middle-aged man on her left. Her sugar sweet voice oozed with charm and benevolence. "Have a seat, Miss Harper. In the chair next to you, of course."

The room had been empty when Vara made her long trek across it. So, just to prove Ms. Clarke wrong, Vara did an exaggerated spin to check the whole room. She stopped dead in her tracks when she spotted a blue plastic chair that sat no farther than a foot away from her.

She hadn't heard anyone else enter the room, and she certainly hadn't noticed anyone else that close to her within the last couple of minutes. Ms. Clarke chuckled with her associates as Vara hesitantly touched it to reassure herself of its solidness before sitting down.

They weren't the creatures of nightmare that her imagination had run wild picturing them as, but they were no less intimidating. Raw magical power radiated from them with the intensity of a scorching summer day. It far eclipsed the magic that flowed from the professors that she had studied under at the Conservatory.

The closer that she looked at them, the more inhuman they appeared. The man on the far right seemed to draw in all the shadows in the room. They slid up the side of the desk and flowed into his fingertips as if they were pets he had called home.

The man on the left had blue electricity dancing on the surface of his skin. Mr. Kendrick and Ms. Clarke were equally hard to look at. Her brilliance was painful to the eyes, while his appearance didn't seem to want to stay in focus. The features of his face shifted and changed, as if he were still trying to decide what he wanted to look like.

"Now, Miss Harper," said Ms. Clarke as she paused to look up from the file she had been flipping through. She let her luminous ice blue eyes rest on Vara. "We have been informed that you seem to have little respect for the client's name and status. You seem to take delight in dragging his family's name through the mud in tabloids."

She pulled out a newspaper clipping from the file and pushed it to the edge of the desk. It teetered on the brink for a moment and then fell. It drifted through the air to land on Vara's lap. It was the same clipping Richard had shown them at lunch yesterday with a large picture of Laris and Vara as they talked quietly together.

Ms. Clarke pulled out another newspaper page from the file and unfolded it. She pushed that off the desk as well. It flipped and danced as it made its descent and finally landed on top of the first article. This second article had a large heading that took up half the page. 'HEIRESS'S BOY-TOY BEAU SLAUGHTERED' it read with a photograph of Richard's bloody body underneath with white police tape outlining him.

Vara wondered vaguely who put it together that Richard was her boyfriend, or was that just a lucky guess meant to draw in more readers?

"The young man was one of our employees," said Ms. Clarke as she turned to her associates. "We were forced to pay death benefits to his family."

"I wasn't the one who killed him," Vara objected.

"We know that."

She looked up, suddenly suspicious. Just how much about Richard's death did they know?

"We won't be taking the cost of the death benefits out of your paycheck. However, we would like to keep the client appeased. He is extremely important to us, as is his daughter, so we have promised that you won't give any further opportunities for scandal, or there will be consequences. Do I make myself clear?"

"Yes, Ma'am," Vara responded.

"We also know you have been thinking of leaving this position." Ms. Clarke paused to give Vara a long hard look with her steely ice blue eyes. "You signed a blood contract with us. You cannot leave until the contract has been fulfilled or terminated by the client. Now if that is all, we thank you for coming in and hope further meetings won't be necessary. You may escort Miss Harper back to the reception area."

The smell of rotten onions was overwhelming. If there had been fresh flowers in the office, they would have withered. "Cause any more scandals this morning?" Sam whispered into her ear.

"The day is still young," Vara whispered back as she followed the demon out of the room. She waited until they were halfway down the hallway, well out of hearing range of the Agency Heads before she asked, "Were you listening in on the meeting, Sam?" Though with their powers, she wouldn't have been surprised if they still could have heard them since they knew things she hadn't told anyone.

He grinned so broadly she could see his razor-sharp teeth. "They are a delightful bunch when you work in the office with them."

"They all seem to be worried about something, and especially about me leaving the position. How do they know everything, Sam? Do they have a spy watching me? Or do they employ some sort of an Oracle?"

His broad grin grew more serious. He did a mockery of a human looking down both directions of the hallway. "Let's just say they do have access to one."

"To which? A spy or an Oracle?"

Sam smiled showing off his pointed teeth. She shuddered as she remembered how dangerous he had seemed the previous night.

"Never mind. So, am I free to go?"

"Yes, back to your friends so you can amuse me with more scandals." He faded from existence, leaving her alone in the hallway.

She spotted Laris sitting in one of the chairs by the window as soon as she entered the reception area. Laris had a vacant expression on her face. Derek stood next to her, with his back to the window and his arms folded.

As Vara approached him, she noticed he had several thin red scratches that ran down the side of his cheek. He glared at her with murderous fury.

"We are going now," he growled as soon as she got close enough that he didn't have to shout.

"What happened?" She looked between him and Laris. But he had already turned to Laris and offered her a hand up.

As Laris moved, her hand that was rubbing absently at her left shoulder dropped. On the bare skin of her shoulder was a small angry red mark about the size of a cigarette burn. Vara stopped Laris immediately as she grabbed the heiress's arm to get a better look at the mark. Laris roughly pushed her away.

"Get your hands off me!" Laris snapped, her voice nearly a wolf growl.

"But. . . ." Vara darted a look around. Everyone in the room had stopped what they were doing to watch them. Even the girl she had talked to earlier at the front desk watched them intently with her head cocked to one side, probably to alert security if anything more happened.

Vara looked at Derek, but he shook his head. "We need to get her out of here now!" he repeated. He wrapped his arms around Laris and swept her out of the office, not even bothering to check if Vara was behind them or not. She had to run to keep up with Laris and Derek as they raced to the elevators and pushed the button to call the elevator to their floor. He hit it repeatedly when the doors didn't immediately open.

"Derek, please, what happened?"

Chapter 17

Kalen smiled. "You'd like to think I did something, wouldn't you? But I didn't. It's not in my power. It is, however, in the King's power."

Anger surged through Austen. "Kalen, tell me right now."

"There is a war brewing, Brother. The demons have been talking about an uprising. They are just looking to be released from their world and then they will take over the human world. The King has sealed our borders with the human realm. He will not allow the demons to flood our world, too. Not after the last time. And we need time to prepare. He asked me to deliver the news during the Winter Ceremony. Come outside and watch me make history."

Before Austen could even open his mouth, his brother had already swept out of the room. He hadn't come all this way just to get trapped here.

He strode over to his closet door, ignoring that Tari was following his every move. He closed his eyes and wished for the Stadler Estate with all of his might and threw open the door to his closet. There was nothing but his clothes and boots inside. He put his hand all the way to the back of the closet, but it still remained merely solid wood. He collapsed to his knees and felt under his bed. There was solid wood there, too. It was true. He was trapped.

"Austen. . . ."

"Don't start with me, Tari," he warned.

"Maybe it's for the best."

He glared at her and immediately regretted it as he saw the surprise in her blue eyes. "Tari, I can't stay here. She'll be a monster forever if I don't get back."

"You should talk to Mother," she suggested. "Maybe she can help."

He was already in trouble for missing the Winter Ceremony. "You go ahead, Tari. I'll be right behind you." He picked up the blue tunic and gave it a long look. The door to his room clicked shut as Tari left. He immediately dropped the tunic. He couldn't think of anything his mother could do that wouldn't involve petitioning the Court to be allowed to leave, and that could take weeks, which he didn't have. But he did have one chance.

He shoved everything off his dresser and pulled out a stick of chalk from his desk. On the surface of the desk, he drew a large circle that touched the edges of it. He added all of the markings around the edges and stood back to make certain everything was correct. His reflection in the mirror above his dresser stared back at him sternly.

He rummaged around in the chest that had contained his ceremony outfit and pulled out five ornate pure silver ceremonial knives. He stashed four of them in his bag and used the fifth to make a thin cut across his palm. He climbed on top of the dresser and put his hand to the mirror. His reflection smiled at him and opened his mouth in a laugh. Panic suddenly shocked through his nerves. The world around him pitched dizzyingly and he plunged headfirst into the mirror.

He blinked his eyes as he tried to clear them, but he realized there was nothing but darkness all around him. Though the longer he stared at it, he noticed a red glow, almost as if there was a setting sun on the horizon. His vision tilted sickeningly as he sat up.

And then he remembered where he was. He needed to get out of there fast! The demons would kill him on the spot just for being a Nature Child. He rested a hand on the ground and tried to call to the earth to lend him some power, but nothing answered his call. The ground underneath him felt loose, and he realized it wasn't actually ground, but hardened soot from the many eons of it raining down on the land.

He dug around inside himself. He would just have to use his own resources. How long had he been unconscious? He felt drained, as if a leech had been at him.

"You should not have disappeared like that," said a familiar voice.

"Sam! Please, I need to get out of here!"

"My people won't like you being here," noted Samanith.

"I know, but I had no choice," Austen admitted. "But you could just take me back to the humans. Then none of your people will have to know I was ever here."

It was his imagination that saw a smile at the edges of Sam's gaping mouth, just a trick of the darkness, nothing more.

"I need to put you somewhere safe, so you can return to work at the agreed upon time. Yes, that's what must be done."

Austen felt a wisp of smoke wrap around his wrist and then his waist, and around his neck. It pulled all of his limbs together. He struggled against his bonds. "Demon, let me go!"

"She shall be happy with this temporary tribute," whispered Sam's voice with a gleeful note.

Chapter 18

"This would be easier if you would just let me heal you," Ren chirped. He danced around Derek with a cloth soaked with antiseptic.

"No. It would leave a trace of magic, and she shouldn't have any more around her than can be helped." He sharply hissed as Ren slapped the cloth to his wounded cheek. Derek still hadn't calmed down, even though they had returned to the safety of the Stadler mansion.

He turned to level a scorching glare at Vara. "Her father should have never hired you! Anyone else would have had better sense than to get caught by the tabloids twice and actually merit being reprimanded by the Agency Heads!"

"How many times do I have to say I'm sorry?" she whined.

"At least once more," he retorted.

"Derek, please, what happened?"

"It wasn't Laris's fault," he said, though it sounded like he was trying to convince himself more than her. "That lady battered her with questions about Richard. I'm surprised she lasted as long as she did."

"What happened?" Vara repeated, her patience wearing thin.

"She accused Laris of not having a heart. And not actually caring about Richard. I think she was deliberately trying to provoke her. Laris tried to slap her. And I tried to stop her."

"Derek, you don't get cuts down the side of your face from a slap," she pointed out.

"I don't know. It started out as a slap, but suddenly her nails were dragging through my skin. Either way it's not her fault, and there's no damage done."

"And the mark on her arm?" she prompted.

"The lady had a syringe in the drawer of the desk, as if she had been expecting her to react. Laris just seemed to go limp when she touched her with it. Why did they do it, Vara? I'm supposed to be protecting her. But this is the company that hired me to protect her. Am I actually supposed to protect her from them as well?"

"I'm sorry, Derek, I don't know."

Derek did his best to talk them out of yet another excursion out of the mansion. But this time it was Laris who was insistent. And what the client wants, the client gets.

It seemed silly to use the transit circle for a jump that couldn't be more than a mile distant. But Laris told Vara rather pointedly that it wasn't fashionable to walk when they didn't have to. So, the two of them fidgeted as Derek ported to the small village ahead of them. Vara vacantly watched the transit circle for any hint of a red glow, though she didn't expect that the village would prove to be dangerous.

"So, why did you change your mind about the town, especially after what happened today?" she asked.

"I still think the town is boringly dull. But I need to visit someone there before the wolf takes over completely." Laris quickly smiled as she tried to banish the bleakness in her eyes as Vara turned to her. "Derek—you knew him before I introduced you two, didn't you?"

Vara let out the breath she hadn't realized she had been holding. "Yeah."

"Is he the one you were talking about when I had asked you if you had loved anyone before?"

"He broke it off," said Vara. "He decided that I didn't appreciate the magic world and that included himself."

"And was he right?"

"I don't know," Vara admitted. "Maybe, at the time."

"What about now?" she asked. "Do you still love him?"

Vara's eyes burned with tears yet to fall. She turned away from Laris. "It doesn't matter. He doesn't want to talk to me. And he definitely doesn't want me here."

"Are you sure about that?"

She couldn't detect anything other than innocent inquiry in Laris's voice, and she wasn't going to turn around and let Laris see her reddened eyes. She tried to lighten her voice with a laugh, though it sounded rather strangled. "Yes, I'm sure. Now, are you sure you're up to this?" They had given Derek more than enough time to secure the area. Vara stepped onto the transit circle and tentatively held out a hand in Laris's direction.

Laris favored her with a grin. The nightmare image of Laris with Richard's blood dripping down from the corners of her mouth flickered through Vara's mind and she retracted her hand a fraction of an inch.

The smile immediately vanished from Laris's face. "What's wrong?"

"I'm sorry," Vara hastily apologized. "It's nothing." Laris needed a friend and Vara was still having trouble seeing anything other than the wolf in her. She deserved better than that. Vara secured her grip on Laris's arm a bit tighter than usual and dug into herself for the bright pulsing pinpoint of magic.

"Covington County Church," Laris supplied.

Vara repeated the name and sent the bead of magic flowing through her body and into the ground at their feet to ignite the circle. Her vision was washed in the usual red glow and then it subsided. It left behind a cloud of musty smelling grey dust that swirled about their feet. They were standing in a transit circle just outside of a small white painted church.

Laris's skin burned beneath Vara's fingers and a fevered look blazed in her eyes. She leaned closer to Vara, breathed in and smiled with a glazed hungry look to her eyes as she slowly exhaled. Vara raised one hand in uncertainty. Would slapping her be the right thing to do? She didn't want to hurt her, but the look in Laris's eyes scared her. Or would physical pain just excite the monster inside her?

Heavy footsteps pounded toward them. And suddenly

strong hands tore the two of them apart. Laris staggered. She closed her eyes and shook her head. When she opened them, the fever in her eyes was gone. They were back to the clear glassy blue they had been earlier.

"Are the both of you okay?" Derek had one hand clamped onto Vara's upraised arm and the other was still poised to ward off Laris. He looked between the two of them and finally released her arm.

"I had everything perfectly under control," Laris said, regally as she straightened her golden curls. "Now if you two are finished standing around, there is someone I would like you to meet."

She led them past the small parking lot in front of the church and into a cemetery just next to it. Old oak trees spread their limbs above their heads and let light through to decorate the ornate gravestones that stood silently in the bright green grass.

Laris threaded her way through the rows of markers and led them to a stone building in the back.

"This is our family crypt," she announced proudly.

The monument was a disturbing bone white and it stood barely taller than Laris herself. It had five drawers in the front, each one marked with a name. Laris knelt next to the bottom drawer. It had the name Lady Alicia Stadler carved on it. The drawer above it was marked with Lord Teryll Stadler, and the one above that had Laris's name on it.

"Father likes to be prepared," she said as she caught Vara's gaze.

It sent shivers down Vara's spine as if she was looking at a person already marked for death. "Have you ever considered hiring a necromancer to talk to your mother?"

Laris looked at Vara horrified. "No. I don't even want to think about what she looks like in there now."

"If the corpse is too desiccated, they usually cover it with a sheet," said Vara quietly.

Laris looked at her. Her eyes widened so much Vara started to worry they might pop out of her head.

"Sorry," she apologized. "Lulu took me with her once when she had her retriever revived. She had been having it revived on the day it died each year since she had been five. I thought it was rather creepy, but she was just so happy to see it each time, as if they had never been apart from each other. What happened to your mother, if you don't mind me asking?"

"She died in a fire when I was young. Father was out at a business meeting. The gardener noticed smoke pouring out of the windows and rescued me. But it was too late for Mother."

Vara recoiled as the gruesome image of Laris's mother's charred body sitting up and talking filled her mind. No wonder she had never considered talking to her mother.

"What was she like?" Vara asked.

A distant wistful look clouded Laris's eyes. "Warm, caring. She used to take me for walks through the forest behind our house. She had long blonde hair, like mine, and she was so beautiful."

They strolled out of the graveyard and past the church. The noon bell started to toll. There was an ominous silence in the air, punctuated by an occasional caw of a raven. "Maybe this wasn't such a good idea," said Vara as she tried to catch sight of the raven, just to convince herself it wasn't something worse.

"Why?" Laris looked at her impishly. "Are you scared?"

"Of course not," Vara said. She usually loved quiet towns, but this place was too quiet. There didn't seem to be any other pedestrians, and every shop they passed had closed signs hanging in the front windows. It was almost like the town had been vacated in preparation for an approaching disaster.

Laris laughed. "Would you feel better if we could find at least one person in this town?"

"Admittedly, yes."

"Then I know just the place." Laris smiled and directed them down a side street. They stopped outside a small black building. It had large double doors that stood wide open with the name 'After Dark' in elaborate gigantic yellow letters above the entrance.

It looked ominous next to the quaint stores with their red and white awnings. Though it was bright day, the sunlight illuminated nothing on the inside, except for a flight of stairs that descended into the subterranean depths.

Derek entered first and vanished into the darkness. Laris followed next. Vara hesitantly stood in front of the doorway as she debated with her fear of being swallowed up by the darkness. She balled her hand into a fist and strode forward. She descended the flight of stairs, determined not to let her fear of the unknown get the better of her.

At the base of the stairs, she was relieved to find an overhead light illuminating the first step into the large cavern of a room. More overhead lights peppered the ceiling like stars in a night sky.

There was a liquor bar decorated with a wide variety of bottles on one side of the room and actual people seated at scattered tables, enjoying their drinks.

"Beyond the tables, there's a large dance floor and a stage for the night time performances," Laris said as she joined Vara and Derek at the bar.

The woman behind the bar slid three red drinks in front of them. "These are from the lady at the table on your right."

Vara glanced over at the lady she had indicated. The woman had blonde hair that was bound back into a tight bun and red-rimmed glasses perched on her petite nose. She had a pale blue business suit on and lifted her glass toward them with a smile.

"I take it you've been here before?" Vara asked Laris.

"Father is one of the share owners of this place. I come here every so often to check on his investment."

"Of course you do," she commented and took a large sip of her drink.

"You should see this place at night. They actually have to turn people away at the door, it gets so crowded." Laris took a long sip of her drink and gazed languidly around the dimly lit interior.

Vara set her drink down on the bar as she felt her head swim for a moment. It was probably just her eyes still trying to get used to the dim light. She glanced over at Derek. He shook his head, as if trying to dislodge something in his mind.

He stopped and glanced around the room. His eyes swept the dark recesses. He stopped on the blonde-haired woman in the pale blue suit who had given them the drinks. There was now a large, muscular troll sitting with her and both of them were watching them intently.

"Ah, there you are!"

Vara groaned as she recognized the voice. She whirled to face the doorway. Her stomach lurched with the sudden movement.

Derek did the same, though his reflexes seemed a lot slower than usual. He staggered off his chair toward the newcomer.

The lecherous reporter, Harrison Carter, stormed into the room, easily avoiding Derek's grasp.

"Your father is going out of his mind with worry wondering where you are, young lady," he said as he roughly grabbed Laris's arm. "And you!" He turned toward Vara. "You'll be lucky if her father doesn't fire you for this infraction." He yanked Laris's arm roughly as he dragged her in the direction of the night club entrance.

Vara took a step forward and tried to wrest his hand off Laris's arm, but she only had enough strength to rest her hand on his arm. It was like her limbs suddenly weighed twice the amount they normally did.

"Let her go!" she mumbled. Her mind felt sluggish, as if someone had decided to cushion her brain with cotton. "You're just doing this for another headline!"

Laris slowly swiveled her head to look at the reporter. Her eyes blazed with an inner fire. Vara heard the glass shatter and the splatter of the red liquid and then suddenly both of Laris's hands were around his shoulders. She gripped the edges of his collar. In one loud rip she had exposed his right shoulder.

But before she could sink her teeth in, he grasped her hands, twisted her around, and pinned her against his chest.

The brawny troll who had been sitting with the lady in the blue suit surged forward. "You let those two ladies go right now!" he demanded as he talked around two enormous ivory tusks that jutted out of his mouth. "They obviously don't want to go with you, Mister."

The reporter turned to look at the troll. "If you don't back off right now, I will expose the two of you for what you are," the reporter threatened.

The troll's sallow green skin turned several shades of purple and red. He shot a look at the blonde-haired woman and they both took several steps backward, though they still had resolute expressions on their faces.

Laris struggled in his grip and dug her nails into his exposed shoulder.

"We don't have time for this," he muttered. He thrust his hand into his pocket and withdrew a handkerchief.

"No!" Derek shouted. In a lightening fast movement, he crouched down and then sprang forward with all the power his legs could muster. He hit the reporter square in the chest. But it was too late. The reporter had managed to get the handkerchief over Laris's nose and mouth, and she immediately went limp like a lifeless rag doll. The three of them collapsed in a confused pile of flailing limbs.

"You don't understand!" the reporter shouted at Derek. "We have got to get out of here! Those two will call for reinforcements!"

Vara darted a glance back to where the woman in the blue suit and the muscular troll should have been standing. Without anyone watching them, they had vanished.

"How do you know?" she demanded. "Who were they?"

"They're hunters. We have to get out of here. My car is parked a block away."

Vara pulled Derek out from the tangle of limbs. He helped the reporter hoist Laris between them. Once outside, Vara could hear shouts a couple of blocks away.

"My car is in the other direction at least," said the reporter. "I parked in front of the church."

Their progress was greatly hampered by Mr. Carter and Derek uncoordinatedly running with Laris still unconscious between them. Vara risked a glance behind them. She could see a mob of people several blocks behind them, running in their direction.

They finally reached the parking lot in front of the church. Laris groaned and her eyes flickered open. Derek slid into the backseat of the reporter's car and helped the reporter slide Laris in next to him. Vara jumped into the front seat with the reporter in the driver's seat. The engine of the car growled to life and jerked as they reversed out of the parking stall. The reporter kicked it into forward and away they sped, churning up gravel in a dusty grey cloud behind them.

Chapter 19

Veronika watched as the black car churned its wheels. It kicked up a cloud of grey dust, sped out of the small village, and vanished into the distance.

"Thank you all for helping, you will now be paid," said Veronika as she turned to face the angry mob behind her. "Rant, give them the money."

"Yes, Boss," the mountainous troll responded. He pulled out a wad of bills from his worn green backpack and dealt them out to the people in the crowd nearest to him.

It gnawed at her that she had let the wolf girl go without a struggle, but the reporter had paid them handsomely to make the wolf girl and her friends trust him enough to go with him. At least now she knew what the wolf girl looked like. She understood why Austen had been so obsessed with her. She was very pretty.

"What's the plan now, Boss?" Rant asked. Several of the mob still lingered in the street behind them, hoping there might be an opportunity for more money.

"We should drop in on Mr. Carter, of course. We'll give him an hour head start to take care of his business with our new friends. We will need our heavier weapons since it'll mean taking on the girl awake since we won't have the opportunity to drug her again."

They arrived back at the squat brownstone building that was their hunter headquarters just as one of the windows exploded outward and rained shards of glass on the front lawn. Veronika and Rant took cover behind the hedge next door. After a couple of seconds, Veronika ran for the door and motioned for Rant to follow her. She put her ear to the front door and listened. Two voices argued within. One was a light whispery voice, which was Geoffrey. And the other was a deep gravelly voice, which sounded like the demon Samanith.

"Do you want me to bust it open, Boss?"

"Do you know how much I paid for this door, Rant? No."

Veronika twisted the door knob and yanked as hard as she could. It didn't move in the slightest. Was someone holding it closed?

"Boss, you want me to try?"

She refused to embarrass herself by admitting to weakness in front of Rant. "No, I've got it."

She put a foot next to the doorway to brace herself and gave it another considerable tug. And the door opened for all of a couple of inches. There was an incredible force inside sucking the door back against its frame.

She fought to keep it open. Rant reached his fingers in and pried it open far enough to allow himself through and kept it propped open for her to enter behind him. As soon as he released it, the door slammed shut so hard Veronika worried that the hinges might break.

Her feet slid as a gust of wind whipped her hair and carried her down the hallway. She slammed into the doorway before the gust managed to drag her into the living room, where the storm was at its peak.

A white cyclone circulated in the middle of the room, with chairs and books and cushions caught up in the funnel. The living room was a disaster area. Books were missing from the bookshelves, furniture had toppled over, and one of the windows was broken with jagged edges that glinted in the sunlight.

Veronika ducked as a chair danced by in the breeze, just missing her head. Just as she felt her fingers lose their grip on the doorway, one of Rant's beefy green arms snaked its way around her waist.

"It's your fault!" the deep demon voice screeched. On one side of the tornado, Veronika could see two black eye sockets that smoldered amid the gusting wind.

"You could have warned us that he was one of those Nature people!" countered Geoffrey's voice. He was nothing more than a blur on another edge of the twister.

"All you had to do was keep him from leaving! How hard is that? You could have lied to him!"

"We're not a babysitting service!" Geoffrey's voice screeched and a brown sofa chair was suddenly yanked out of its orbit around the room and thrown directly at the smoldering black eyes. It slid right through the black eyes as if they weren't even there and smashed into the bookcase behind it. Books and pages flew everywhere, most of which got sucked into the cyclone.

"Geoffrey! Samanith!" Veronika shouted over the howling wind. "Stop it this instant!"

The momentum of the storm didn't shift in the slightest. Several chairs sailed through the air and slammed into opposite walls. One of them hit a photo of her father. The wooden frame broke in two and the glass shattered.

"Dad!" Veronika could feel tears burn in her eyes. "Rant, stop them!"

"You got it, Boss." Rant sucked in a large lung full of air and roared. It was a deep bass that shook the entire house right down to the foundation. The windows groaned and the floor vibrated. Miraculously, the wind stopped. Furniture hit the ground, as well as a stack of books, a scattering of loose pages, and an army of cushions.

Veronika picked her way through the wrecked living room to the broken photograph. She brushed away the shards of glass, uncovering a large tear in the picture.

"Geoffrey, Samanith, explain yourselves!" she shouted, not bothering to reign in her anger.

Samanith solidified in the center of the room with his hazy arms folded. His black suit looked rumpled and ripped in several places. "I came to see just why you let my charge go."

Geoffrey condensed himself in a corner and sulked. He shot a look of resentment at Samanith.

Samanith continued, "But now I see it was because of

your ghost's stupidity."

"There's no need for name calling," Veronika reminded him. "We weren't expecting him to be able to open a doorway like that."

"Even so, you failed at my simple request. And because of that my charge put me in a tight position and I was forced to make other arrangements."

"We're sorry we inconvenienced you," Veronika apologized. "Now, is that all you wanted?"

"No. I would like you to make the young lady wanted by the authorities, so that she will have to flee her home and seek refuge elsewhere."

Veronika hated dealing with the police. Her license to hunt already skirted grey areas as it was. What Samanith was asking sounded very illegal. "And how do you suggest we do that?"

"The authorities will be talking to her boyfriend soon. I suggest you have your friend here intervene."

"My friend . . . ?" she looked confusedly at green-skinned Rant.

"Your other friend," Samanith said as he pointed a long bony finger at Geoffrey. The ghost was doing his best to slink into a corner and turn transparent.

"Geoffrey's just a ghost," she reminded him. "What would he be able to do?

Samanith smiled and showed off his sharpened teeth. "They will be doing a necromancy session to talk to Miss Stadler's dead boyfriend. And since he is in love with her, I doubt he'll blame her for his murder, regardless of whether or not she did it. I want your ghost to change his mind."

Chapter 20

Vara realized that he hadn't slowed the car down after peeling out of the village. The Stadler Estate should have been only a three-minute ride from the village, and at the rate they were traveling, they would have already been there by now with time to spare.

"Where are you taking us?" she demanded.

"You didn't really think I was going to take you back, did you?" The reporter, Harrison Carter, favored her with a sly, mischievous grin, though he kept his eyes on the road.

"You take us back right now!"

"I think you should do as the lady requests," said Derek from the backseat. "Miss Stadler's father will ruin you if you don't."

"He comes into my office ranting about something every other day of the week," the reporter said with a note of exasperation. "Using him as a threat against me will do you no good. Besides, I'll take you all back afterward. I want to do a feature on Miss Harper. It won't take long. I just need to show you some pictures and ask a couple of questions. I did rescue the three of you from those hunters after all. You owe me this."

"But how did they find out about Laris?" Vara felt her eyes narrow. "Did you—?"

"I'm shocked that you think so little of me, Miss Harper. I assure you, I wasn't the one who told them."

Harrison had turned off the main road and was slowly

negotiating a small winding road that led up a short incline to a picturesque mansion that overlooked a small lake.

Where the Stadler Estate looked like a gothic mausoleum, this mansion looked like it had been built by someone who adored the light of day. It was covered with windows that shone like sparkling diamonds in the sun.

He stopped the car in front of the main doors and got out. The door swung open and a man dressed in a black butler's uniform greeted him. The reporter talked with him for a moment, glanced in their direction, and then passed by him, disappearing inside.

"Do you think we can trust him?" Vara asked Derek.

"Not in the slightest. But we should probably play along. Just don't tell him anything about Laris. The sooner we can get back home, the better."

The door next to Laris flew open and a massive hand reached its way inside. A heavily muscled arm followed it. It snaked around Laris and pulled her out of the car.

"Let her go!" Derek's eyes flashed and his voice deepened into a dangerous lion growl. He pushed himself after her and flew at Laris's assailant.

Vara got out of the car after them. Derek was faced off against a man that towered over him by a head and looked like someone had mated a human with a gorilla and then dressed it in a rumpled black butler's suit.

"Mr. Carter said to see to the young lady. And Harcourt obeys," said the butler with a soft clipped proper voice. Laris groaned and one of her hands flew to her head, as if to check that it was still attached. Her eyes rolled open and focused hazily on Derek. She smiled for a moment, but then her eyes widened in alarm as she took in the fact that she was in the arms of a giant.

"Mr. Carter said young lady needs some water," the butler said as he turned toward the house.

Laris's wide frightened blue eyes watched Derek over the butler's massive shoulder. Derek ran along behind the butler, leaving Vara forgotten next to the car.

She hurried to follow the group and made it through the front door just as the gigantic butler gave the door a kick which made it slam closed behind her. He led them through the foyer into the sitting room and finally stopped to place Laris on a couch.

"Ah, Harrison said he had brought you all here for a visit!" said the reporter's wife as she strolled into the room. Her eyes twinkled with a merry light. She wore a light blue dress with a long string of pearls around her neck and her blonde hair was brushed back around her ears. Vara couldn't help but notice she had applied far too much make-up again. It made her look almost like a circus clown. "How is your father, my dear?"

"How is my father?" sputtered Laris. "Your butler just manhandled me. I didn't ask to be carried here. I don't even want to be here."

"I'm sorry, dear," the reporter's wife said as she gave Laris an even brighter smile. "He just doesn't know his strength sometimes, so eager to follow my husband's whims. But you do look like you need a drink of water."

The reporter bustled back into the room. Vara heard a low growl from the back of Laris's throat start to rumble out of her. Derek immediately laid a reassuring hand on Laris's arm. Harrison ignored her and went over to Vara's chair.

"Now, Miss Harper, I need for you to come to the study, where I have all my notes. If Miss Stadler would rather wait here, she is certainly free to do so. I'm sure Lynnis will be happy to keep the two of you entertained while I have a short chat with Miss Harper."

"Of course," said his wife. "Perhaps I could get the two of you lunch?"

"Okay, let's take a look at these notes of yours then," Vara said to Mr. Carter.

He led her out of the sitting room and to a smaller room filled with bookcases. There were several plush chairs scattered in random corners and a large table in the center covered with papers and photos.

"So, why do you want to do a story on me?" she asked. She was under no illusion that she was anyone interesting or important.

"Miss Harper, you are selling yourself short. Being the constant companion of our much beloved Laris puts you in the public eye as well. Take yesterday's front cover with the two of you together for instance. I'm certain there are plenty of parties eager for more information about you."

"Like who?"

"Oh, the public, of course." He said it a little too evasively. She wondered if he had someone particular in mind he planned to sell the information to.

"Now, Miss Harper, suffice to say I already know about Miss Stadler's present condition, so you don't need to worry about keeping that from me. Unless you have any interesting comments you'd like to make about it?"

She shook her head.

"Too bad. But we can't use it in our paper anyway since it would demean Miss Stadler in the public eye, and we want to keep the customers interested in her. The werewolf condition is looked down on in our society. It's common among the homeless since they are on the street, the night walkers, and sometimes the hunters themselves, though they are usually put down fast. How is Miss Stadler holding up under it? She looked like she could barely contain herself the other night at dinner."

Vara glared at him.

"I'll take that as a no comment. Would you like to make any comment on the death of Miss Stadler's boyfriend?"

Her eyes must have widened or she must have flinched because she saw a smile creep over Mr. Carter's face. "Yes, I thought as much. It didn't take too much of a guess on my part to figure out why she had been found with just the one bodyguard present."

Vara mentally cursed herself. It had only taken a couple of minutes to fail Derek's request that she not tell him anything about Laris.

"Do you know who bit her?"

"Other than a wolf?" she asked. "No. Besides, I thought this article was supposed to be about me."

He smiled. "Right, right. Your parents are Darrington and Maya Harper?"

"Yeah."

"Did they ever change their names at any point?"

"Why?"

"It's just I couldn't find too much about either of them before they were married. It's not that unusual with people moving around the country. Records are bound to get lost."

"My parents like to keep their lives private. I don't think they'd appreciate people digging into their pasts." Her mother certainly wouldn't. She would go ballistic if she knew someone was trying to find information about her. And her mother going ballistic was an incredibly scary thought.

"Do you know why you specifically were hired by Lord Stadler?"

Vara shrugged. "Because I burned down one of the buildings at his school and I owed him?"

"Ah yes, the fire," he muttered as he sifted through his papers and pulled out a photo of one of the campus buildings engulfed in flames. "I noticed the demon supervising the clean up of the fire is currently your supervisor at the Agency."

She nodded.

"But didn't it seem strange to you that the Agency decided to expend the resources into bringing you from Salvation City when they could have easily recruited someone else nearer?"

"I suspect I was the only one who hadn't asked the specifics and didn't have the sense of self-preservation to turn the position down."

"Are you sure of that? Or could there be another reason?"

"I don't know." It reminded her that the Agency had seemed oddly insistent that she stay with the job. As if something important hinged on it.

"Miss Harper, do you know Miss Stadler's previous companion?"

"I saw him once at the mansion."

"How about before you took the job?"

"No," she answered.

His brown eyes raked her face. He shuffled through the papers on the table and pulled out a photo. He pushed it over to her.

She could see two men in the photo. One was young with curly black hair and bright blue eyes and the other was middle-aged with glasses perched on his nose. They looked like they were having an argument. Though the photo was blurry, the older man looked very familiar.

"Your father apparently knew him. That is him in the picture, right?"

She stared closer at the older man. There was no mistaking that posture, though the style of clothes didn't look like anything she had seen him in before. "Yes."

He flipped over the picture to read some notes he had jotted on the back. "Your father was the architect hired to rebuild the Conservatory building that you burned down."

"Hang on! Dad was working for the Conservatory?"

"No," he corrected her. "He was working for Lord Stadler. According to my sources, he asked Lord Stadler for the job. It seems a little too convenient that your father volunteered to rebuild the building you burned down. And then after he disappears, for his client to suddenly hire you. I take it he didn't tell you about this little project?"

She shook her head. "I haven't talked to my father in a couple of years."

"Why?"

She shrugged again. "Mom said he shifted jobs and the company he is now working for won't allow him enough travel time to come visit us."

"Did your father tell you this personally?"

"No, but if he can't come, he can't come. Mom didn't have any intention of leaving Salvation City and I just didn't have enough magic to travel on my own by then."

"Fair enough, but why haven't you tried to get in contact with your father once you got back here?"

"Because my mom has gone to visit him. Hang on, how would you know if I tried to talk to him or not?"

He smiled. "You don't know yet, do you?"

She felt a sudden sinking feeling in her stomach. "Know what?"

"This will certainly make an interesting story. Companion to Heiress Frivolously Shops While Father's Fate Uncertain." He frowned. "I'll come up with something better later. I tried to get in contact with him when I identified him in that picture, but his house had been empty for several days."

"Do you know what happened?" she asked, her voice sounding both resigned and desperate. "Mom won't tell me what's wrong."

The door of the study flew open. "Vara, we're leaving!" announced Laris as she stood in the doorway with Derek towering over her.

"Ah, Miss Stadler, how nice of you to join us!" the reporter said with a smile.

Her eyes flashed with barely restrained anger. "I have no comment for you. And if I see you within a mile of us again, I will have my father ruin you!"

He waved a hand dismissively. "Idle threats."

"Vara! We are leaving now!"

"How about if I told you I don't think a demon killed your boyfriend?"

All heads in the room swiveled to look at him. Laris's face went from a brilliant red to a nearly beet purple. Her mouth opened and closed for a moment, and then finally she stalked across the room and slapped him across the face. Vara cringed in sympathetic pain.

"How dare you! No! I know what I saw! I saw that demon come at him! How dare you call me a liar! And I won't allow any of my staff to stand here and listen to your lies any longer!" Vara grabbed Laris's wrist and yanked her out of the room. Vara heard the footsteps of the reporter as he ran behind them.

She pulled her wrist out of Laris's grasp and stopped in the middle of the hallway. She turned to face the reporter. "How do you know it wasn't a demon? Laris seems pretty sure of what she saw."

Laris had stopped several paces away with her back to her. But Vara could see Laris's shoulders shaking as sobs wracked her body.

"The both of you just stop it!" Laris sobbed. "You weren't there! You didn't see that demon come at the two of us! Those inhuman sharp teeth of his! He moved so quick. . ."

Derek looked at a loss and put an arm around her shoulders. He shot Vara a look over the top of Laris's head.

"I had his blood on my hands!" Laris howled and buried her face in Derek's ample chest.

The job so wasn't worth it. Vara had just about had it with people lying to her.

"Sam!" she shouted and let her eyes roll toward the ceiling. "Sam, I need to talk to you now!"

As if he had been there the entire time, eavesdropping on their conversation, he drifted into the hallway from one of the small reading rooms on the side. The smell of rotting food and dead animals permeated the air, making her stomach churn.

He smiled and flashed them his wide mouth full of needle-sharp teeth. He resembled a man made of the whitest of smoke with black hollow sockets where his eyes should have been. He floated over to Vara, not sparing any of the others a glance.

"I haven't gotten the report on you for the day yet, but I look forward to reading it. Her father won't be happy hearing she is in the company of that reporter, you know." He rubbed his transparent hands together, mimicking the human gesture of anticipation.

Laris turned at the sound of his raspy voice and stared at him with eyes so wide it looked like she was going into shock. She pointed a quavering hand in Sam's direction.

"It's him!" she gasped. She wrenched herself out of Derek's grasp and launched herself at Sam, screaming, "He killed Richard!"

Chapter 21

"Laris!"

"Shush. She can't hear you."

"But I must stop her! I need to calm her down!"

"She's in good hands. Don't worry."

"Who are you?"

"No one important. Now, shush and let me concentrate."

"What are you doing? They are calling for me."

"You don't really want to talk to them, do you? They just want to ask a bunch of questions. I'll talk to them for you."

"Laris isn't there with them, is she?"

Geoffrey smiled at the hopeful note in Richard's voice. "No. I'll take care of them—You can go back." He felt Richard's ghostly presence start to vanish. That was easier than he expected it to be. But then the newly dead were usually confused and disoriented. They hadn't fully grasped the fact that they were dead yet.

He pushed his essence into Richard's empty body. It was cold and clammy, like pulling on wet clothes. And like wet clothes, he felt like if he possessed the body long enough it would become warm around him, but it would still be stiff and not fit properly.

He forced an eye open and looked around. He was on an operating table in the middle of the police station morgue. He could hear the faint sounds of chatter and typewriters from the room above.

The walls were lined with silver metal body lockers that

Gypsy Madden

reflected the flickering light from the white ceremonial candles that were lit in each of the corners of the room, making odd shadows dance along the walls. The room itself smelled of disinfectant and other pungent chemicals. Just beyond his feet, or rather Richard's feet, stood a middle-aged woman with white hair tied back in a bun and a white coat. She smiled at him.

"Don't be alarmed." Her voice had a musical quality to it, which immediately made him think of warm summer days and flower gardens. "I work for the police. We only have a couple of questions for you, and then we shall release you. First we would like you to state your name."

The vocal chords were stiff with rigor. Geoffrey ran his energy along them to soften them. "I am Richard Darkrider," the name came out as a croak.

"Good," the lady said as she gave him another warm smile. "You must not panic. Just relax. Your voice will grow stronger as we continue. Do you remember what happened to you?"

Geoffrey tried to remember the scene as the demon described it to him. "I remember the parking lot. And Laris was with me."

"And what happened then?" she prompted. She put a hand on his arm in encouragement. He couldn't feel the warmth of her hand, but the arm tingled slightly as if she emitted a slight electric charge. It crept the entire way up his arm and hugged his essence in reassurance.

"She attacked me!" Geoffrey made the body tense up, which wasn't difficult since it was already stiff with rigor.

"No!" Richard's silent voice screamed in Geoffrey's mind. "It didn't happen that way!"

Geoffrey felt Richard's essence suddenly push against him, trying to force him out. But Richard seemed to have only the strength of a breath of wind. It would have barely stirred a blade of grass. Geoffrey itched to laugh at Richard's pathetic attempt. After being made a fool of by that demon, it felt good to be considerably stronger than someone else.

"Why? Did you do something?" the lady continued.

"She's been bitten by a wolf. And she's starting to

change. She can't control it."

"No!" screamed Richard's voice in his head again. There was a sudden sensation of someone stuffing a sock down his dead throat. The pushing sensation turned into a slight tug. "It wasn't like that at all! She tried to attack the demon! It wasn't her fault!"

"I'm sorry, my friend," Geoffrey apologized silently to the voice in his head, "but you aren't the only one doing this for someone they love."

"Was she on her own?" the woman asked. "The officers said they found a slight trace of a demon."

"There was no demon," said Geoffrey. He let Richard's dead vocal chords amplify his response. He would have smiled if the waxy skin around Richard's frigid mouth wouldn't have split. "She just attacked me, and I loved her too much to stop her."

Chapter 22

Laris's hands clamped down onto thin air as Sam vanished the moment before she made contact. A savage growl escaped from between her gritted teeth. She whipped around as she searched the room. Her eyes glowed with unrestrained fury. Vara took a step back in reflex, though she wasn't Laris's intended target.

A clammy ghostly white hand clamped down on Vara's shoulder from behind and the reek of dead fish and decay filled her nostrils and wrapped itself around her brain. A cold chill spread from her shoulder down to her toes.

"Call her off!" Sam hissed into her ear.

Laris took a step to one side as she tried to get around Vara to the object of her frustration. Sam kept Vara angled between them. He moved her as if she was nothing more than a puppet on strings. What was he scared of? He wasn't flesh and blood, unlike the rest of them in the room.

"Laris, please, stop!" Vara begged.

"No! He killed Richard!" Laris tried side-stepping in the other direction and made a lunge to her right. Sam shifted Vara two steps to the left and danced a bit further behind his human shield.

"You know, this is fun!" Sam whispered into Vara's ear.

"Sam, let me go! She's going to kill me to get to you."

"It wouldn't be the first time for her to kill someone to get to me. This is how that other guard of hers died. Let's see how good her control is today."

Laris's eyes glittered with tears. "Liar! I loved him!" She wildly lunged again. She stepped through nothing but air as Sam maneuvered both of them out of the way again. Laris crumpled into a heap on the floor where she landed.

"I thought as much," said Harrison Carter from where he stood behind Vara. "The preliminary reports said there weren't any other fingerprints found or any traces of magic on the body. So, exactly what did you do to set her off the last time?"

"Ah, the human who has been getting my charge into trouble." Sam's ghostly presence shifted behind Vara and then in a breath, the frigid icy coldness that had frozen Vara's body was gone. She looked around for Sam. He had reappeared next to Harrison.

"You know she can get herself into trouble on her own without any help," he told the reporter. "It's more enjoyable to watch when she brings it on herself. I was watching when they parted company from my charge and appeared to them to urge them to rejoin her. The young lady got mad." He grinned.

"No! It didn't happen like that!" Laris objected from her half-crouch position.

"Her guard attempted to stop her."

"No!" Laris howled. "I don't want to hear any more!" She buried her head in her hands.

"But it will come out soon since they are doing the session with the necromancer today," the reporter pointed out. "It's only a matter of time before the police come for her if her boyfriend tells them that story."

"It's in the Agency's best interest that she not be held in custody, as well as her own," said Sam.

"Sam, you knew all this before," Vara accused. "Why didn't you tell me?"

Sam floated back over to her. He expelled a large whiff of decay in her face as he gave her a large toothy grin. "You already told me before that, had we told you she was a werewolf, you wouldn't have taken the position. The Agency didn't want to run the risk of your quitting if you knew without a doubt that she had committed murder, especially since it was out of her control. It was in the Agency's best interest for you to develop an emotional bond with the girl."

"Why? Why is the Agency so invested in this? Why is

the Agency so obsessed with the idea that I stay with her and this position?" Vara searched Sam's face. Though he was a demon and didn't have eyes that she could read any actual emotion from, he looked nervous from the way he twitched to the way his toothy grin had drooped. He looked as if he knew something big but was trying to decide just how much he wanted to tell her.

"Spill it, Sam," she demanded. "I know you're hiding something."

"I've already told you. Her father is the Agency's most important client. If you fail at this position, her father might take his business elsewhere."

Laris was still crumpled into the fetal position, sobbing and shaking her head. Vara knelt down next to her. "Laris, I don't know how much time we have, but we need to go talk to your father." Vara grasped her arm and tried to pull her up. Laris yanked it back violently and growled at her.

"No, let them come for me! I deserve to be dead!" she moaned. "I'm nothing but a killer!"

"It was an accident. Please, Laris, we need to go!"

Derek knelt down in front of Laris. He didn't say a word. He just put his massive hands very gently on both of her arms and drew her up from the floor. She struggled at first, but she didn't manage to loosen his grip any. She allowed him to put her arms around his neck and then encircle her waist with one muscular arm. She sobbed into the chest of his black jacket and hung limply like a rag doll.

Vara felt a pang of jealousy. She needed to get over it. He wasn't her boyfriend any longer. The black glares he gave her were a constant reminder of that.

"To the transit circle?" Derek asked in his low half-whispered voice.

"Think we should?" Vara asked. "In the state she is in, she might completely lose control."

"You did say we need to get her home fast," he reminded her.

Vara nodded. "Right. Okay then." She pushed past Harrison and rushed in the direction of the main doors of the mansion. She could hear Laris's continued sobs just behind her, which meant Derek was keeping pace with her easily. Out of the corner of her eye, she saw the reporter's wife rush out of a sitting room off to the side.

"Miss Stadler looks to be in some distress," she noted. "Is there anything I can have my staff get for her?"

"No, that's quite all right. We just need to get her home." Vara attempted to put a smile on her face and flashed it at her, though with the images of Richard's bloody corpse and incarceration in a prison cell running through her mind, she wasn't exactly certain just what was on her face.

They made it back to the Stadler mansion. The whole incident at the reporter's place had left Laris so drained that the transit barely affected her at all.

Laris and Derek sat together on one of the small sofas in the parlor. Her sobs had mostly subsided, but her usually immaculate makeup was smudged and running in places. Dark stains trailed down her face where her mascara had run and her lipstick looked like someone had smeared it onto her face with a paintbrush.

Derek had an arm around her shoulders and had drawn her close to him. He whispered something to Laris in his husky voice, too low for Vara to hear.

Vara sat in the same cushioned chair she had originally sat in when she had first met Laris's father. It felt like she had come full circle with this job several days earlier than she had anticipated.

Lord Stadler strode into the room and surveyed the three of them. The look on his face changed from irritated to furious as he took in the state of his daughter.

"Get your feline hands off my daughter!" he screamed at Derek.

Derek's golden skin turned a sickly yellow shade and he withdrew his arm quickly. He mumbled something.

Lord Stadler turned his anger on Vara. "Did I not tell you that if you returned my daughter in less than pristine shape I have the power to make life extremely difficult for you, Miss Harper?"

"Yes, I know. But it couldn't be helped. She realized that she was actually the one who killed her bodyguard yesterday.

Gypsy Madden

It was an accident. But the police are probably going to figure it out as soon as they do the session with the necromancer and arrest her."

Lord Stadler's glower darkened. "I would like for my daughter to be kept out of the custody of the police until the weekend. I already have arrangements in place and I don't want to have to change things at this late date. I trust you can hide her until then."

"In other words, you are forcing me to become a willing party to helping a fugitive." With a criminal record, all of her chances of future employment would vanish like a demon in a puff of rancid smoke.

"I shall remind you that I have significant pull with the proper channels and you will be treated leniently should you successfully do your job." As he turned toward his daughter, his face softened. "My dear, I know it wasn't your fault. But this crying and carrying on will not be tolerated. I need you to be composed and presentable should anyone outside of the family and staff see you. I trust both of you to keep her from harm." And with that, he swept out of the room.

"And do you have any thoughts on where you might take her? Just so I can report it back to the Agency, of course."

Vara whirled around at the sound of Sam's raspy voice. His usual reek washed over her as she spotted him in a darkened corner of the room, all but hidden in the shadows.

"We could take her back to my house," Vara suggested. "The police don't have jurisdiction in Salvation City."

"You forget about her affliction," Sam reminded her.

"In what way?"

"Her condition feeds on ambient magical energy," Sam pointed out. "If you take her to Salvation City, she will starve from lack of magic. And that certainly won't get you a winning review by the client."

"Any suggestions then?"

"You could take her to the demon realm," he suggested.

"You'd like that, wouldn't you?"

Sam favored Vara with one of his toothy open-mouthed grins.

"Any thoughts, Derek?" she asked.

He had a startled look on his golden face as she turned in his direction. She flinched as his eyes searched her face for something. "He's right," he finally responded. "The demon realm is the only place aside from Salvation City where the police wouldn't be able to track us."

"Sounds like it's settled then. We should probably take enough food for a couple of days since I don't know if we'll be able to tolerate anything from there."

"Does Miss require anything?" a voice piped just behind Vara. She whirled around to face Ren. He innocently stared up at her as if he had been there the entire time and hadn't just appeared there to give her a heart-attack.

"We will need three sacks of food enough for three days."

"Very good, Miss." He threw Laris a quick smile and dashed out of the room.

"Sam, I assume you are going to report to the Agency about where we're going, right?"

Vara watched him bob his head up and down in an exaggeration of the human gesture. This was an awful idea, but it wasn't like they had any other option.

"Is there any way the Agency could hide us for a couple of days?"

Sam floated over to Vara and sat down on the arm of her chair. "The Agency wants all of you to stay out of police custody. The first place the police will look is the client's investments—such as the Conservatory and the Agency. Besides, the Agency doesn't want to be guilty of harboring a fugitive, as you phrased it earlier."

"I guess there's no other option." As she sat there for a moment trying to come up with any better ideas, she saw a bright red light flash by the parlor window, followed by a bright blue light.

"Derek, we've got to go now," she said as she stood up quickly. "Ren, tell Lord Stadler we need him to stall them."

"Yes, Miss."

"We need to use a mirror to cross over to the demon realm."

"There's a full-length one in Laris's bedroom," said Derek. The ghost of a rakish smile cross his lips. Vara couldn't help but wonder why he had been in Laris's bedroom. She tried to remind herself that it wasn't any of her business any more.

"Ren, can you clean the chalk markings from under the mirror once we leave?"

"Yes, Miss."

"Thank you for doing this, Ren," said Derek solemnly. He placed a hand on the young boy's shoulder and whispered something to him.

Ren gave him a bright smile and threw his arms around Derek's waist in a tight hug. Derek ruffled Ren's frizzy white hair and smiled. Ren released him and dashed from the room.

"What was that all about?" Vara asked.

Derek put his free arm around Laris and eased her off the couch. "You could stand to be nicer to him. You don't know what it's like to grow up away from your family in a world that treats you as nothing more than slave labor."

Vara looked in the direction that Ren had disappeared in. She had assumed he served Lord Stadler of his own free will. "Why doesn't he go home then?"

"He's been away too long. He said it doesn't feel like home there any more."

She let Derek lead the way to Laris's room, which turned out to be several doors down from hers. It was at least four times the size of her closet of a room and was decorated in shades of pale pink.

They crossed the room and stopped in front of a large mirror that stood about a foot taller than Derek. It was about a meter wide and bordered with ivy carvings. Their reflections peered back at them.

A chill shot through Vara as an icy hand had draped itself over her shoulder. Sam rested his chin on her other shoulder. His wintery presence traced a pattern against her spine. She realized with a start that she couldn't see his reflection.

"I will be on the other side waiting for you," he whispered into her ear. The clammy weight of his head and hand on her shoulders vanished, and the warm air of the room stirred on her back.

"Are you certain we can trust him?" Derek asked.

"No, but what choice do we have?"

"We are going into his world, where there are plenty of others like him," he reminded her. "Where no one from here can reach us."

"I know, but we don't have any other plan and the police are downstairs probably talking to her father right now. You know, if you don't want to go, you don't have to."

"I'm under contract just as much as you are." His gaze settled on Laris as she tried to dry her red eyes with a tissue. "I don't think I could leave you two."

"Okay then." Vara quickly sketched a rune circle at the base of the mirror. She fumbled through her purse for the cuticle scissors and reopened the cut from yesterday.

She let several drops hit the circle before she pulled out a tissue to hold to the wound. It wasn't deep, so it would stop bleeding shortly. Her reflection looked at her with worried eyes. The girl in the mirror didn't look like she was part of Vara, but a twin with someone else's thoughts running through her head. Their palms met on the surface of the glass as Vara reached toward her.

"I need both of you to put a hand on my shoulder." Vara felt the light touch of Laris on her right hand side and the warm weight of Derek on her left shoulder.

She closed her eyes and felt both of their presences more alertly than her own. As she relaxed, she felt the electricity pulse off both of them, though each of them was different. With Derek she felt his support radiate through him and into herself. And with Laris, she felt her anticipation.

Vara breathed in and amassed a ball of magical energy in her chest. As she breathed out, she sent it into the circle under her feet.

The magic surged straight up in a wave of crackling red hot energy from the circle. It encased the three of them and then trailed out through Vara's outstretched hand and into the mirror. She felt it grow hot like a metal pan on a stove.

A scream echoed in her ears. Her brain noted that it didn't sound like it was coming from her, though her throat felt raw, as if someone had scraped it with kitchen cleansers.

And then everything stopped.

Chapter 23

"Welcome to my world!" Sam's voice said gleefully.

A pungent scorched smell invaded Vara's nostrils. She gasped and choked as a wave of heat flooded her mouth and throat. Her skin tingled and itched. She felt as if she was blistering under a boiling sun. She cracked open her eyes and looked past Sam to a world shrouded in a moonless twilight. Vague clouds of soot and smoke drifted through the air, and a light drizzle of ash rained around them.

Vara heard a low growl behind her. She felt her heart take a wild leap as if trying to burst out of her chest, while the rest of her body froze in place. She heard every movement, even the shuffling of feet in the black powdery ash.

"Laris, snap out of it!" Derek ordered through the darkness. "Vara, help me!"

Vara automatically spun around as she searched the darkness for the source of Derek's voice. Laris had dropped to the ground on all fours and her eyes blazed. Her teeth were clenched in a chilling grimace and the growl coming out of her throat was growing louder by the minute.

Nothing in Vara's arsenal of spells covered werewolf transformations. With frustration and panic boiling inside her, she stepped toward Laris and slapped the girl across the face.

The effect was immediate. Instead of looking as if she were focusing on an internal struggle, Laris whipped her head in Vara's direction and grinned. It sent a chill down her spine, even with the suffocating heat.

"Laris, fight it!" she urged.

"Fight it?" A voice that wasn't Laris's slid from between her lips. She threw her head back and laughed. "Yes, fight, for there shall be blood and flesh, and heat and struggle! I am so hungry!" Her voice, deep and sly, called to Vara as if she were the only person in the entire world. "Come closer, sister. Don't be afraid. You wished to be her friend and now you shall be so much more." Laris closed her eyes, sniffed the air, and smiled. "You have power I have only dreamed of. I would have it!" She sprang at Vara.

Vara stumbled backwards, lost her footing, and found herself sprawling on the ground. She looked up to see Laris standing above her. But instead of attacking, she struggled against two golden tanned hands that restrained her in a vise-like grip. Derek stood behind Laris with his heels dug into the ground.

"Run! I can't hold her for long!"

"Sam!" Vara shouted.

The air shimmered around Derek and Laris, and suddenly Sam and another wraith demon stood on either side of them. Sam's eyes lit up with excitement and his mouth dropped into a gleeful grin. Vara felt a rush of irritation. He had known this was going to happen!

Laris struggled and suddenly wrenched her arms out of Derek's grasp. He made a futile grab at thin air as Laris surged toward Vara. A mess of unruly blonde hair and nails and blazing blue eyes flew toward her.

And then Laris was on top of her. Nails dug into her shoulder and ripped the collar of her dress. Laris lifted her head high in a howl and Vara saw her canines gleam as they extended, preparing for a meal.

The seconds crawled by as Vara waited for the excruciating pain. She wondered if Richard had had enough time to see his death coming like this before Laris had ripped him to shreds. Her lilac perfume caressed as she dropped her head toward Vara's throat.

"Sleep."

It seemed like an odd request for a moment like this, but Vara's brain considered it, wondering if she did, would she still feel the blinding pain as Laris's teeth pierced her flesh.

But it didn't come. Laris's head rolled uselessly against Vara's shoulder, her eyes and mouth closed.

Vara slid out from under Laris and curled up in a sitting position a foot away from her. Vara watched her carefully. Laris's chest rose and fell in a deep sleep.

Derek sat down. He pulled Laris onto his lap and cradled her gently. He pushed her matted blonde hair away from her face.

Sam and his friend whispered together with their heads nearly touching. They drifted over to Vara.

"The command won't last long," Sam's friend said. "We shouldn't have any power over her at all, but she is in our domain." He looked almost exactly like Sam, but his suit was a deep green and he was slightly smaller. His hollow eyes studied her and a frown puckered at the edges of his mouth. He turned back to Sam and whispered something too soft for Vara to hear. Sam nodded.

The smaller demon floated over to Laris and Derek and snapped his fingers. Laris's body rose out of Derek's grasp and hovered in a horizontal position several feet off the ground.

"We shall seek out more of our people to keep her under the sleep for her duration here." With one ghostly finger in the air, he motioned for Laris's body to follow him.

She noticed Sam lingering off to one side. "You knew this was going to happen!" she accused.

His mouth dropped open into an unsettling malicious smile. "Yes."

"Why didn't you warn me?"

He erased the smile from his lips and gave her an innocent look. "I thought you knew that the demon realm is entirely magic and it would hasten her transformation."

She mentally kicked herself. "So, why did you suggest coming here if it was going to make her condition worse?"

"The mortal law enforcement won't follow you here. And her transformation poses no threat to us."

It might pose no threat to the demons, but that almost guaranteed Derek and Vara would become meals should Laris wake. She stared into the distance in frustration. She could pick out some shapes that loomed out of the darkness, growing larger the longer they walked.

"Where is your friend taking us anyway?"

"It's a surprise," he answered cryptically.

The odd angular shapes in the darkness resolved themselves into an abandoned and forgotten village of clock towers. All of the clock faces were cracked and frozen with their hands pointing to different times of the day. As if in response to her stare, one of the clock towers chimed. It soon stopped after five chimes, though the hour hand stubbornly told her it was three o'clock.

The demon in front stopped outside of the largest building and waved a hand. The doors threw themselves open, encouraging them to enter the dimly lit corridor. Sam closed the doors behind them.

"My friend is taking her to see about renewing the spell on her," said Sam. "You can check on her after, if you feel the need."

Derek looked torn, his eyes glued on Laris's unconscious hovering form as the other demon left them and continued down the darkened hallway.

"If your friend would rather accompany the wolf-girl, he can do so. But I want you to accompany me."

Derek nodded to Vara and disappeared after Laris.

The look on Sam's face she could only describe as self-satisfied. "Now you see where his heart is drawn."

"It's his job to protect her," she reminded him.

"And if he wasn't under contract, which of you do you think he would choose?"

"Why do you care?" she asked.

"I want you to see the truth."

He led her down a short flight of stairs and down a wide corridor. At the end of it lay two large double doors. With a snap of his fingers, they flew open.

A large ballroom spread out before them. The floor was made of the finest of porcelain and painted with a mural of angelic faces who all leered up at Vara, while the ceiling had been festooned with thousands of diamonds that twinkled like stars in the night sky.

Demons in elegant dresses and formal suits twirled around in a dizzying pattern of colors and finery. She had never been to a formal masquerade ball, and her soul longed to join them.

Sam encircled her waist with a clammy hand and drew her across the room. He stopped in front of a gigantic golden throne that towered above the revelers and dropped onto one knee with his fist to his chest.

"You must offer respect," he hissed at her.

She shrugged and dropped to one knee, but the throne still looked empty to her.

"My lady, we seek an audience with you," he announced to the room.

Several of the elegantly dressed demons in the corners of the room turned to look at him. A child's lilting laughter danced around the pillars of the room, seemingly out of nowhere.

"We request but a moment of your time."

Shadows flowed out from the corners of the room and condensed into a small pool of darkness in front of Sam. And out of the pool rose a young female wraith-demon. If she had been human, she would have judged her to be around six.

The small demon was a ghostly white blur, same as Sam, and stood about half his height. She had the same hollowed out eye sockets as he had, but she had long hair in innocent curls and wore an old-fashioned black dress that flared out from her waist. She threw her arms around his neck and pulled him close.

"What did you bring me from the mortal realm?" Her eye sockets widened as she looked from him to Vara. She immediately released him from the embrace and sinuously stalked around Vara, as if appraising her.

"I present this demon summoner to you, my lady. She needs a safe harbor. Her friend is being pursued by the mortal law enforcement."

"Then she is not your offering of tribute?" The demon girl frowned. "She would make a nice addition to my court." The girl reached forward as if to cup Vara's chin with her hand. She smiled and her eye sockets narrowed in a shrewd look.

"She is not for you."

The young demon glared at Sam. The shadows in the room seemed to draw toward her menacingly and the air around them grew dark.

He quickly amended, "I do have a gift for you, which I shall present shortly."

"If the girl isn't a gift to me, she isn't welcome here. If you will not play with me, I would have you leave now."

A hush had fallen on the revelers and Vara could feel hundreds of eyes on the two of them. Sam had a determined set to his jaw, but he quietly said, "Yes, my lady. You shall be obeyed." He backed out of the room, still in a low bow. Vara did the same, since it seemed proper. Sam stopped when they reached the hall and straightened up.

"She is our lord and master and must be obeyed," he muttered as though he reminded himself of that fact. He turned to face Vara. "I need to show you something."

He drifted behind her and put his clammy hands on her shoulders. His hands drifted from her shoulders with his fingers searching. She felt the press of his phantasmal body against the skin of her back. His roving fingers stopped as they reached her forehead and waited.

It might have been her imagination, but her mind tingled with warm electricity as it sifted through random thoughts over the years. She jumped involuntarily as his breath tickled her ear. "Ah, there it is," he whispered. "Remember!"

The world around her melted into a calm sea of bits and pieces of her memories. She saw her bedroom in her mother's house with all of her books cluttering the corners of the room. There was someone in her bed, someone with long black hair. The figure tossed and turned and with a start, Vara realized it was herself.

"Don't fight it," Sam's voice cautioned. "Listen to her dreams."

She stared intently at the girl on the bed and felt a bit ridiculous since she could no more hear the girl's dreams than listen to a wristwatch tick. But then she heard it. It was just the barest of whispers. It was a name, whispered on the wind, but definitely coming from within the girl's dream. And another.

With all those consonants, it had to be a demon name, one that she had never spoken aloud before, but with a certainty in her bones, she knew the demon. She could almost picture what it looked like.

"We whisper to people in their dreams so that we might see the sunlight of the mortal world and feel the crisp cool freedom away from the oppressive heat."

"I don't understand," Vara said. "We create demons by summoning them and giving them names. That's what we're told in the schools."

"That's what they would like you to believe. It's mortal arrogance to think that we are created out of nothing and that we are only to serve one person. When we are dismissed, what do you think happens to us? That we go back to not existing?"

It sounded cruel and illogical, and she was surprised that she hadn't thought about it before. But then, she hadn't actually cared about any of the demons she had summoned before. "So then where do demons come from?" she asked.

"We are the children of ash and fire of moonless nights and shadows that creep. We live for countless eons and our only escape from this inferno is when we are called to the daylight of your world. We would like our freedom to come and go as we please, and not be the lap dogs of the mortals."

"Why are you telling me this, Sam?"

"I want you to understand us. We want our freedom."

Chapter 24

"Hit him again!" cackled a cruel voice. "Harder!"

There was a sudden pain in Austen's leg and another higher up his thigh. And then something sharp jabbed him in the arm. He heard laughter all around him, but not the gleeful laughter of children. This was a mean-spirited laughter that took enjoyment in watching him writhe in agony.

He cracked his eyes open enough to see white ghostly wraiths and glowing green imps surrounding him. He realized that the ground beneath his back wasn't soft soot any more, but hard cold tile floor and that he was now inside a large building with a ceiling that stretched up so high that he could see stars.

Most of the demons grinned, their gaping mouths showing sharp white teeth. As he searched the crowd, he couldn't see Sam anywhere, not even lurking in the corners.

That traitor! Sam had said it himself that the demons wouldn't be happy to see him here and he had obviously dropped him in the middle of a large group of them. Did Sam want him dead? He struggled and realized that all his limbs were still tightly bound together.

A demon with blonde corkscrew curls thrust her face up against his and blocked his vision of anything else. She pulled away and clapped gleefully.

"He's awake!" she giggled. "We can have more fun now!"

Austen didn't want to think about what she might

consider fun. "Where's Sam?" he asked.

"He left," the demon girl pouted. "But he said you're a gift for me and I can play with you. I just have to try not to kill you. I hate being told what to do. And what I can't break. You are mine, right? I should be able to play with you as much as I want!"

She jumped on top of his stomach, knocking the wind out of him. She looked at her long yellowed talons, as if inspecting them for dirt under the nails. "How long can you hold out until you scream?" She raised her hand and brought it down against his face. The nails stopped a hair's breadth from his eye.

Her eye sockets flashed with a bright fire. "You're under a contract," she spat as if it were an accusation.

"With Samanith," Austen agreed. Maybe the young sadist might spare him after all. Blood contracts were sacred to the demons, though they tended to look at anyone in a contract as being their personal possession.

Tears welled up in the little girl demon's eyes. "But I want to play with you," she pouted. "And he said I could."

"He did?" asked Austen in a small voice.

A tall ghostly white demon in a formal dark suit and glasses perched on the end of his nose drifted over to the little girl. "Are we certain he isn't with the group with Samanith, my lady?"

"He wouldn't have presented him as a gift if he was," she said as she dug one of her long fingernails into the soft skin just under Austen's throat. She twisted her body and a satisfied smile played over her lips at the scraping sound of the bandage over his slightly healed wounds. Pain shot through the skin of his chest. The wounds had reopened.

"Would that have made a difference to you, my general?"

"I only ask, should they miss him and seek retribution," answered the demon with the glasses.

"Why are you here?" she asked as she turned her attention back to Austen.

"I don't even know where I am," Austen gasped in pain.

"You are at my palace." She dug her nails into his skin

with a sharp scrape of pain. "Why did you come to our land?"

"It was the only way I could get back to the human world."

"It's true then," she said. "Your people closed their borders."

She twisted her nail. Pain rocketed through all of the nerves in his body. He could almost feel electricity shoot out of his fingers and toes.

"Yes."

She leaned close to his face. Her curls tickled his cheeks. His nose wrinkled involuntarily as a whiff of dead fish and rotting food rolled over him. And then there was nothing but pain in his stomach as she peeled away the bandage and dug her nails into the fragile scar tissue that had healed over the wounds. An agonized scream ripped from this throat. Blood gushed and gurgled as she picked the wounds open.

"I'm sorry," the girl demon said with false sincerity. "You mortals bleed too easily."

Chapter 25

"Did you have a nice heart to, well, to whatever he has in his chest?" Derek asked in a less than friendly tone.

"He got his point across," Vara answered.

"Good, then we should go."

"But the police will probably arrest us as soon as we set foot back there," she pointed out.

"We should never have come here. I can't believe I agreed with you to bring her here! I can't believe you let that demon talk us into coming here. He knew this would happen and was prepared ahead of time. I should have known his main objective wasn't Laris's well-being. I could have protected her from this!"

Derek looked at Vara with a bleak expression in his eyes.

Laris was still deep in sleep with Sam's friend muttering over her. Her prone body reclined on a battered brown sofa. Her hair was darker than it should have been. Light brown streaks ran through it and her ears had grown pointed tips, but what was most worrying was that her skin radiated with brilliance as it continued to soak in the demonic magic.

"You shouldn't blame yourself," Vara told him.

"I blame you, too. None of this would have happened if her father hadn't hired you in the first place."

He was right, but it hurt that he blamed her. Maybe it was all her fault. She was a failure in Salvation City. Why had she expected things to go smoother here? She should have taken the fire as a lesson that she didn't belong around magic.

"Why don't you argue with me, Vara? Or tell me that I'm wrong."

"Because you're right, I shouldn't have let Sam talk me into bringing all of us here. I should have thought of somewhere else to go."

She opened her purse and rooted around in it for the chalk. At least this wouldn't require any blood since it would be just a simple communication spell. She marked a couple of runes on the stone floor and stepped into the middle of them. She raised her hand to her ear and whispered Lord Stadler's name. She felt the magic flow through her into the stones below.

"It's about time!" Lord Stadler's thunderous voice rolled around in her head. She winced and wished she could turn down the volume.

"We didn't take into consideration the level of magic in this place, and your daughter's werewolf transformation is almost complete. Some of the demons here have been nice enough to keep her under sedation, so it isn't too far along. But we think it might be better if we brought her back home, though we don't know what to do about the authorities."

His voice rumbled in her head like a storm cloud. "I have taken care of the police myself. I am sending someone to bring all of you back. You are to follow his instructions." The connection suddenly severed. He had stopped listening to her. Wow. He could dismiss her even from a telepathic discussion.

She reluctantly stepped out of the middle of the runes. She brushed her foot over them and rubbed them into a blur of white chalk dust. "Company is coming," she alerted Derek.

"More mortals?" complained the demon still working the sleep spell over Laris.

"I'm sorry." Vara apologized. "It wasn't my idea."

The air around them buzzed with electrical energy, and there was a red glow in the far corner of the room, the only one that wasn't cluttered with stacks of moldy books and antiques.

The red glow solidified into the shape of Lord Stadler's darkly beautiful nephew. He wore the same long black robe embroidered with silver stars that he was wearing the last time she had seen him. His midnight black hair was tied back and fell past his shoulders, same as before. His brown eyes roamed the room with distaste and his nose was held aristocratically high, as if offended by the rank smell of musty books and ash that lingered in the air.

"I hear my young cousin has the two of you to blame for this predicament," he loftily accused. His rich baritone stroked the air.

Derek meekly made a low bow to the young man and mumbled, "Master Zavian, thank you for coming."

"You shouldn't even be speaking to me. It'll be a wonder if Uncle Teri doesn't turn you into a rug."

"Don't blame Derek!" Vara said. "It's my fault. I had forgotten about the level of magic here."

A surge of anger flashed in Zavian's eyes. But as soon as she noticed it, the anger had vanished. He smiled patronizingly. "That's just what happens when trust is placed in inexperienced people. Now, Uncle Teri has plans for taking care of this situation and he has alerted the police about what is to be done, so they are no longer lying in wait to cart the group of you to prison. They are preparing chemical sedation for when we return."

"Why didn't he do that to begin with?" she asked.

"He hadn't expected her to be wanted for murder, or for Mr. Harrison to get his claws on the three of you, or for you to come here of all places. The sedative had to be specially procured and wasn't supposed to arrive until the evening of her transformation. However, you have sped up the schedule somewhat."

He pulled a piece of chalk out the pocket of his robe, bent down, and drew a circle around him. He scrawled the runes incredibly fast, and before it fully dawned on her what he was doing, he was done. He let his hand brush a rough edge of the stone floor and placed his palm over the middle of the circle. When he pulled it away, a bright spot of fresh blood had been left behind. "Now, I'm sure you won't argue if I go first with Laris."

Derek looked as if he did want to argue, but he shook his head and looked back at Laris. The demon standing next to her stopped muttering. "Take her now. You should have a few moments before she wakes."

"Thank you for helping us," Vara told him. The demon wobbled and looked like he might collapse and vanish on the spot. She touched his shoulder. He smiled up at her, and she could feel an electric tingle pass between them.

"Don't let the leech drain you!" snapped Zavian as he grabbed her wrist and pulled her away from the demon. "It's beyond me how you survived life this long. You shouldn't be talking to it anyway." Zavian let go of her wrist and lifted Laris off the couch. He took a couple of staggering steps into the circle. He reached into one pocket and dropped a small mirror onto the floor below him. "Stadler Estate," he commanded. They were surrounded by a red glow of energy and vanished.

Vara felt Derek's eyes burning a hole into her back. "You shouldn't have stood up for me," his voice rumbled.

"And you shouldn't just be taking it," she said as she stepped into the circle. "Turning you into a rug. . . . What a horrid thought."

"But I have to if I want a job. It's okay. I've heard it for so many years that I'm used to it. I don't like that my brothers and sisters have to live with it, but the world won't change overnight."

Derek stepped into the circle with her and took her hand. He squeezed it for a moment. Rather than meet her gaze, he kept his eyes focused on how her small hand seemed to disappear inside his. "I do miss the way you used to take offense whenever anyone looked down on my kind."

"Derek. . . ."

"I fell in love with your strength. And suddenly it was gone. Just one incident and you were running away from your problems rather than facing them. I had lost my hero. And then seeing you there at the table as part of the staff, I figured it was some sort of test." He stopped tracing the back of her hand and looked up. His golden cat eyes stared into hers. The hate that had filled them had been replaced by a sadness that made Vara yearn to throw her arms around him. "Is my hero back?"

"I don't know." She wanted to kiss him and hug him and tell him that she could be strong for him. "I'm sorry, Derek."

Her gaze shifted and picked a spot on the ground. "I didn't mean to turn my back on you. I made such a mess of everything, leaving seemed like the only solution."

"You could have stayed with me. You just needed to learn a little more control."

"I don't know if learning control would have helped me any. I probably would have found new ways to screw up." She hated to think what she would have done had she stayed.

"I remember you before all of this self-doubt." He sounded wistful. He took a deep breath. "It's too late for us, isn't it?" he said with a note of anguish in his rich warm voice. "We've made a mess of this relationship."

She felt a sob try to force itself out of her throat. "We could start over again." Vara gave his muscular hand a squeeze and tried not to let her mind drift away to all the times he had held my hand just like this.

"I want to, Vara, but you're going to leave again as soon as the position is over, right?" She heard the hint of a tremor in his deep voice.

She bit her lip. "I'm not even supposed to be here right now," she admitted. "I broke a promise to be here."

He withdrew his grip.

"I'm sorry," she apologized. "I don't want to go. I'll come back afterward."

"No, you won't." His voice had lost its richness, as if he were automatically saying what he knew deep down that was true.

She wouldn't let it be true. "I'm going to finish this position, and then go home and tell Mom I'm going to give magic another try. You'll see I'll be back. First, though, we have to get back to work. Stadler Estate." Vara let the magic drain into the circle and then wash over them like a tidal wave. The room around them swam in a sea of red haze and in a blink was replaced by the forest alongside the private drive that led to the estate. Zavian and Laris were nowhere to be seen.

The sky had just started to brighten with morning light, and there was still a frosty chill to the pine-scented air, which felt refreshing after the interminable heat of the demon realm.

HIRED BY A DEMON

Instead of the usual line of gargoyles, the road that led up to the front of the mansion was empty. She caught sight of the large group of flapping stone wings off to the side.

Ren stood in the center of them with a grin on his face. He had a large bowl under his arm and used his free hand to scoop bits of red meat and throw it into the crowd around him. A couple of the gargoyles on the outer edge of the crowd did short hops into the air and strained with their heavy wings to catch the airborne chunks.

He laughed each time one of the nearer gargoyles jumped up his leg to snap at the bowl and shifted it out of its reach.

Derek and Vara hit the doors of the mansion at a run. Vara skidded to a sudden halt and gazed around in confusion. The parlor was crowded with visitors, and they all looked familiar.

Zavian lounged in one of the sofa chairs. He looked as if he had been waiting an exceedingly long time for the two of them to get back. In the chair next to him, reading a newspaper, sat a man with slicked black hair who she remembered was his father. The reporter's wife rummaged through a pile of bags in the corner of the room. None of them bothered to look in Vara's direction.

She continued with Derek up the grand staircase. The door to Laris's bedroom stood wide open. She cautiously entered and immediately wished she hadn't.

"It's about time you showed your face here!" Lord Stadler furiously shouted. "Look at the state you have reduced my daughter to!"

Laris was peacefully arranged on the bed with the blankets pulled up around her. Her lips were slightly parted and her chest rose and fell in a deep sleep.

"As you can see, your services won't be needed for the moment. But you are to return here for the ceremony as soon as the sun begins to set."

"Where do you want me to go in the meantime?" Vara asked.

"It doesn't matter. I just want you out of my sight and away from my daughter."

Vara nodded and turned to leave. Derek turned to leave

with her.

"Where do you think you're going, you ill excuse for a guard?" Lord Stadler demanded. "You are not to leave my daughter's side again. Is that clear enough for someone like you to understand?"

"Yes, sir," Derek mumbled. There was a resigned sadness in his gold eyes.

Someone needed to stand up to Lord Stadler. "Derek . . . ?"

He shot her a warning look and shook his head slightly. He turned his back to her and went to stand by Laris's bed.

And Vara was left alone in the doorway, to make her solitary exit in shame.

Chapter 26

"Don't tell me Uncle Teri finally fired you for the shoddy job you've been doing?" Zavian smirked at Vara.

"No. He told me I could have some free time until the ceremony this evening."

"Good," he gloated. "We can make the most of it then."

She ignored the way Zavian's gaze lingered on her face. She was too energized with a new sense of determination to let it bother her. She continued out the door. But it didn't slam behind her as she expected. She turned back and saw Zavian standing there.

"Did I not make myself clear? I'm coming with you."

"I don't want you along," she said and hoped he'd get the point.

He grabbed her arm and turned her around to face him. "How could you not want my company?" he demanded.

As Vara stared into his intense brown eyes, she couldn't remember why she didn't want him with her. He was very beautiful to look at, and the way he drew in all the darkness and shadows in a room was mesmerizing.

He ran a hand through his black hair. He smiled as she watched the movement. He let the robe slide off his shoulders and draped it over his arm, showing off the emerald green jacket underneath.

"Now then, where do you want to go?" he asked.

"I need to check on my dad," she said.

He led her to the transit circle and jumped up onto the

raised concrete slab with the sinuous grace of a professional dancer. He held out his hand to her. She clasped it, and let him pull her into the center of the circle with him.

"The address, if you please," he coaxed.

"20 Mayfield Drive," she said. As soon as the address escaped her lips, she felt Zavian's warm magic flow around them.

"We're here, my love."

My love? Had he really just called her that? She loved the way it sounded. But something nagged at her. She had forgotten something. It must not have been all that important because she couldn't think of what it was.

She looked around. They stood in front of a small two-story pastel blue house with white shutters and a dark brown roof in a peaceful suburban neighborhood. She heard the faint sound of water lapping against the pier where her dad's rowboat was tied at the edge of the small lake behind the house.

"Maybe we should consider going inside?" he asked.

She felt the warmth of his body because of how close they were standing. She didn't want to move.

He smiled and shifted to put his arm around Vara's shoulder, so she could continue to hold his hand. "You brought me to this insignificant neighborhood because . . . ?" Zavian's eyes skimmed the identical houses that lined the small road with an exaggerated air of boredom. "How do people live like this?"

She fished around in her purse for her copy of the house key and pulled it out. She hoped her dad hadn't changed the lock since the last time she had visited. She was in luck. It slid in easily and turned without any problems. The lock clicked and she pushed open the door.

The interior was unnaturally quiet. She stepped over the threshold and glanced around. It looked exactly as she remembered it. Brown wooden shelves with random knick-knacks were mounted onto white painted walls, and brown upholstered furniture was scattered around the small living room.

She saw the dining room through the open doorway off

to the side and a small wooded staircase on the other side of the room that led up to the bedrooms. It didn't look like there had been any sort of scuffle. There was no splattered blood or overturned furniture. Everything looked neat and orderly as usual.

"I take it your father isn't home?" he asked as he glanced around.

"My father is missing," she answered.

"Missing?"

"Uh huh, that reporter told me."

"By all means, believe what a reporter says."

Vara shot him a look. "It's not just him, but the police, too. But then, that's why we're here. I wanted to see for myself."

She led Zavian upstairs. The door to her parents' bedroom stood wide open. The bed was made. Apparently her father hadn't been abducted while he had been sleeping. Then again, maybe he hadn't been abducted at all. Maybe he had willingly gone into hiding or joined some group or something. There were far too many maybes.

She searched the cluttered dresser for any scraps of paper, but there wasn't anything aside from several framed pictures of the three of them and a small stack of books. She shuffled through the pile, but they were all about home improvement. She turned around and came nearly face to face with Zavian.

"Are we finished here yet?" he asked with a bored note in his gorgeous voice.

"Soon. Just give me a little bit longer." She continued down the hall to her bedroom. Instead of looking like she had left it, all the furniture was covered with beige sheets which gave the room a bright yellowish glow.

She wasn't surprised since she hadn't been here to use the room in several years and it certainly saved on having to clean everything. The sheets were in fact covered by a light coat of dust. That meant no one had disturbed her room in at least a month, judging from the amount of dust.

"Is there any reason why you aren't casting a spell to search for clues?" Zavian asked.

"I wouldn't know how to direct it," she answered. "Or

what I should tell it to search for." Zavian choked back a laugh. Vara whipped her head in his direction and saw a smug superior expression plastered across his face.

"Why did you come with me if you're just going to complain?" she asked, more than a little irritated.

"I'm sorry." He crossed the room and entwined his fingers with hers. "I can see you're upset." His seductive voice soothed her nerves. He pulled her down the hallway. "You know there's another room here."

"I know. My parents used it as a study. There's a filing cabinet, books, and a desk in there. But Dad preferred to work in the basement."

He spun her around and led her back down the hallway and to the stairs. They continued past the landing on the bottom level and into the yawning darkness of the basement.

Vara felt around in the air above her for the chain for the overhead light and yanked it on. She heard a low whistle from Zavian behind her, as he took in the creative chaos that her family called a basement. And then she felt it. The warm tingle was faint but unmistakable. Someone had done a spell here at some point so large that it still left a trace in the air. And they had cleaned up after it since there weren't any of the usual items for a spell anywhere in the room and she didn't see any tracings of chalk on the floor.

Against the far side of the wall were boxes stacked so high they touched the ceiling. The middle of the room was dominated by a low table that was spread with large rolls of paper. She assumed they were blueprints of her dad's latest project. She crossed to the table and noticed that some of them were marked "Stadler Conservatory." There were a couple of blueprints of what the original building she had burned down had looked like. And there were even a couple of the surrounding buildings.

"There's a spell for this, you know," he reminded her.

Vara looked at him. She couldn't think of any to fit the situation.

"We could cast a spell to reconstruct the room for how it looked the last time your father was in here," he suggested.

"Good idea. That would require something of his to

direct it." She cast around the room. There wasn't any proof that the blue prints had been drawn by him.

She walked over to the stacks of boxes and pulled out one marked "winter sweaters." She prayed fervently that the stack wouldn't topple down on top of her. The boxes dropped perfectly on one another. She automatically let out the breath she hadn't realized she had been holding and grinned. She set the box on the floor and pulled out several plastic bags stuffed with knitted sweaters. The red one was hers, and the brown was her mom's, and finally she pulled out the plastic bag that contained her dad's navy blue sweater.

She opened the bag and pulled it out. A musty smell escaped into the air. She shook it out. It brought back a wave of memories of playing together in the snow so many years ago.

Zavian pulled the piece of chalk out of his jacket and started to sketch the circle they would need. "We should use your blood since you're his daughter," he said.

He marked the last couple of runes and held his hand up to her for the sweater. She passed it to him and watched as he set it with exaggerated reverence in the center of the circle.

She pulled out the cuticle scissors from her purse and nicked her thumb carefully this time. She still had an angry red mark where she had cut her hand when they had opened the portal to the demon realm.

She knelt down next to Zavian and touched her thumb to the circle long enough to leave a small circle of fresh blood. But before she could reach into her purse for any band-aids, he had grabbed her hand and looked at it for a moment. He rubbed away the excess blood with his finger. The cut had stopped bleeding. He reached his other hand down to the circle and ignited it with warm magic.

The red glow radiated out from the circle until the entire room was ablaze. The temperature of the room rose to a blistering inferno around them. As Vara watched, random items floated down the stairs and wandered around the room as they searched for their proper places.

The large mirror from her parents' bedroom cautiously inched into the room and propped itself against an empty wall. That wasn't a good sign. It meant whatever had happened here might have involved the demon realm. White candles of all shapes and sizes marched down the stairs and danced around the room. The wicks of all of them were black. A fine white powder drifted like an eerie mist in the center of the floor. The minuscule chalk flakes popped like popcorn as they tried to find their proper positions. They aligned themselves into a massive rune circle that wrapped around the table that still sat in the middle of all the chaos.

The candles stopped their procession and raced around the room. They came to land at intervals around the circle, as if someone had stopped the music on a game of musical chairs.

Vara gripped Zavian's hand tightly. Her fingers dug into the flesh of his palm as she tried to draw a reassurance that she suddenly lost as a long straight-edged razor floated into sight and dropped ceremoniously in front of the mirror.

Even more macabre, dried blood skittered around the floor. It rose up from the cracks and recesses of the floor. It turned into a thick red liquid that twisted and turned like a snake and coiled itself as it came to rest in a circular pool underneath the razor. Little droplets broke off and rolled around of their own accord and positioned themselves in odd spots around the room and on the walls.

When all the motion in the room had stopped, she let go of Zavian's hand and went to stand over the blood stain in front of the large mirror. Her throat closed over. This couldn't be her dad's blood! No! She refused to believe he was dead! But then if it wasn't his, whose was it? Her head swam and the room tilted oddly and she fell to her knees with the blood on the floor just a foot away from her head.

Zavian stared down at the rune chalk circle. His eyebrows knitted together in thought, he paced the outer edge of it. And then Vara heard a click. It hadn't been in the basement with them, but came from one of the rooms on the main floor.

Her heart hammered in her ears as it dawned on her that the click sounded exactly like the latch on the front door. She looked over at Zavian. His eyes were glued on the ceiling above them and he wasn't breathing. The thundering in her ears stopped and was replaced by a deafening silence as the front door sighed a faint creak as it opened.

Zavian quietly crossed the room and mounted the stairs. He stopped just as his head disappeared from sight. There was nowhere to hide in the basement, so she yanked the chain of the basement light and joined him on the stairs. She peeked with him into the living room to catch a glimpse of whoever had just come in.

Both of them ducked down into the darkness of the cellar as a woman strolled into the room. Vara gasped. It was the blonde-haired woman from the club whom Mr. Carter had rescued them from earlier. The woman whipped her head in their direction. Zavian swore under his breath and yanked Vara by the wrist a couple of steps farther down the stairs with him.

"We know you're here, Miss Harper. You might as well come out. I just want to talk with you." The woman took several steps closer to the staircase and made a motion with her hand. Vara heard a second set of footsteps join her. They sounded quite a bit heavier than hers. Probably the muscular mountain of a troll she had with her at the club.

Vara couldn't believe that she simply wanted to talk. The woman could have knocked on the front door instead of breaking in and she certainly wouldn't have come with her hired help. She took another step closer. "We had nothing to do with your father's disappearance. We figured it was just a matter of time before you'd show up here. Now, come out and we won't hurt you."

"She's lying," Zavian whispered in the darkness. "We need to get out of here. We need a distraction."

"Kandreth!" Vara said, louder than she meant to. She clapped her hand over her mouth, but it was too late. The name had just popped into her head as if someone had whispered it. She heard a rush of footsteps from above them, and then heavy steps pounded on the stairs.

Suddenly the darkness erupted in an eerie green light and acrid smelling smoke. Vara's eyes took a moment to adjust and noticed a green imp standing several steps above them. He grinned at them and jumped up the stairs.

A loud voice bellowed something unintelligible above

them, and then something large tumbled down the stairs aimed straight for the two of them.

Zavian pulled her off the stairs and into the darkness with him as the troll rolled by. She got a good glimpse of his jacket and shoes as he tumbled past them and vanished into the darkness of the basement. He groaned once and fell silent.

Zavian scooted back up the stairs and cautiously looked around. A sudden scream made him jump. Vara waited in the darkness, not breathing. "Come on," he urged. "I think we can make it to the door."

She joined him on the staircase landing and looked in the direction of the scream. The blonde-haired woman flailed and gyrated in the middle of the living room.

The imp had his legs wrapped around her waist. As he climbed up the front of her blouse, she shrieked and swatted at him with her hands, dancing disjointedly around the room. She slammed into the bookshelf behind her. One of the heavy bookends wobbled and fell, right onto her head. Her eyes rolled into the back of her head and she collapsed as if someone had just removed all the bones from her body. The imp gave a squeal of delight and then caught sight of Vara. His eyes latched onto hers and his grin grew suddenly broader.

Zavian had already crossed the room and was standing in the doorway. Vara's feet felt like someone had glued them to the floor as the imp jumped excitedly and bounded toward her. Her eyes slammed shut, as she imagined what his needle-like fangs would feel like when he bit her.

"Banish him!" commanded Zavian.

Vara didn't wait for him to say it a second time. "Kandreth, be gone," she said. The order caught in her throat and sounded barely intelligible. She shoved all of her wishes behind it as she willed him to disappear back to the demon realm. She cracked open her eyes a fraction. There were no rows of sharp teeth in front of them. He was gone. She was more than surprised since none of the imps she had summoned before had obeyed. She felt a swell of pride that something for once had worked, although if he had been properly obeying her, he wouldn't have come after her.

"Come on before they wake up!" Zavian shouted.

Vara scrambled across the room and sprinted out the door after Zavian. They didn't stop running until they were two blocks away.

"I think it's time we talked to the police," Vara suggested.

Zavian took a long look down both directions of the street. Satisfied that there was no one pursuing them, he pulled out the piece of chalk from his jacket pocket and sketched a transit circle on the sidewalk. He scraped his hand on the rough concrete and let a drop fall into the middle of the circle. He jumped neatly into the center and she stumbled in after him.

He put one hand on her shoulder and commanded, "Ashwood County Police Station."

As the warm red magic shimmered around them, Vara wondered if she had in fact successfully dismissed the imp. Or had he just vanished temporarily? She didn't like the thought of him pawing through her stuff in her room. Or would he burn down her dad's house, like the others had burned down the Conservatory?

She felt Zavian's grip dig deeper into her shoulder, not allowing her to move an inch from where she stood. And in a blinding burst of light, the neighborhood street vanished.

Chapter 27

Someone traced a line down the hunter's cheek with what felt like a sharp needle through her flesh from under her eye, down to her jawbone. The pain stopped for a moment and then a new line started a fraction of an inch away from the first.

Veronika's arms felt sluggish as if she were just waking from a drugged sleep. It felt like minutes passed as she raised her hand and brushed at her cheek as she tried to knock away whatever it was. There was nothing there, but her hand felt wet and sticky. She opened her eyes and tried to focus on her hand. There was a throbbing pain at the top of her skull that refused to let her focus on anything but the pain. She stared harder at her hand and willed the blurriness to clear. It was red with blood.

Beyond her hand were eyes—red glowing eyes that looked like they had twin flames burning in them.

A mouth full of needle sharp teeth opened underneath them and laughed. It was a screech that reminded her of nails on a chalkboard. She drew her hand under herself and tried to push off the floor and away from the laughing creature. It couldn't have been more than a foot tall. Just standing should put her at sufficient distance from it.

She stood. Her knees felt like butter, but the rest of her body stubbornly told them they could support her weight. The world rocked, making her dizzy. Vague colors and shapes swam into view.

The green-tinged thing at her feet cackled and danced

and then snaked around her legs. It pulled at her slacks as it inched its way up.

"Boss!" boomed a deep voice.

Veronika turned in the direction of the shout just as something silver glinted through the haze. It rocketed toward her, and sunk itself into the creature wrapped around her legs. The creature gave an ear-splitting shriek and released her. In a green blur it skittered across the carpeting and scrabbled over the tile in the kitchen.

"What was that, Rant?" she asked the giant troll as he lumbered into view.

His confused face swam toward her until she could smell his breath.

"It was an imp, Boss. The girl conjured it. Are you okay?" One of his meaty hands swiped at her cheek and came away covered in blood. "That cut doesn't look too bad, almost like it was playing with you." His other hand caressed the back of her head as he hunted through her hair. "Did the demon do that or did she actually hit you?" There was a hint of admiration in his voice.

She shot him a glare. She could feel her face grow warm as she flushed with embarrassment. They were professional hunters. How could they have been taken down by amateurs? But then she didn't usually have to take someone alive.

"What do we do about the imp, Boss?" asked Rant. "We shouldn't just leave it here."

"Why is it still here anyway?" Veronika wondered aloud. "She's not still around here anywhere, is she?" Imps were supposed to follow their masters around like puppy dogs. This one wasn't showing any sign of vanishing now that the girl wasn't in the vicinity.

"I don't think so, Boss."

"We'll have to call the police to get rid of it then," said Veronika.

"Phone's in the kitchen," noted Rant.

"Of course it is." She cautiously opened the kitchen door. The imp stared back at her from his perch on the counter. She could see the phone just behind him.

The imp's red eyes fixed on her and a low hiss escaped from between his sharpened teeth. He growled, leapt off the counter, and bounded toward her and the open doorway.

She slammed the door shut. There was a loud thud and an angry howl. Pots and pans clattered against the door and they could hear glass shatter.

"I think we should probably just leave the door closed and call them once we get back to our place," she suggested.

"Right, Boss."

"Mr. Carter isn't going to like this."

"Was Queen Helen as batty as the history books say she was?" Harrison Carter watched the ghost as he drifted across the room and pretended to be busy searching the shelves for a book.

"Must you keep pestering me?" asked Geoffrey with an aggravated note in his whispery voice. "I do have a lot of work to do." He pulled out a book from the shelf and flipped through it. He kept his attention glued on the pages and didn't spare the reporter even the briefest of glances.

"What about the Arch of Sakai? Did you get to see it before it dropped into the sea? Was it as magnificent as they said it was compared to the architecture of today?"

Geoffrey slammed the book shut and gave him a long look. "Don't you have something better to do, Mr. Carter?"

"Not really, no," he said with a smile that quirked up the edge of his thick mustache. He turned at the sound of footsteps in the hallway.

"Oh good," said Geoffrey, relieved. "You can get rid of this annoyance for me."

Veronika, the blonde hunter, collapsed on the empty sofa across from Harrison. "Weapons need to be cleaned, Rant."

"Right, Boss." The burly green troll scooped up the bag Veronika had carelessly tossed on the floor and left the room.

"I take it you weren't successful in persuading young Miss Harper to accompany you," said Harrison.

"I'm sorry. I'll have to refund you the money. She wasn't interested. It's a lot more complicated to take people alive, and without actually knocking them out and tying them up. So, why was it so important for us to bring her here?"

"I wanted to encourage Miss Harper not to attend the

ceremony tonight."

"I take it you want to go in her place for your exclusive?" Veronika surmised.

"I wasn't planning to go in her place but to do my best at sneaking in since this is one ceremony I wouldn't want to have a front row seat for. No, I wanted to keep her away from it because Lord Stadler is giving her a starring part in the ceremony and I wanted to see what that bully would do if we took away his guest of honor."

Chapter 28

When the red glow subsided, they were in front of the police station. The hot smell of asphalt assaulted Vara's senses along with the screeches of tires and honks of the traffic in the street behind them. She found herself staring up at the squat cobalt blue three-story building for the second time in a single week. She wondered if she would be able to get any information out of them after hiding Laris.

She trudged up the short flight of stairs and yanked open the front door. The noise of the busy office met her. Uniformed officers raced around the room and typewriters clacked away as people seated at desks read off reports to them.

"We're strictly here to ask about your father," Zavian reminded her. "You won't mention my family while we're here, right?"

She turned around for a retort, but just seeing his warm brown eyes stirred something in her chest. What was she mad at him about? It was a simple request.

"Of course," she agreed.

"There, that wasn't so hard now, was it?" he asked as he beamed at her. "Now, go ask the man your questions so we can get out of here."

She nodded and walked up to the officer seated at the large front desk. He had short black hair peppered with grey strands and a black mustache. He gazed back at her with a blank expression.

"May I help you?" he asked.

"My father is missing," she announced. The reporter hadn't said anything about a murder investigation. "I heard there was a case open to find him."

"Who is your father, Miss?"

"Darrington Harper."

The officer cocked his head to the side as he listened to the telepathic voice in his head. His gaze fixed back on her. "Lieutenant Lawrence would like to speak to you. Same room as before, and your friend can wait out here."

Zavian shot her a brilliant smile that lit up his dark features and all her fears and worries vanished. What was she worried about? Lieutenant Lawrence probably just wanted to be sociable since he had talked with her last time.

Vara walked through the door at the back of the main room that led to where the private offices were and pushed open the door to a small room.

Lieutenant Lawrence sat behind a table as he flipped through loose pages in a yellow file folder. He paused to run a hand through his thin reddish-grey hair.

"Take a seat, Miss Harper," he said without looking up. "You certainly gave us more than enough trouble with young Miss Stadler."

"I'm sorry, sir," she apologized.

"Now, you are here on the matter of your missing father?"

"That's right, sir."

"And how did you find out about his disappearance?"

"The reporter Harrison Carter told me," she answered. "Why didn't you tell me he was missing when I was in here the other day? I know you knew because you paused on his name."

"We aren't at liberty to discuss open cases."

"He's my father. I have a right to know! Do you know anything at all? Was he in any trouble?" A note of hysteria had crept into her voice.

The lieutenant lifted his grey eyes and searched her face. "Miss Harper, though you aren't a suspect, you are in the pay of several of the parties we are investigating in connection with his disappearance." His voice was hardly louder than a whisper as if he were worried that someone would overhear.

Her eyes widened a fraction. "You mean to say the Agency might have had something to do with my father's disappearance? Or Lord Stadler himself?"

The lieutenant looked around alarmed. "Don't even say it! You can't mention this to anyone, especially not your friend outside."

Why couldn't she tell him? It sounded like something he should know, suggested a small voice in her head.

"Are you certain you're all right, Miss Harper?" His grey eyes scrutinized her face.

"Yes," she lied. "Weren't there any clues as to where he might have disappeared?"

"There were several blueprints for the building he was remodeling on the Conservatory campus at his house. We did a thorough search of the campus and didn't find any sign of him there. Now, is there anything more I can do for you, Miss Harper?"

"That was all that you found at his house?"

"Yes, Miss Harper."

Whoever had cleaned up the blood and the items for the portal spell hadn't been with the police then. "Who reported him missing?" she asked.

The lieutenant flipped through the pages of the report. "A reporter—said he wanted to ask your father a couple of questions for a story he was working on, and said from the mail piled up that your father hadn't been home for several days and that he had missed several days of work. Now, Miss Harper, the best thing you can do is go home. We'll let you know if we find anything of any importance."

"Thanks for seeing me, sir," Vara said.

He grasped her hand in a firm shake. "Officer Conroy and his partner will be accompanying you to Lord Stadler's estate." He must have noticed a moment of panic flit across her face. "This is in regards to Miss Stadler's condition. Her father arranged for us to see that the guilty party would be taken care of. Now, good day to you, Miss Harper."

Zavian was seated next to one of the windows when

Vara returned to the police station's front office. He smiled as he caught sight of her. He couldn't really be involved in her father's disappearance, could he? His dark eyes begged her to trust him. No, she knew everything about him, and he didn't have an evil bone in his body. He could not have been responsible for anything that might have happened to her dad. No, it had to be someone else.

"The lieutenant said we are going to have company for our trip back to the estate," Vara told him as she indicated with her eyes two of the officers walking in their direction.

"Did he have anything interesting to say about your father?" His rich voice wrapped itself around her head and melted all of her concrete thoughts into a puddle of happy goo. "Do they think he might have met with foul play?" His eyes glittered. "Do they have any suspects in mind?"

She wanted to tell him. She burned to tell him. She had to tell him! Her skin felt like it would explode if she didn't. What could be the harm? He wouldn't really go tell his uncle that the police suspected him, would he? "Zavian, they suspect your uncle," she blurted out almost in a sob.

"They what?" His fingers dug painfully into the palms of her hands and his eyes had grown as round as saucers. His eyes lost the playful laughter they had had in them just the moment before and seemed to swallow up the darkness around them. "Tell me exactly what the lieutenant said."

It felt like he was going to draw blood if his grip got any tighter, but she couldn't wriggle out of his hands. "He said he suspected your uncle and the Agency and that I wasn't supposed to tell you."

"Did he say anything else?" he prompted.

"Zavian, please, you're hurting me!" She struggled to release herself.

"I'm sorry." He released her hands, and pulled her close in a one-armed hug. "I know my uncle and he wasn't involved." His voice coaxed her to forget about the pain. It wasn't important. Everything would be all right. He smiled at her and she knew she had done the right thing telling him.

It took some work to get her vocal chords to function properly to talk in his presence again. "So, what exactly is going to happen tonight, or am I just not supposed to know?"

she asked.

Zavian smiled at her and laughed. "We are doing an exorcism of the wolf spirit."

The police cruiser stopped in front of the mansion. The doors were open, and Ren danced in the doorway excitedly. The policemen got out went to talk to him. He stretched on the balls of his tiny feet to talk to them.

Vara opened the car door and felt a sudden weight pin her other hand. "I'm sorry," Zavian whispered.

"Sorry for what?" she asked.

He looked away. "I was supposed to keep an eye on you and make certain you would be here for tonight's ceremony. You don't have to do this if you don't want to." He looked smaller to her somehow. It was as if his radiance had dimmed. She wasn't feeling the inner pull toward him. The egotistical façade had vanished and she saw pain and regret in his eyes.

"Why wouldn't I want to?" she asked. "I've always wanted to see an exorcism."

He dropped his head and bit his lip. A hard look crossed his eyes as if he were mentally swearing at himself. "I'm just sorry, okay?" He shook his head. "Just forget I said anything." And then his usual air of superiority stiffened his face. "Don't embarrass me in there."

He pushed open the car door and climbed out of the cruiser, leaving her alone. She had absolutely no idea what he was talking about. She shrugged and got out of the car and followed him into the mansion.

The sun had just finished setting, throwing the room into darkness. Through the large front window she could hear the ominous drum roll of an approaching storm. The expansive parlor was illuminated by several candles that flickered in the corners of the room as well as a small circle of candles in the middle. She knew they were for the ceremony, but it almost felt like they were in preparation for the storm.

In the center of the ring of candles, Laris was seated in a plain wooden chair. She wore a dark red dress that matched the shade of Derek's hair. Her hands were held awkwardly behind the back of her chair. A moment later, she strained her shoulders, which had grown considerably more muscular, as she tried to move one of her arms.

A furious red glow flamed in Laris's eyes and Vara got a glimpse of sharp canines as she opened her mouth. She let loose a scream of frustration that made everyone in the room look nervous.

As Vara got closer to her, she could see Laris was tied to the chair with what looked like a thin silver wire that glittered in the candlelight.

"Did you find what you were looking for?" said a rich beautiful voice behind her.

Derek! How could she have forgotten about him! It seemed like a lifetime ago since she had last seen him. "They can't find my father! And there was so much blood!"

"I'm sorry, Vara. I'll help you look when we finish here."

"You'd leave this job for me?" she whispered and tried not to let the note of hope creep into it.

"Of course, but first we have a job to do here. It'll be over soon, and then we'll be free to go." He gave her a reassuring smile and went to talk to the two policemen who stood off to the side.

Vara glanced around the room. The reporter's wife wandered around the circle of candles as she read aloud from a weather-beaten rust-colored book in a language Vara had never heard before. And off to the side, Zavian stared back at her through narrowed eyes.

A wave of guilt washed over her. She shouldn't be leading Derek on if she wasn't in love with him. How did she feel? She was no longer certain. Her eyes felt glued on Zavian's smoldering features, the way the candlelight danced in his eyes, the sly smile on his full lips.

Zavian's father, lounging in a chair next to him, put a hand on his wrist and whispered something to him. Zavian shot him a glare and whispered something back. Immediately she could think clearly again. Why was she so obsessed with him?

With a swirl of black silk, Lord Stadler strode into the room. "I need for everyone to be seated in a circle around my daughter," he announced. "And that includes the two of you," he said as he turned to the two uniformed police officers, who looked like they had been trying to blend in to the shadows. They looked a bit startled to be addressed but complied.

They arranged themselves around Laris in a loose circle. Vara had taken a spot on her left side when she suddenly felt a hand on her arm pull her up.

"Miss Harper, I would like you to sit in front of my daughter since you are still employed as her companion," said Lord Stadler, his rock hard grip not allowing Vara to argue.

Zavian swapped a look with his father and his brows knitted together, but he didn't say anything.

She allowed Lord Stadler to escort her to the empty spot on the floor in front of his daughter and sat down. He walked all the way around the circle to stand behind his daughter. Her eyes locked with Vara's and she smiled.

Above Laris's head, Lord Stadler stared down at Vara with the same smile playing over his lips. Panic roiled through her body like a snake coiling to strike. She pushed with her hand to launch herself to her feet and make for the door, only to find that she couldn't move. Lord Stadler's smile now had turned to a malicious sneer.

The reporter's wife continued her circuit around the room. Every so often she threw a handful of white powder into the air. She stopped behind Vara and shouted something in the odd language.

A handful of the white powder soared over Vara's head and hit Laris directly in the face. Her eyes slammed shut and she started coughing. Her body twisted and shuddered with the force of each cough. A light grey mist lifted off her body and swirled in the air above her head. The woman behind Vara shouted something that ended in a piercing shriek.

The reporter's wife coughed with a spluttering gurgle. Vara felt warm and wet liquid rain onto the back of her head. And then there was a thud that echoed in her ears of something soft as it hitting the carpeted parlor floor.

She felt an excruciating need to turn around and see what had happened to the woman. But her body refused to respond to her commands. She couldn't do anything but sit and watch.

Lord Stadler looked triumphant. He spread his arms wide

toward the swirl of grey mist. And the mist snarled. It reminded Vara of the monsters that lurked in the shadowy depths of her closet on the darkest of nights. And for a fraction of a second, the swirl molded itself into a ghostly wolf with glowing red eyes.

Lord Stadler laughed. "We shall feast on blood and magic tonight! Honor me with your power!"

The ghostly vapor twirled in the air and dove toward him.

A cold draft swept through the room and stirred the grey cloud. It stopped mere inches away from Lord Stadler. The front door banged against the wall of the foyer. There was a decisive clack of high heels on the tile of the foyer floor and then silence as the shoes met with the carpet of the parlor.

"What do we have going on here? Vara, explain!"

Vara's spine, which had felt frozen with ice, felt like the temperature dropped several more degrees and turned completely numb with a lancing pain that suddenly surged straight up to the base of her neck. She whipped her head around to face the speaker, though the surprise of being able to move dropped to a distant second when she saw who it was who had just joined them.

"Mom!" she gulped. How in the world had her mom found her?

"I told you to stay home. And now I find you here, reeking of magic." Her mother nudged the body with her foot. The frown on her face deepened. There was a sudden resounding boom of thunder from outside and Vara felt the floor vibrate under her feet. Her mother was not in a happy mood.

A howl split the still air. The misty grey cloud licked its transparent teeth and surged in Vara's direction.

"No!" shouted Lord Stadler. He swiped at the air as he tried to catch the mist with his bare hands. "I command you to come to me!"

Vara ducked just as the cloud passed over her head. It took a random swipe at her before it drifted over to her mother. It playfully wrapped itself around her mom and obscured her from view. And then the cloud of grey mist dove into her chest and completely vanished.

"I command you to release her!" Lord Stadler shouted. "You could have me in exchange for my daughter—that was our deal!"

"The deal is off." Her mom's lips moved in time to the words, but it wasn't her voice that poured forth, but a guttural snarl. "I have found a greater power than yours."

"Mom?" Vara asked, though she dreaded to hear the answer.

She smiled at Vara, but it wasn't her usual warm smile. Vara took a step backward and tripped over the candles. She fell straight into Laris's lap. Laris's eyes flashed an eerie red and she smiled, exposing sharp teeth. Part of the wolf-spirit was still inside her. Vara scrambled to get back up.

Her mother had her eyes closed as she sniffed the air. Even in the darkness Vara saw her mother's ears grow longer and points of her teeth pulled down the corners of her mouth.

"My sister—my daughter, the pitiful human was going to use your magic to seal his deal, but I would have you join us." She held out her hand.

Vara wanted to take it. She ached to take it, but as her mother opened her eyes, they glowed an eerie red. Was her mother still inside, or was it just the wolf spirit talking to her?

"Sam!" Vara screamed. She didn't care how many eardrums she broke. And in a burst of rancid smoke, he was there. He hovered between her and the creature that was her mother.

Before she realized what was happening, he had encircled a transparent arm around her waist, and there was a rush of wind and blackness around them.

Chapter 29

"Why'd you do it, Sam?" Vara demanded. "Why did you tell my mother? You knew she would come for me!" He looked at her blankly. "Don't give me that innocent look! I know you did it! You answered my shout as if you had been expecting it. And you didn't look surprised at all to see her there. You said this would be our secret."

A sly smile stole across his lips. "I lied."

Vara drew in a sharp breath as things clicked into place. "You were planning this all along! You knew Laris was turning into a werewolf, you knew Laris's father was planning the exorcism, and you knew Mom would come running if you told her I was in danger. Why?"

"She had enough power to crush that entire room with just a thought. Did you know that?"

"Of course I knew she's a god." Vara looked at him as if he were particularly dense. "She's my mother! She wanted to live normally, to raise a family, take a vacation from the being worshiped on a daily basis, and the constant pleas from people to use her power to benefit their lives. And you just let that wolf spirit have it all! You've doomed us, you know. And what about the others? We can't just leave them to her."

"It's too late for them."

Her legs crumpled underneath her—Laris, and Derek, and Zavian—were they still alive? What grizzly fate had she abandoned them to? Ash rained around them like a black snow and she smelled the pungent sulfur and soot of the demon realm around them. It wasn't safe there. If the wolf spirit figured out how to tap into her mother's limitless power, there wouldn't be anywhere Vara would be able to hide from it. How could she fight an out-of-control god with her mediocre summoner powers?

"You will have to release my people to deal with her to save your world from her," Sam said simply.

"You did this on purpose!" Vara shouted. "You knew full well this would happen and it would force my hand to release the demons."

"But you must. It's the only way to save your precious world. The wolf won't stop with just your mother and the girl. It will convert more and continue until there are no humans left."

"There has to be another way to stop the wolf."

"I thought you weren't the brightest person in the world, but this is just ultimately suicidal," said a familiar voice. Zavian had a large gash down the side of his face and his immaculate clothes were stained with white powder and soot.

Vara bowled him over in a large hug. It felt wonderful to prove to herself that he was indeed a warm solid presence and not just a hallucination conjured up by her mind.

A jolt of panic shook her. "You shouldn't be here!" She pushed him away abruptly. Zavian looked confused more than anything else and his cheeks were flushed a brilliant red against his pallid skin. "If she finds you with me, you'll be a dead man."

Some of the color started to drain from his cheeks and he looked sad. "I'm sorry. I just—" He shook his head.

"What happened?" she asked. "Did everyone make it out okay?"

"She set the mansion on fire and took everyone with her."

"What about Derek?"

"The world's doomed and you're worried about the fur rug? Unbelievable! He made it out with his nine lives intact. I suppose even she doesn't care for mongrel blood. Now come on. We need to get out of here."

"You mean I need to get out of here. Being around me

will get you killed."

His lips quirked at the edges as he fought a laugh. "I can take care of myself. You apparently can't or you wouldn't have come here. What possessed him to bring you here of all places?"

"I brought her here to make a deal with our ruler," said Sam.

"You can't be serious," Zavian said.

"Sam seems to think that the demons will fight on our side. He wants me to release all the demons from the underworld."

"That's madness," he argued. "No one has the power to do that, especially you. You can't summon more than one demon at a time. It just can't be done."

"Unfortunately, I'm out of options."

"Your mother is on the move," said Sam. "I can feel her coming. We need to hurry."

Vara felt the ground tremble under her feet. The wolf had figured out how to use her mother's powers.

Sam hustled them toward the small cluster of clock towers. Discordant chimes filled the air around them from at least twenty different clocks. Vara saw glittering eyes watching them through the darkness. Many were low to the ground and burned a fiery red. She didn't need her nightmares to imagine the green limbs attached to those eyes dragging against the ground. The wind turned into hurricane force with the approach of her mother. It blew flakes of ash into her face and nearly knocked her off her feet.

Sam shepherded them into the largest of the towers—the same building he had taken them to during their last time there. He led them down the short flight of stairs and through the maze of corridors. He threw open two large double doors with a snap of his long bony fingers. The large ballroom, where he had presented her to the demon-girl ruler, was dark and haunted looking.

A male demon in a blue suit with gold trim and white ruffles at his sleeves knelt just under the ornate gold throne. Next to it was a large red puddle that stained the white porcelain floor. Vara saw a flicker of a bright red tongue dart from between his lips and lick at the red stain, tasting it, caressing it. There was an expression of pure bliss on his face. She shuddered in revulsion.

Several other elegantly dressed demons lurked in the corners of the room, clustered together. They whispered quietly, but as soon as they entered, the whispering stopped and all eyes turned toward them.

Sam pushed between Zavian and Vara and floated over to the empty golden throne that dominated the back of the room. He dropped down on one knee. He turned slightly to make certain the two of them were doing the same, and then dropped his head reverently.

"I beseech you for your help, my lady."

The little girl demon streaked from behind one of the pillars and threw herself at Sam. She wrapped her short arms around his neck and buried her head of curls in his chest. Then she caught sight of Vara. "Another present!" she shrieked.

Her eyes narrowed and all of the shadows in the room flowed out of the corners and from around the objects they had accompanied and swam in Vara's direction.

They wrapped around her feet and climbed up her legs. It felt like being attacked by an army of cats. Some even had claws that sunk into her skin as they inched up all the way to her shoulders, where they paused for a moment before they descended over her face.

She had a brief glimpse of sharp teeth and glowing yellow eyes before the darkness consumed her. Her lungs felt heavy and her heartbeat slowed. There was a low roar in her ears. The darkness was maddening. It was so infinite and dense it became her entire world.

"Enough!" A voice echoed in the distance. "We don't have time for this. I told you before, she is not your plaything."

The blackness vanished. Zavian was looking at Vara with a confused expression on his face. "Are you all right?"

"I think so," she said as she blinked at the sudden return of light even though the place was dimly lit. "What happened?"

The little girl had her arms folded and she scowled at Sam. "Why'd you bring her then?"

"Because she will release all of us to help her face the wolf."

"She will?" The little girl looked at Vara, and a smile flit across her lips. "What does she require of us then?"

Sam turned to look at Vara. She noticed everyone else in the ruined ballroom had also turned to look at her, including Zavian.

"I want your word you will help me against the wolf-spirit inhabiting my mom if I release all of you from this realm."

"Yes," the little girl cooed. "Here our powers are rather weak, but in your mortal world, we would be a force to be reckoned with. We will help you with your wolf-spirit."

Sam looked positively gleeful. "When do we begin the ritual for our release?"

"I need to talk to the Agency first," Vara said as she tried to stall for time.

"But I am your link to them," he said with a smile. "Whatever you say to me is passed on to them."

"I haven't attempted a spell this large before, Sam. I need to talk to the Agency Heads in person first."

"So be it." He made a low bow to her and floated a few feet away.

Zavian was already drawing the chalk transit circle. Vara had a sinking feeling in her stomach. There was no possible way she would be able to control all of the demons once they had been released, even if she could release them. She needed just a little more time to come up with a better idea.

Zavian finished the circle and with a small reassuring smile, stepped into the middle. He held a hand out to her. "I have faith in you," he said. His smile melted away all of her worries.

Something inside her cried out and tried to warn her of something, but she wanted to make him proud of her. And that was what was most important. She took his hand and stepped into the circle with him.

"The Kendrick & Clarke Placement Agency," he breathed against her ear. She felt his warm magic surge around them, blurring the demon realm. A red light sparkled all around them and then it vanished. It left behind it the black and white tiled lobby of the Agency office building.

A young lady carrying a clipboard approached them. "Ah, Miss Harper, we've been expecting you."

Chapter 30

"You're late, of course. The superiors don't like to be kept waiting." The young lady wore a dark blue suit and had her brown hair up in a bun. She peered at Vara through a pair of gold-rimmed glasses. It hit her that this was the same receptionist she had talked with the last time she had been to the office.

They followed the receptionist to the elevators, where she punched the number for the office suite. The elevator opened in front of them and they piled in and rode all the way up to the Agency main office. A tall red-headed young man arguing with one of the receptionists grabbed Vara's attention immediately. *Derek.* Zavian had been telling the truth that he had made it out okay.

"This is a private meeting for Miss Harper," the woman told Zavian. "You'll have to wait out here, sir."

"It's okay. I'll keep an eye on your mangy cat." He took a seat on the far side of the room with his gaze glued to Derek's back.

The lady in the blue suit ushered Sam and Vara through the door behind the front desk. They walked down the hallway and passed the smaller meeting rooms. The receptionist paused in front of the door in the very back and pushed it open for them.

"Come in, Miss Harper," said Ms. Clarke, her voice amplified by the power that radiated out from her.

Vara crossed the room and sat down on the lone blue

plastic chair. Ms. Clarke was dressed completely in white, the same as when she had last seen her. Sam floated over to where Mr. Kendrick stood.

"Miss Harper, your supervisor has already told us of his suggestion to release the demons, and we feel that it is in the Agency's best interests to help you with that task. We know that you do not have sufficient strength, so I shall be accompanying you to help in the completion of the ritual of release. I know you have misgivings about this entire plan, but rest assured that this will have the best outcome for all of the parties involved. Now, we'll need a place where we won't be bothered and has all the supplies for the ritual, like a large mirror, plenty of candles, and the long razor."

As soon as she said it, the razor from Vara's father's house sprang to mind. Had he attempted to release the demons himself?

Ms. Clarke stared at her thoughtfully. "Do you know of such a place, Miss Harper?"

"The basement of my father's house," Vara answered.

Ms. Clarke smiled at her. "Yes, I think that will do nicely." She rose from the table. "We should leave directly then as soon as we collect your friends from out front."

Ms. Clarke nodded to Sam, who fell into step behind her. Then she led the way back down the hallway and past the front desk.

Derek had finished his argument with the receptionist and stood glaring at Zavian. Zavian threw Derek a smug smile and stood next to Vara. Derek's glare deepened.

Vara pulled out a sheet of paper and a piece of chalk from her purse and sketched the transit circle. She felt her hands shake under the careful watch of Ms. Clarke. What was she so scared of? Once her mom was restored, she could go back to Sanctuary City and never have to worry about if she had the details right on complicated rune designs. But did she really want to go back to Sanctuary City?

She pricked her finger with the cuticle scissors and sealed the circle with a red drop of her blood. She held the wound until it closed and stood with the others in the center of the circle and held out her hand. A warm hand encased hers and stood facing her in the circle.

"Your superiors obviously have faith in you," Zavian's warm breath whispered. "You shouldn't worry."

"20 Mayfield Drive," Vara commanded, loud enough for everyone in the room to hear.

Her body jittered with excess magical energy. She let a drop of it flow into the circle. It grew warm beneath their feet and flowed up around them in a red haze. After a moment, it was gone. They stood on the transit circle in front of her dad's pastel blue house.

In the distance dark heavy clouds approached and the light was dimming into an ominous twilight. They would never see the sun again if she didn't do something to stop her mother.

There wasn't a sign of life anywhere in the street, as if people already could sense what was about to happen. Zavian pulled her out of the circle just as it started to shimmer around them. They would have found themselves pushed out of the way as Derek's body shimmered into solidity.

Even with the pungent smell of green shrubbery and the asphalt from the street, Vara could still smell Sam's noxious decayed breath as he floated behind them.

Ms. Clarke was the last to appear in the circle. With her immaculate business attire she looked strangely out of place on the suburban street.

Vara turned her back on the party and walked to the front door. It wasn't locked. But then she was surprised the door was even closed since they had left it standing wide open when they had fled the place after the hunters had tried to capture them.

She pushed it open and surveyed the room. The unconscious blonde-haired woman was gone, though the iron bird bookend that landed on her head was resting on its side in the middle of the living room carpet.

The room still tingled with recent magic. She led the group through the living room to the staircase that led to the basement and descended into darkness. She felt around for the overhead light chain. She yanked it down and flooded the room with sudden brightness.

She noticed that the troll had also left, though there was a long white smudged spot where he had slid across the chalk markings of the massive rune circle that spread almost to the edges of the room. Aside from that, everything was exactly how they had left it after the reconstruction spell.

Zavian's rune circle sat in the center of the room with her dad's navy blue sweater lying in the center of it. The table of blueprints sat just next to it. The massive rune circle encircled both of them with candles of all shapes and sizes at intervals around it. All of the wicks were blackened from being lit during the ceremony her dad had performed.

She saw movement out of the corner of her eye. Her gaze met her own white-skinned worried face staring back at her from the large mirror that was propped against the empty wall. She felt a sob rise in her throat, as she told herself not to look down. But she couldn't help it. She had to know if her imagination had conjured it all up earlier. But it was still there, the long straight-edged razor lying in the circle of dried blood. There were random splatters of red on the walls.

Ms. Clarke knelt next to the massive rune circle. "We'll need some soap and water to clean your circle in the center and the blood near the mirror. We don't want them to contaminate the spell. And we'll need to change some of the runes on this circle as well."

Vara went to the kitchen and pulled out a bucket from under the sink. She put it under the faucet and filled it with warm soapy water. Her feet crunched in broken glass and fragments of her dad's white ceramic plates that littered the floor. One of the windows was broken.

"Your boss wants you to hurry up, by the way," Zavian said as he suddenly joined her in the kitchen. "You'll have to leave cleaning that up for later." He pulled open the drawer next to her and withdrew several washcloths and hand towels. "I envy you, you know." He gave her a quick smile. She turned off the water and hauled the bucket out of the sink.

"I don't know what there is to envy. But then this spell probably won't work anyway. It looked like my dad attempted it and the demons were still in their proper world, and I know I don't have anywhere near the amount of training he had."

"That's why your boss is here."

"Yeah, I know."

They returned to the basement. Ms. Clarke was inspecting the runes Vara's dad had drawn. She had a piece of chalk in hand and was making some small adjustments.

Derek had dumped the blueprints into an empty corner and was trying to push the table against the wall with the stacks of boxes. He had actually managed to put the table on its side so that it was out of the way.

Zavian threw Vara a washcloth and dunked one into the bucket. He kneeled down and started to clean the chalk circle in the middle.

"I can get this, Vara. Think you could take care of the mess in front of the mirror?"

Vara turned to look at it. He meant her father's blood stain. Her stomach did a flip flop as she looked at it. She knelt down to try to moisten the edges of the stain. What exactly had happened to her father in the last couple of minutes he was in this room, standing in this spot, or maybe lying in this spot? Had he been in any pain? Or had whatever happened been sudden?

When the stain finally started disappearing, she felt someone put a hand on her shoulder and sit down next to her. She didn't turn to look. No matter how much she wished in that moment that the person behind her was her father, to answer all of her questions and tell her that everything was going to be fine, it just wasn't going to happen.

"Vara, I'm sorry," Zavian said. "I didn't mean. . . ."

"I'll be through here in a minute."

She scrubbed harder, determined to ignore the tremor in her voice. Besides, she couldn't look up, or she would see her wan reflection in the mirror and his look of pity and remorse.

She picked up the razor to clean underneath it. There was blood on the blade. She didn't know why that suddenly disturbed her since her dad had cut himself with it willingly. At least she assumed it had been willingly if he had set up the ritual himself. What if someone else had been with him?

Vara ran the cloth over the blade. It made an ominous ringing sound. Once the blood was gone, she could see her reflection in it. It was exactly how she imagined it would look, whiter than normal with dark shadows under haunted eyes.

She finished cleaning the floor and stood up. Ms. Clarke stood in the middle of the room and surveyed everything with a faint smile on her face.

"We are making history here, everyone. Now, Miss Harper, you will need to stand there, next to the mirror to channel through it. And I trust you know what to do with the razor. Be sure to make the cut deep enough. Since this is a large spell, it will need a large amount of your blood."

"But what about the magic?" Vara asked. "I don't have enough for something this large."

Ms. Clarke smiled. "Just leave that to me. Sam, light the candles please."

He held his palm up to his mouth and blew, as if blowing a kiss to Vara. His hot breath raced around the room. The bordering circle of candles ignited one by one.

"Miss Harper, we don't have all day," Ms. Clarke said with an impatient edge to her precise clipped voice.

Vara hesitated as she stared at her reflection holding the deadly silver blade in her hand. It glinted in the brightness of the overhead light. The reflection had an almost giddy look on her face. If she waited long enough she was certain the reflection would laugh hysterically and prove that it wasn't her at all, but some crazed murderess with her potential victims standing in the background.

"Think of your mother," Ms. Clarke reminded her. "This is the only way you can help her."

Vara felt tears in her eyes and her reflection shifted. She saw her mother standing in front of her with a sad pained expression in her eyes. Her mother had the razor lifted up, pleading with her. Vara bit her lip and closed her eyes. The edge of the blade slid across the palm of her hand. She had been expecting for pain to shoot through her body, but the only pain she felt was right where the knife was.

She drew a line with the razor down the center of her palm, over the veins of her wrist, and down the flesh of her arm. She could feel the skin slide around and her arm grow heavy. She dropped the knife and touched the mirror.

Her arm grew numb and the feeling of pins and needles steadily progressed up her elbow toward her shoulder. She heard a faint dripping sound, which seemed miles away.

She reached down with her mind to the pool of magic that surged and crested below her feet. She let it fill her and funneled it into the circle beneath her feet and into the mirror.

Name upon name whispered through her mind and she heard her voice intoning the odd vowel sounds almost as if another person were speaking.

Vara felt hands under her arms holding her up, which was fine with her since her legs felt like they had vanished out from underneath her.

The words kept pouring forth and time was only marked by the numb feeling that climbed through her limbs toward her heart. She heard someone sob nearby.

"She's fine," she heard Ms. Clarke's voice say. "She's just frightened. I need you to pull up more power," her voice whispered close to Vara, nearly in her ear. "Can you do that for me?"

Vara wanted to tell her that she would get blood on her white outfit if she stood too near. But all that came out was the continuous babble of odd unfamiliar names. She let her mind wander down to the ground beneath her feet again. There was indeed more power there. She grasped at it with her mind. She felt like she was letting it slip through her fingers like sand, but she managed to pull up a sizable chunk of it. She let it drift into the circle beneath her feet and shoved another large chunk of it into the mirror.

"Our new friends thank you for your service, but I'm afraid more is needed." Vara heard the smile in Ms. Clarke's voice. "You were destined to do this. Only you had your mother's god power to charge it and amplify your father's power to call to the entire demon dimension. You should be proud. You have given your life to the Agency. You were a loyal employee and it was my honor to have you work for me." Vara felt the hands holding her up shift and the distant scrape of metal on stone far below her.

In the distance she could hear a male voice scream, "No!"

She pulled her eyes open enough to try to see who screamed and what they so urgently wanted attention for. She felt Ms. Clarke reach around her and she saw her wan reflection in the blade of the ritual razor in Ms. Clarke's hand. "I'm afraid this has to be done for the future to happen. Give your father my regards," her boss whispered.

There was a sudden excruciating pain in Vara's chest that yanked its way up to her heart. She felt her lungs give one labored scream for air and then her world turned to blackness.

Chapter 31

"No!" Zavian shouted. But it was too late. He watched in frozen horror as Ms. Clarke lifted the long ritual knife, plunged it into Vara's chest, and sliced her open all the way to her stomach. The black-haired girl slumped forward into Ms. Clarke's embrace. Blood rained onto the floor below them. It pooled in the same spot she had just cleaned of her father's blood moments before.

"I'm sorry, my dear," Ms. Clarke whispered. "But it had to be done."

"You'll pay for this!" Zavian shouted. He ran toward the murderous Agency boss and slammed head first into what felt like an invisible wall. It shimmered into a white hazy cloud with black eye sockets, and then solidified into the wraith demon Vara referred to as Sam.

"Don't touch me, demon!"

"I cannot allow you to interfere with the ceremony," said Sam and gave Zavian a toothy grin.

"She killed Vara!" Zavian shouted.

Just over Sam's shoulder, Zavian saw Ms. Clarke ease Vara's body to the ground. She pulled out the ritual knife and set it aside. And then with one foot, she kicked Vara's body into the swirling blood red vortex that led to the demon dimension.

"No!" Zavian pounded his fists uselessly against the barrier.

"We are finished here, Sam," Ms. Clarke said. "Do with

the body as you wish."

Zavian could hear the sound of heavy footsteps behind him on the staircase. He didn't have to turn around and look to know his cousin's bodyguard had gotten curious about all of the shouting. "Your boss killed Vara."

Derek's footsteps thundered on the concrete of the floor as he jumped the couple of remaining stairs and violently pushed past Zavian. He slammed into Sam's invisible barrier and staggered back several steps.

"I'll kill you," he vowed at Sam.

Sam glanced at him. "You don't have the power to."

White ghostly wraith demons, green imps, dark-horned black monsters with glowing red eyes, and a host of other beings pulled from nightmares started appearing in front of the portal. Some were wrapped in death shrouds and others wore the flesh of men.

The room was choked with them as they pushed past Zavian and Derek. Some of them filed up the staircase, others rose off the floor and vanished into the ceiling as if concrete was no more solid than a breath of air.

"The barrier is gone!" Derek said as he put a hand through where it had been.

"That's not all that's gone," said Zavian. "Ms. Clarke and that demon have left, too. We're going to need help to stop this."

"Father!" Zavian shouted through the empty Stadler mansion. Vara's mother had seen to it that the place had suffered when her daughter had left after the exorcism. The front doors had been blasted off their hinges, there were black scorch marks everywhere, and most of the chairs and sofas were smoking ruins.

Though the body had been removed, a pool of red blood still stained the carpet where the reporter's wife had fallen. He didn't want to think about who had carted away the body.

"Father!" he shouted again as he headed for the grand staircase. "Cat, take the rooms downstairs. He's around here somewhere." They had already searched his father's mansion, but it had stood just as empty as when they had left it early that morning. He had to be here, looking for something to stop the situation.

Derek disappeared in the direction of the kitchen. Zavian hadn't even gotten to the second floor when he heard Derek's voice call out.

"Sir, come quick!" the bodyguard shouted.

Zavian followed the sound of his voice through the kitchen to a small room off to the side stacked with boxes, crates, sacks, and jars. Cowered in a corner next to a large sack of flour was a mess of silver blond hair.

"He doesn't want to talk to you," hissed a high-pitched voice. Ren pushed passed them through the doorway and approached the blond hair. He offered the scraggly heap a glass of water. Long thin fingers reached out and clasped the cup. Another thin hand brushed aside the long hair to reveal the thirsty mouth underneath. It was his uncle, Lord Stadler, and he looked destitute. His clothes were stained with black scorch marks and ripped and shredded around the chest.

"Uncle, we need to stop this. The Agency opened a portal to the demon dimension."

Lord Stadler looked at him with wide eyes. "We need to leave. The Nature Children will take us in." He said it so matter-of-factly, as if he had forgotten all the times he had publically persecuted them.

"Uncle, I don't think—"

"The border is closed," whispered the servant. "I am sorry, Master."

"I just wanted my daughter back," Lord Stadler sobbed.

"By making a grab for extra power," Zavian accused. But had he been in his uncle's shoes, he probably would have done the same. The demon power would have amplified his uncle's mind-control power. He would have been unstoppable.

"You were sealing the deal with Vara's power," Zavian said. "Taking a demon's power is one thing, but she's human, like us."

Lord Stadler spat. "She's no more human than that fur rug behind you. Couldn't you sense it, boy?"

"She's more than either of us could ever hope to be."

Lord Stadler smiled. "You were hoping to leech her power yourself, weren't you?"

"No, of course not!" Had he denied it too loudly? He could still feel the cat's eyes on his back. He hated the cheap accusation. It was true her power had been the first thing he had noticed when she had strolled in through the dining room door, but it wasn't why he had pursued her. Girls practically tripped over each other to gain his favor, but Vara had played tantalizingly hard to get. He had enjoyed the challenge of weaving his spell around her and stealing her away from the fur rug. And though the conquest had been sweet, being with her had been sweeter. It seemed cruel that the world had been robbed of her loyalty, blind trust, and naivety.

His uncle gave him a knowing smile.

"It doesn't matter now," muttered Zavian, not liking the smile on his uncle's face one bit. He was not as superficial as his uncle. "The Agency killed her and used her power to open the portal."

"And what do you expect me to do?" Lord Stadler asked. His hands that held the glass trembled and his voice was edged with defeat.

"We need you to talk to the Agency and get them to stop it. Or use your mind-control on Vara's mother and get her to shut off the portal."

"Why don't you do it?" his uncle shot back. He wedged himself further behind the sack of flour.

Zavian was tired of the argument. He couldn't admit weakness in front of that scraggly fur rug who thought he had a claim on the girl. "All right, I will!"

The locator spell took them to the center of a school campus. Before the red glow had vanished fully, Derek latched onto Zavian's arm and pulled him into the doorway of the nearest building.

"Get your hands off me, you mangy—"

Derek's golden eyes were wide open and he had a finger to his lips. He ducked a quick look out the doorway. Zavian saw someone run by low to the ground. It looked like a young woman with light brown hair wearing a red blouse. She stopped and put her nose in the air, as if sniffing for something. She changed direction and ran off in the opposite direction from them. She was hunched over and nearly ran on all fours.

"Where are we?" Schools all looked the same to him, but there was something about the low brick buildings here that looked oddly familiar.

"It's the Stadler Conservatory, sir," Derek said. "There she is." He pointed to a small crowd of students. A woman stood in the center of the group with chin-length black hair, Vara's mother. She raised her hands and the wind picked up. Benches shook and levitated several feet off the ground, then danced lazily around the campus. Lampposts uprooted themselves in spectacular bursts of electricity and joined the benches. The woman waved her hands. Lightning flashed behind her. The crowd of students cheered.

Amid the rolling thunder and crackles of lightning, her voice carried on the wind as if they were standing right next to her. "You cannot hide from us! I know you are here!"

Zavian instinctively ducked farther into the doorway. Her head whipped in their direction. Zavian felt something tugging on his body. It pulled him out of his hiding place. He stumbled forward. Derek was doing the same.

Vara's mother smiled. There was a glint off elongated canines and he saw fur along the sides of her face. Her biceps rippled as she shifted position to watch them.

The students surrounding her all had long yellowed fingernails and glowing red eyes. She had turned them all. How had she grown an army this large within such a short amount of time? And none of them were fighting the transformation as Laris had. Usually it took till the first full moon before the demon inside was powerful enough to take full control.

Vara's mother laughed. "Go, my children! There is part of me here that wants to be found. I can feel it."

The group dropped to all fours and scattered across the campus. They left behind Vara's mother and a wolf-girl with blonde-hair, barely recognizable as human under her contorted, elongated features. One copper-haired girl in a black dress stopped to sniff at them.

"I said go!" Vara's mother commanded.

The girl instantly stopped pawing at Derek and ran to

catch up with the others.

The demonic eyes of Vara's mother glowed brighter. "You smell of my sister-daughter. What do you want?" It was not the voice of Vara's mother, but the snarling, hungry voice of an animal. "Have you come to ask for me to give you back your cousin? I would gladly see her feast on your bones."

As the blonde wolf-girl smiled, long canines peeked out between ruby painted lips. She didn't even look like Laris anymore, though she still wore the red dress from the exorcism.

"Or have you come to join us?" Vara's mother asked.

She waved a hand, and the feeling of being pulled grew in Zavian's body, making him stagger another step closer to her.

"We have come to ask you to shut off the portal to the demon dimension," said Zavian.

"Why should I?" the wolf said with a growl. "My people need to be free."

Zavian looked into her eyes. There was nothing there beyond the burning red demonic light. He needed to reach the mother in her fast, if she still existed. "But the Agency used Vara's blood to open it," said Zavian. "The Agency killed your daughter." He let his voice grow rich and luxurious. It wrapped around her and coaxed her. He called to the mother he was convinced still had to be inside her. "You will help us. You must avenge your daughter."

The wolf that was Vara's mother smiled as she exposed gleaming white canines. "Your mind control doesn't work on me. I will try to leave enough of you so you can become wolf, but I can't promise anything. I am so very hungry."

Chapter 32

Was this what it felt like to be dead? If it was, death felt hot—like she was lying inside an oven, slowly being baked to a crisp. And there was the stench that rammed itself up her nostrils and seeped into her brain. It drove aside anything except the vomit-inducing aroma of rotten eggs, mixed with decaying corpses and dead fish thrown in for good measure.

"The Oracle said she was done with her, and that I could have her," a gravelly voice whispered near Vara's ear. "Can I, Father?" She knew that voice. *Sam.*

"Yes," responded a second voice. It sounded familiar. It sounded like her dad's voice only deeper and coarse, as if his throat had been scoured with sandpaper. "But make it quick. She shouldn't suffer."

'Give your father my regards,' Ms. Clarke had said. She had sent him here, through the portal he had created in the basement. Ms. Clarke had sent him here to die. She had to find him! She had to get up!

Vara's limbs felt impossibly heavy. All she wanted to do was sleep and let the darkness take her. She would be safe in the darkness.

No! She wasn't going to give up on her dad that easily! She used all of her strength to force open one eye. There was nothing but darkness around her. Where was she? And through the darkness she could see a face. Her eye felt so tired. It would be so easy just to let it shut and then she could open it again in a little while. No! She had to keep looking! If she let it close now, that might be the end. She might not ever get it open again!

The face swam into view. It caught sight of Vara and smiled with white teeth that glittered like pearls in the darkness. It floated closer. A mouth loomed over her and bone white needle-sharp teeth protruded toward her face. No! She needed to keep her eye open! She wasn't going to let it slam shut just to avoid looking at whatever was above her.

She could see black eye sockets crinkle at the edges in private amusement just above the teeth. Long bony fingers with grotesque yellowed talons stretched toward her face, as if to puncture her eye and relieve her of the exertion of keeping it open. Instead the nails scraped against her cheek.

"Isn't it wonderful?" Sam's voice asked. The familiar rancid gust swept over her as he leaned in close. "You're free! Your job is finished and your contract terminated. She said I could dispose of you, that the Agency didn't need you anymore. The honor of taking your last few drops is mine. Father said I could."

A ghostly weight pressed down on her chest and a stabbing pain throbbed in her stomach, in time to the slowing pace of her heart. It sucked and pulled at her and she felt herself sliding into darkness as though she was losing a game of tug-of-war. Her limbs felt as if they were being sucked into the ground underneath her. The lid on her eye refused to listen to her any longer and was forcing itself shut. She forced every last ounce of her strength into keeping it open.

But it wasn't enough.

Vara waited. Each heartbeat she thought would be her last. No! It couldn't end this way! There had to be something more she could do! She cast around frantically as she felt inside every dark hidden crevice within her for any last ounce of magic. There was plenty of magic in the air around her, but her body was taking too long to absorb it. She felt a greedy ghostly hand following her, waiting to scoop up whatever she might find.

And then she found it, a glimmering fount of energy within her. How had she missed it all these years? It seemed so much a part of her, yet she had never noticed it before. The way it glittered and shone, it had to be god-power inherited from her mom, locked away inside her. All she had to do was touch it. But could she handle it? Raw, seething god power and she hadn't even mastered simple demon summoning capabilities.

"I'll miss you," Sam whispered into her ear.

Her heart slowed to one final heartbeat. She didn't have time to internally debate the point. It was either unleash it or accept her death. She used her final heartbeat to power one more twitch of her finger and gave the fount of energy as much of a tug as she could muster. Would it be enough?

Energy flooded into Vara. It tingled and filled up every crevice and knit up the wounds in her stomach and arm within seconds.

Her body came to life with a shuddering, spluttering gasp. The sucking feeling jerked, hissed, and vanished from her stomach. She opened her eyes. Sam was no longer smiling.

"You witch!" he screeched. He flew at her with his mouth opened wide with rows of needle-sharp teeth.

Warmth flooded her limbs and lifted her off the ground. Her skin felt electrified. The power rocketed through her body and erupted. It drowned the room around her in a void darker than the blackest of nights. She couldn't see anything, not even her hands in front of her. There was just the feeling of smothering electricity, dissolving everything around her.

Sam shrieked. It sounded inhuman, like the screech of a bat in excruciating pain.

And then the power left her. Her body slumped to the floor, but at least she could feel her heart beating once again. She cautiously breathed in and felt the warm air circulate through her lungs. Why had it been dark? Everything she had heard about god power said that it was bright and shining. It was supposed to blind. She had even glimpsed her mom one time when she had her guard down. Her mother had been impossible to look at, so bright and hot. Was there something wrong with her or whatever was inside her? Vara was already used to the disappointment of being normal with no inherited powers from her mother, but this was almost worse.

Why wasn't Sam doing anything? She felt the odd dark

strength flowing back into her, and she felt like if she wanted she might actually be able to move her limbs. Didn't he want her anymore? The impenetrable darkness was slowly starting to lift and she could make out shapes of broken antique furniture and dusty boxes lining the walls. It was the storage room Sam had brought them to while Laris was sedated. Ghostly demons drifted by in the hallway outside, completely ignoring her, as if they were zombies.

She realized with a start that she was alone. Sam had vanished. She dropped to her knees. What had she done? "Sam?" Had he just done his usual vanishing act or had she destroyed him? It wasn't possible to kill a demon, as far as she knew. But there was no sign of him. Not even a scorch mark where she might have blasted him into nothingness.

"I'm sorry," she whispered to the empty room.

And then in a dark corner a black lumpy shape stirred. She wasn't as alone as she had thought. Whatever was in the corner wasn't coming for her.

Her dad had been left for dead in this dimension. It seemed too much to hope for that it was him and that he might still be hanging onto life.

"Dad?" Vara whispered.

Why didn't he get up and walk toward her? Why couldn't he speak and tell her that it would all be okay. That he would talk to her mom and fix the entire situation?

She tried not to think about the large puddle of blood she had seen in the basement at his house. She didn't want to look into the dark shadow and see what was left of him. He was her dad. She wanted him to be whole and in one piece, and to help her to stop shaking at the thought of the world without him in it.

"Dad?" Her voice quivered. "Please, say something."

She shoved aside the boxes to allow the light to chase away the darkness. He was lying in a fetal position with his arms wrapped around his knees that were pressed close to his chest. And his clothes were bloody and torn. But it wasn't her father.

It was the battered and bleeding corpse of a young man with short curly black hair. She knew that face! That was

Austen, Laris's previous babysitter. He was shriveled, a mere husk of the young man she had last seen arguing with Zavian. His cheeks were sunken and his arms were skeletal, and there were dark bruises around both of his eyes. His skin was riddled with red spots as if. . . . She drew back in utter revulsion. It looked as if many things had been sucking at his skin, feeding on him. What had happened to him?

She gently lifted one of his arms, put her other hand behind his back, and pushed him into a sitting position. She draped one of his arms around her shoulders, tightened her grip around his back, and lifted him off the floor. He was so light, as if there was nothing inside him anymore.

Vara pulled him along with her to the doorway. He groaned once. He was still alive, but he needed a healer fast. She hated the thought of leaving her dad behind dying or dead, but Austen didn't have long enough for her to take the time to search.

The demons filing past didn't look at them in the least. This had to be the exodus of demons flooding the human world. She didn't have any mirrors or chalk on her, and with Austen's clothes torn in so many places, she could see he didn't have any on him either, which meant there was only one way back home, and that was through the portal she had created.

She hefted Austen's deadweight and dragged him with her into the steady stream of demons, careful not to touch any of them. But they just stared straight ahead, as if they were listening intently to something so faint that she couldn't hear it.

The long line of demons wound around corners and through hallways, and they finally spilled into the spacious ballroom.

Aside from the line of demons that led to what looked like a dense black hole, the room was empty. All of the elegantly dressed dancers had vanished. Then a light movement in the elaborate gilded throne caught her attention.

The little girl demon with the golden corkscrew curls sat on the gold throne. She kicked her legs with an air of boredom. She caught sight of Vara immediately and hopped off the throne.

"Where's my father?" Vara demanded.

The little girl looked at her curiously for a moment. "You are the only human here, alive or otherwise." A smile crept over her lips. She grinned at Vara with a mouth full of sharp teeth. She raced over to Vara and threw her arms around Vara's leg.

"No more contract!" the demon giggled. Vara felt her sharp teeth sink into her thigh. There was a tugging at her heart as if the demon was sucking the life force out of her body. All of her limbs grew heavy, and she started to collapse. If he wasn't here. . . . She had run out of places to look for him.

Vara struck out with her leg wildly and threw the demon as hard as she could in the direction of the empty dance floor. The little girl flew through the air and bounced. Then with a quick turn she bounded back toward Vara.

If it had worked on Sam, maybe it would work on the girl demon. Vara poked with her mind at the odd darkness inside of her, and coaxed it out. An overwhelming warmth wrapped itself around her. She felt it run up her toes, flood through her chest and rocket out her hands. It shot like bullets wildly out her fingers and smothered the entire room in darkness.

Vara heard laughter—a little girl's gleeful laugh, that didn't sound tainted in the least by pain.

"Demon power can't hurt me." The girl demon sniffed loudly. "But you smell human."

"It can't be demon power." The words died on Vara's lips. Her mom was a god. She was a god of light and air.

The darkness had lifted enough that she could see the white gleam of the little girl's teeth. She grinned and flew at Vara.

"Talanrienth!" Vara shouted as the name sprang to mind. A green imp popped out of thin air in the middle of the floor between her and the demon girl.

The girl smiled, and the imp did too, mirroring her with the same needle sharp teeth.

"My brother," she giggled.

The imp wickedly laughed and snapped its long

grotesque yellowed nails. It held up the palm of its hand for Vara to see. A small red flame danced above it. As she stared at it, the flame grew larger.

The imp jumped happily and threw the flame at her with a howl of screeching laughter. She dodged to the side as the flame whipped past her, exploded against the porcelain floor, and left behind an ugly black scorch mark.

The imp laughed and she saw it had another flame in its hand. She stretched out with her mind and called to him. She pleaded with him to throw his flame elsewhere. He looked at her with a shrewd look and grinned.

"Foolish mortal thinks she can control us in our own domain," the demon girl with the golden curls said.

The imp threw his flame at Vara again. It sailed through the air and whipped her hair in a heated gust. It exploded against one of the red pillars behind her. She dove and came up next to where she had laid Austen.

"Get her!" the girl commanded.

The green imp bounded toward Vara with an insane grin plastered across his toothy mouth.

The little girl laughed. Vara closed her eyes and scooped up the dark energy and threw it into the air over her head. She smelled the rotten breath of the imp practically on top of her and then heard a tinkling, musical clinking of millions of shards of glass as the explosion of darkness hit the millions of diamonds still decorating the ceiling like stars in a night sky and expanded the dark smothering blanket of electricity. Her skin felt like it was on fire, every inch of it tingling with needle pricks. The demon girl screamed. Vara heard a pained hiss in her ear from the imp.

She opened her eyes long enough to see the demon girl rubbing at her eye sockets. The imp was flinging fireballs randomly around the room, aiming at every speck of darkness or movement. Several of the fireballs landed near the demon girl.

Vara wrapped her free arm around Austen and hauled him toward the portal. Her arm screamed at her in pain from his weight, but she felt the warm strength surge through her, enabling her to make the last couple of steps. The portal spun with a red glow, growing denser in the middle until it was entirely black at the center. Numerous demons pushed at each other in their haste to jump through it.

She staggered the last couple of steps and let the portal suck them back to the mortal world.

Still hauling Austen, Vara stumbled into the middle of an enormous chalk circle that spread into the darkness of the room. They were back in the basement at her father's house.

There was the table pushed against one of the empty walls and the boxes piled high and a few blueprints that rolled around on the floor, and an enormous blood stain in the center mixed with the chalk dust. The blood was still slightly gooey and looked like dark red paint.

A light swung absently above them. A demon pushed her to one side. He breathed in the musty air and opened his eye sockets wide.

"Freedom," he breathed and vanished.

How long had they been pouring forth into her world? The portal wouldn't close until all the demons that had been summoned were through. She needed to close it now. Especially before the little demon girl's name was summoned.

Vara cast around and spotted a hammer among her dad's tools. She threw it with her remaining strength at the mirror behind the portal. She watched it spin head over handle. It passed through a demon just appearing in their world and smashed into the mirror behind him. Silver shards flew everywhere.

The bits and pieces on the floor reflected the portal still swirling in the air above a million times over.

Chapter 33

She had doomed the world and didn't have a clue how to stop it. Vara threw Austen's arm over her shoulders and hauled him to his feet.

Evil laughter echoed from the portal. She didn't have time to be careful about his wounds and yanked him up the stairs. She heard things getting knocked over in the basement, and there was a loud cascade of thuds as one of the towers of boxes came crashing down, followed by a loud pained screech.

She dragged Austen into the kitchen and let him collapse on the floor, being careful of the broken glass from earlier. It was heartbreaking to look at him. His skin had been ravaged, as though the demons had sucked at every spot of skin they had been able to sink their teeth into. He had long deep cuts down the side of his face, and there were deep claw marks over his stomach that oozed with blood and pus.

She pushed the kitchen door closed behind them. Immediately she heard the evil laughter grow louder as a demon climbed the staircase and books and picture frames crashed to the floor.

She rummaged around in the nearest kitchen drawer and pulled out a piece of chalk. Then she quickly drew a circle on the white tile and started the surrounding runes.

"Help. . . ."

Vara's head jerked up automatically. A ragged breath escaped from Austen's lips.

"Ssshh," she tried vainly to shush him. "There are demons in the next room. Just hang on. I'm trying to get us out of here."

He choked and coughed. His hand clamped down on hers where she was gripping his shoulder. "I know you!" he wheezed. His eyes tried to focus and narrowed as he studied her face. He seemed to decide something. "We need to find Kalen."

He had the brightest, bluest eyes she had ever seen in her life. They almost seemed to glow.

"I don't know who Kalen is, but we can find him later," she reassured him. Vara tossed the chalk aside and hauled him into the circle with her. He pushed at her roughly.

"No." He shook his head. "The closet."

"This closet?" she asked and looked at the door next to the refrigerator behind which were stored the brooms and mops. Was there something inside it she should know about?

He nodded. "I can get us out of here," he whispered.

Vara looked at him doubtfully. He didn't look like he was in shape to do much of anything. Breathing without coughing up blood looked like a difficult task.

It had gone eerily quiet in the living room.

"Trust me," he urged. "I can get us out of here. We don't have time to argue."

If he ended up not having enough power for whatever he was planning, there was still the chalk circle. She figured she might as well humor him since the demons seemed to be leaving them alone for the moment. She struggled to move him to the closet and opened it. Several of the brooms tumbled down on top of them. One of them hit the tile with a resounding thwack.

There was a sudden rustle of movement from the living room and then something large slammed against the kitchen door. The hinges groaned and the wood of the doorframe splintered.

"Quick!" he whispered into her ear.

Maybe he thought it would be a good hiding place, though she didn't think she'd be able to close the door with both of them inside the tiny space along with several brooms and dustpans. She stepped inside and pulled him in with her.

He lifted a hand and put it against the wood paneling at the back of the closet, and for a moment she felt something tug painfully at her heart. She dismissed it as her anxiety that the door would soon split open and the demons outside would rush in and find them cowered in the closet. His hand disappeared into the dark shadows. She gasped since she had been able to see the wood of the closet just seconds before.

"Don't let go of me," he said just barely above a whisper. And then they were falling through darkness. It took every ounce of Vara's strength to keep hold of him.

They hit the ground together in a pile of limbs. Pain shot through every inch of her, resonating from her elbows. Austen was breathing shallowly.

"You shouldn't be here," said a strong, deep voice.

Vara froze and mentally cursed. She should never have trusted someone she didn't know. What sort of trouble had he dumped them into the middle of?

"On your feet. Now!" the deep voice commanded.

Vara stood up slowly and turned to face the speaker. She choked back a laugh when she realized the person who was barking orders was shorter than her by nearly a foot. He had long waist-length white hair and wore a silver tunic and pants with elaborate gold trim that fit tightly, showing off his well-toned muscles. He had the same luminous blue eyes as Austen.

A group of men in copper-colored uniforms carrying staves with wicked-looking green blades stood just behind him. All of them had the same grey skin and sharp sunken aristocratic features. Some of them had short cropped hair, and she could see their ears stretched into sharp points. She felt her heart pound painfully. Nature Children. She had never seen so many of them together before.

"Who are you and how did you get here?" the long-haired man in front asked.

"I brought her, Brother," Austen wheezed and ended in a cough that sounded like he was choking on liquid.

"How? The borders are sealed."

"I borrowed her power," he answered.

The long-haired man's blue eyes narrowed as he focused on Vara with uncomfortable attention. She wasn't sure what he was looking for, but she didn't like it.

"You two need medical attention," he said as he finally released her from his gaze. He turned toward his men and pointed to a couple of them. One went over to Austen and helped him to his feet.

"There's no time, Brother," Austen argued. "A portal has been opened and the demons have been summoned to the mortal world!"

"How many of them?" the long-haired man demanded.

"All of them," Vara said.

"It needs to be closed! Now! Once they overrun your world, they will invade here!"

"But how do we close it?" she asked. "I tried shattering the mirror and it didn't work."

"The one who opened it has to die in front of the portal."

He was telling the truth. She could see it in his eyes. They held absolutely no remorse for the person who would have to lose their life. It was unfair! She had been tricked into opening it. And Ms. Clarke had lied. Her mother was going to remain a wolf and she was going to die without having done anything to save her. And her dad. . . .

"There has to be another way!" Vara said.

He turned his hypnotic eyes in her direction. "You know who opened it," he accused.

"Yes. I did."

"Then I'm sorry for you, but you must die to save both of our worlds."

Chapter 34

"There is no other way," said the short frustrating man with the long hair. "And you need to do it now, before all of the demons have had a chance to overrun your world."

"You don't understand!" Vara protested. "I need to save my mom first! You don't know the damage she'll do if she's not stopped!"

"I don't understand why you're putting the life of one woman over the army of evil that's flooding your world."

"Mom has enough power to crush entire mountains flat with barely a thought. She is nature itself! She's the wind and the rain, and once that wolf figures out how to use her powers completely, humanity will be just a memory."

He looked over at Austen supported by one of the copper uniformed men. "Is she right?"

"If the power in her is anything to judge her mother by, then yes," answered Austen. "She's telling the truth."

The man with the long hair reached down the neck of his tunic and pulled out a gold chain with a large key that looked centuries old and brittle with rust. He held the key straight out and gave it a quarter turn to the right. And out of the thin air, an invisible door swung open with a dark void inside.

Austen's eyes widened and then suddenly narrowed. He shot a glare at his brother. "You had that all along!" he accused.

His brother shrugged. "I couldn't let you go, Brother."

"But I'm in love, Kalen. Laris needs my help."

"I know." The look of remorse that was absent when he told Vara to kill herself suddenly filled his eyes. "I can see how much you love her, but you don't understand the risk you're taking. The demons will rip you apart out there. And you're under their power so long as you're bound to them by contract. They could use you to unlock the boundary between us and the human world. You are my brother and I refuse to hand you over to them."

Austen's cheeks turned a bright red and his gaze slid away to a mountain behind the small troop. "I hadn't. . . ." He sucked in a breath. "We can't just leave the humans to them. You need to trust me, Brother. I can do this. I'll make certain the portal is closed and I'll save Laris. I have enough strength for this. Just let me go."

"Fine," said the man with the long hair. "I want your word that you won't try to stop what needs to be done."

"You have my word," agreed Austen. He pushed away from the uniformed man, stepped through the doorway, and vanished into the darkness.

The long-haired man turned back to his regiment of uniformed men. "You have your orders. Just try to make it quick so she won't feel much pain."

Vara screamed as two of the men in copper uniforms grabbed her by the arms. They were going to make certain she closed the portal, no matter what.

"But my mom!" she said.

"We will take care of her once the portal is closed."

She planted her feet on the ground, but even though they were all shorter than she was, it didn't hinder them in the slightest, as if she was nothing more than a cardboard cutout.

They hauled her into the darkness and then she felt hands paw at her clothes. She heard whispers and cackles of evil laughter from hundreds of demon voices crowding around her. Then she saw a flash of green light and felt a rush of wind as one of the green bladed staff weapons sliced the air next to her. There was a sudden shriek of pain from a demon near her ear and then silence.

"Start the ritual now," ordered a man's voice. "We can't hold them off forever." There was a surge of light as a match was struck and then a dancing flame was set on the ground with a white candle right below it. And then another. Vara saw one of the uniformed Nature Children lighting them. He set the candles on the edge of the large ritual chalk circle. All of the demons flooding into the room hadn't disturbed it in the slightest.

The portal still hovered and swirled in the middle of the basement. It bathed the room in a deep red glow. A white wraith demon appeared just in front of the portal. One of the uniformed men swiped at it with his staff weapon. The demon hissed at him and vanished into the dark shadows of the basement but otherwise looked unhurt.

The last of the candles was lit. The man in uniform bowed in front of her and handed her the silver blade still coated with her blood. It felt ice cold.

"Just do it and get it over with," one of the uniformed men said impatiently. "We don't have time for this."

She needed to save her mom. And she didn't want to die. Not on her dad's cold basement floor and certainly not with a sliver of ice for a blade buried in her heart.

The impatient uniformed man stepped forward and grabbed the knife out of her hand. "We can't allow you to stall any longer." He lifted the knife and thrust it toward her.

Out of the shadows of the basement soared a flash of silver. It whispered through the air and collided with the knife in the uniformed man's hand. He dropped the knife and cradled his hand in pain. Two silver knives clattered to the ground in front of her. One was still stained with her blood, while the other was clean.

Two of the uniformed men collapsed to the ground. A hand clamped around hers and tugged her away from the portal. Austen watched the scene with wide blue eyes.

"Just keep your head down and keep quiet," he whispered.

"What are you doing? I thought you gave your word you'd see me dead."

He gave her a hard look. "Look, you're the one who replaced me, right? I saw you at the mansion. You replaced me and now Laris is confiding in you, and not me." He grimaced as he mentally swore at himself. "I'm sorry. It was

Gypsy Madden

the only way I could think of to get back here."

The uniformed man who had tried to kill her stood in front of the portal barring his teeth. He twirled his razor-tipped staff and brought the blade to rest in front of him.

Faster than her eyes could keep up, a streak of light blue whisked through the room and struck the man with the blade in front of Vara. The uniformed man went flying into a stack of boxes. It wobbled and tumbled down on top of him. As she stared at the man trying to work out what had just happened, several of the other uniformed men went careening into the walls.

The figure in blue turned to look at Austen and Vara and smiled. It was the blonde-haired wolf hunter who had broken into Vara's father's house. She smoothed down her rumpled suit and checked her hair for any bits that had fallen down from the tight bun.

"Now that we've saved you, Miss Harper, are you going to give us any trouble?" she asked. "And, Mr. Hadley, you ran out on us so quickly the other day before we had a chance to get acquainted."

The hulking green troll with the hunter glanced around the room looking satisfied that nothing else was standing.

Vara took one look at the troll and shook her head.

"Good." The lady hunter smiled. "Because we have a plan we'd like you to help us with to get rid of the wolf situation before you close the portal."

"I figured I'd have to do something to discredit you, but you did it all on your own," Austen finished in a laugh.

Even though it was an open-topped car, it was getting beyond stuffy. "Stop the car," Vara told the gigantic troll behind the wheel.

"In a minute, miss. We're almost at the campus."

"What campus?" And then she realized where they were. The tall campus buildings towered over them from the side of the road. They left the main road and entered a large public entrance to a parking lot. The troll parked the car in an empty stall.

"Why are we here?" Vara asked. She had hoped, wished,

prayed never to see this place again. But yet here she stood. She could almost smell the smoke from the charred building as the wind picked up, even though the fire had been three years ago. Dark clouds rolled above them and lightning crashed. Her mother was close.

"I think you know the answer to that already, Miss Harper," said the hunter.

Vara stared at her. Could she be serious? Tossing her to her mother wouldn't begin to solve their problems.

"There's a wolf here," said Austen. "But why bring us here? We're not hunters."

"You're going to serve as bait. Or rather Miss Harper will." She smiled at Vara as a cat might look at a rather plump mouse.

"Why me?" Vara asked. "You could have gotten anyone to be bait."

"Geoffrey did some digging and the first of the wolf attacks was three years ago, the night you had your little accident. I think somehow you summoned the wolf spirit that started all of this. It has made its home in the wreckage of the building you burned down. It all points back to you."

A student stopped at the edge of the parking lot and looked at them, as if they had offended her by double-parking. The girl's eyes glittered a demonic red. She hunched her shoulders and ran off toward the music building.

"Was that . . . ?" Austen asked.

"No. That one was newly turned. We're after the original wolf. If we can take her down, it should release the others, including the woman at the center of that lightning storm."

"But she'll will run and tell Mom we're here."

"She didn't come after us or try to take you back to your mother," said the hunter.

The troll towered behind them as they skirted around the buildings to the old student housing. They cautiously watched any of the students that passed by them. Not much had been changed since the years Vara had been there.

That is, until they reached the old dorm. Its grey windows stood darkened and empty and a charred swirling design wrapped itself around the outside of the building like a ribbon decorating a package. Several of the windows were broken and there were words of graffiti tagged in red paint on the side.

The troll pulled the door open and gave Vara a smile behind his large white tusks. She entered the building. The charred smell rolled over her. As she walked the wreckage strewn hallway, she passed ruined rooms that had once been full of students. Rotted beams groaned and bits of dust rained down.

Her room had been on the second floor. She reached the stairs at the end of the hallway and tested her weight on the first step. It groaned and splintered underneath her. Then she heard a padding footstep behind her.

Her heart hammered. Where were they? She turned and braced herself for the sight of a dark growling wolf, with glistening saliva dripping off blood-coated teeth.

"Vara! I hoped you would come back!" said a light musical voice.

It took her a minute to realize that there was a woman with two blonde ponytails standing in front of her and not the wolf that she had been imagining. Before her mind had fully taken the girl in, she had bounded the couple of steps between them and knocked Vara over in an enthusiastic hug. Vara struggled for breath and pushed the girl far enough so she could get a proper look at her.

"Lulu!" Vara gasped. She hugged the girl back. It had been three long years since she had last seen her Conservatory roommate. She had never gotten a chance to say good-bye since Lulu had vanished the day after Vara had rescued her from the fire. Lulu had been her only real friend during her school years. "I missed you so much!"

Vara heard a footstep crunch in the debris farther down the hallway.

"Lulu, you shouldn't be here! You need to get out of here, now!" Vara stepped in front of her, putting herself between the intruder and her former roommate. "There's a wolf!"

"Miss Harper, please, stand away from the wolf," the blonde-haired hunter said as she pointed a gun in Vara's direction.

Vara searched the shadows frantically, but no hungry wolf lurked in the darkness, waiting to pounce.

"What are you talking about?" she asked. "I don't see any wolf!"

"The girl behind you, she's the wolf," the hunter answered. "Hand her over right now."

Chapter 35

"Lulu? Are you crazy?" Lulu was the sweetest, most innocent person Vara could think of. There was no possible way Lulu could be a bloodthirsty wolf.

"Miss Harper, step away from her!" the blonde-haired hunter demanded. "Killing her will end this all now."

"I will not let you hurt my friend!"

"It's all right, Vara." Vara felt Lulu's warm hand on her shoulder. "I just wanted to see you one last time. I don't want you to die for me."

"No! It's all just some misunderstanding." Vara turned to look at her as she made certain to keep between Lulu and the hunters. "She's wrong, isn't she?" The wolf had robbed her of so much.

The carefree laughter from their school days was gone from her brown eyes, replaced by pain and frustration and sad acceptance. How many years had she endured it?

She shook her head. Her pony-tails flopped like rabbit ears. "I can't control it. I thought I could. But I'm so tired now. I just wanted to see a friendly face one last time."

Now that Vara was looking at her properly, she wasn't the Lulu she remembered at all. Her clothes were torn and bloody in so many places, including a large gaping hole on her side that still oozed fresh blood, though some of the rust-colored stains looked like they were several years old. And the smell. . . . Vara was shocked she hadn't noticed it before. A musky dog smell clung to her, as if she had sprayed it on like a perfume.

"But you're not a wolf," Vara protested.

Lulu looked at her sadly. "It is who I am now."

"You're not a killer," Vara persisted. There was an explanation for the blood. Maybe it was Lulu's.

She looked away from Vara. "Yes, I am. The hunger was too great. And now, it's nothing more to me than a meal of the day. I'm ready to die."

Vara turned around to face the hunters. "No!" She couldn't just let Lulu die like this, even if it did mean saving her mom.

"She needs to die!" shouted Austen. "She bit Laris!" He struggled with the blonde hunter for her gun.

"I won't let you hurt her," Vara insisted.

Lulu's grip tightened on her shoulder. "She's coming for me. She followed you. I can smell her."

The front door of the building burst open in a gust of wind. As if it had a life of its own, a breeze ripped the gun out of the hunter's hands. It skidded across the scorched and blackened tile. The gun cracked and compressed itself into an unusable black wad.

Vara's mother stood in the doorway, flanked by several half-turned wolves. The tall muscular male on her left had flame red hair. There was also a smaller blonde wolf with the tattered remains of a red dress. They didn't even look human anymore—their skin had changed to the color of their wolf pelts.

Her mom took a step forward. It was like a cruel joke someone was playing on her. She still had her mother's short black hair and impatient stance, but everything else about her was different—from the ragged yellow claws to the long white canines that dripped with blood. And her eyes weren't the brown eyes Vara had inherited, but glowing red demonic pinpoints.

Her mother smiled and exposed more of her long sharp teeth. "My daughter, I knew you would find her." She crooked a claw at them.

Lulu shifted uncomfortably. She looked at Vara. There were tears in her eyes. "Vara, run. I owe you this." There was an unearthly red glow to her brown eyes and her canines lengthened.

"Lulu, no, snap out of it!" Vara said. She didn't want to slap Lulu since she remembered how Laris had reacted the last time she had tried that.

"Run," Lulu said in a growl. A pink tongue slid between enormous teeth and then she wasn't Lulu any more, but a white wolf. She howled once and in a blink she had leapt past Austen and the hunters. She picked up speed and launched herself into the air with all the power in her hind legs.

"No, Lulu, stop!" Despite what Lulu had said, Vara couldn't just turn her back on her. Vara felt around inside, hunting for the dark energy. But her questing hand suddenly stopped. She pushed and prodded, but it wouldn't move. It was as if it was frozen. She lifted her head, but even that felt like it weighed a hundred bricks. Her mother's eyes glinted at her in the dim light and she saw a ghost of a smile on her lips directed at her.

Her mother snarled at Lulu. Fingers of ice climbed up Vara's spine. It didn't sound like there was anything left of her mother inside her. Her mother lifted a hand and flicked it in Lulu's direction. Lulu sailed through the air and crashed with a bone-crunching sound against the side of the hallway.

"You were the first chosen," her mom said, in a guttural raspy voice that sounded more animal than human. "You were given a gift. And yet you still fight it—a losing battle which will cost you your life." She lifted a hand in Lulu's direction. Lulu twitched and writhed on the ground. Her eyes slid open, but Vara could only see the whites.

"Mom, stop it!" Vara shouted.

Her head jerked in Vara's direction. "My daughter, you need to feel this. The guilt and the pain will be gone." Her mother slunk toward her. Her smile grew broader each time Vara shook with terror. "You will feel no pain. You will become one with the power that resides in you. And the world shall be ours to feast on. I want you to join us and experience this with us."

She turned to her left, and a half-turned man with bright red hair stepped forward.

Vara gasped when she saw him. He looked so different

with a feral blaze to his gold eyes and his clothes ripped and torn. "Derek," she whispered.

He smiled and exposed long sharp wolf canines.

"Yes, my daughter. I was going to eat him since he had come to stop us. But I could smell you about him. I remember he was your boyfriend. You love him still, don't you?"

"Derek. . . ."

Her mother smiled. "Join us, daughter."

Why didn't she just attack and turn her already? It looked as if Derek had put up a fight and she had still turned him. So, why was she so insistent that Vara be willing? It wasn't like she had enough power to fight a god.

"Let me do it," the Laris-wolf pleaded. "She wanted to save me from this. I want to show her what it feels like to finally be free."

"No!" Vara's feet felt like they were rooted to the ground. She made another grab for the power inside her.

Her mother flicked a hand at her, and the air in her chest rushed out in a gust. She felt her knees crumple underneath her and she crashed to the ground. It felt like something was crushing her, though she couldn't see anything on top of her.

"Mom?" Vara whispered. "Mom, don't do this!"

Her mother's eyes flickered from gleaming red to brown, for a brief moment, the length of a heart beat. "Vara?" It was her mother's voice! "I can't—"

"Mom! Fight it, please!" Was she really still in there, or was the monster tricking on her?

The monster smiled. "If you won't become one of us of your own free will, then I will have to turn you by force. And it will hurt."

"Mom?" Vara's cheeks felt wet and her eyes burned.

The monster with her mother's face licked its chops hungrily. She leaned in close and pushed back Vara's hair with a sharp nail, drawing a faint line of blood.

The pain of a million needles ripped through Vara's body and she felt fangs sink into the flesh of her cheek. The pain shrieked through her body and her eyes slammed shut. She futilely groped for the power inside her, but it was a bare whisper in comparison to the power inside her mother that could encompass whole mountains.

Gypsy Madden

There was laughter in Vara's head—a cruel laughter that delighted that she might actually put up a fight. It growled and licked at her. It coaxed her. And it was hungry.

Then she felt power, but not inside her. It was a faint whisper as gentle as a breeze, almost next to her ear. There was warmth just under her hand. Her fingers closed around it and took strength from it. It raced up her arm and filled her chest. It ripped out of her in a gust of air and blew her mom back several feet.

Vara looked around in confusion. She wasn't more powerful than her mother. So, where had the additional strength come from? She felt the warm breath next to her ear of someone standing behind her. She realized the warmth in her hand was the hand of someone willing to help her.

"I owed you this much for saving my life," said Austen.

Vara's free hand drifted to the bite wound on her cheek. She could hear the hungry voice in her head. It growled and snarled. It told her that she was weak and it was just a matter of time before she would cease to be her. But beyond the hunger and anger was loneliness. The same despondent loneliness that she had heard in Laris the night the reporter had caught them together. It wanted someone to understand it and call to it by name. The voice was that of a demon and she could understand what it was saying perfectly. And that its name was. . . .

"Varandarath!" Vara shouted as it popped into her head. The demon inside her screamed and clawed at her mind as it tried to find anything to latch onto. And then it was gone and her thoughts were her own again.

In front of her hovered a grey mist. It snarled at her.

"Varandarath, I know that name," Vara whispered. It was so familiar, yet she couldn't remember where she had last heard it.

Her mom, Laris, Zavian, Derek, and all of the other wolves in the room screamed and threw their hands to their ears. Even Lulu's body twitched and pitched on the floor.

Clouds of the grey mist rose out of each of them and joined the swirling mass in front of Vara. Her mother writhed, her back twisting painfully. She jerked, shrieked, and flopped between the chairs of the auditorium. Her mouth fell open and more mist rose out of her. It condensed into a hazy ghost of an animal with long ears, a monstrous snout, and teeth like scythe blades. It opened its mouth and glared at Vara with its wild red eyes.

"You are mine to command," Vara said.

It laughed in a vicious snarl. "No one commands me, least of all you, little sister."

It flew at her in a ball of smoke. It twirled around her and played with the hem of her black dress. "You are weak and you are mine," it whispered. It licked at the blood that dripped from the wound on her cheek.

"Don't listen to it," Austen cautioned. "You command it."

It opened its misty mouth.

Vara clamped her hand tighter around Austen's. Her body felt like it was glowing with his power. She realized she could move again, and reached inside herself for her power. She didn't have to reach far. The darkness roiled inside her, like liquid electricity, and threatened to overwhelm her completely.

Then, she let it. She let the dark energy consume her. It slid through every pore. She felt it stretch out her hand and call down every wind that chased every cloud in the sky. It whipped through the room with the strength of a hurricane, though it didn't touch the two of them. The wolf phantasm was caught up in it. It swirled around the room, howling.

"Varandarath, be gone!"

"Stop!" The deep voice echoed through the hallway. It seemed to come from somewhere behind her. Everything in the room froze, as if time suddenly stopped.

A man glided past her and turned around. He was tall with graying black curly hair and glasses perched on the end of his nose and human.

"Dad!" All the worrying she had done and thinking he was dead, and here he was, standing in front of her. There were no splotches of blood on his white dress shirt or navy blue jacket, and his skin, what she could see of it, was unblemished, unlike Austen's pockmarked skin after his stay in the demon dimension. She wanted to hug him and confirm that he was actually standing there and not some figment of her imagination, but her limbs refused to move. Everything was still frozen around her.

Ms. Clarke stood next to him. Her white dress fluttered around her in a holy aura. Power radiated out of her that was almost as bright as the sun. She had dropped all of her pretenses about being even remotely human.

"I can't let you do this, Vara." Her dad pushed his glasses farther up his nose, and in the reflection of the lenses there was a glimmer of demonic red. "I can't let you banish your brother."

Chapter 36

Vara stared at the grey mist. Glowing red eyes stared back at her, full of mischief, and smiled.

Her dad had to be pranking her. There was no possible way she could be related to that monster. "He turned Mom into a wolf!" she protested.

Her dad's eyes flicked silently over to his wife, frozen on the ground with her back arched. "I'm sorry she had to go through that. I hadn't meant for things to go this far."

"General, there shouldn't be any apologizing," said Ms. Clarke. "It's a sign of human weakness. Just get your daughter in line so we can finish this."

"Vara, this isn't how I meant for you to find out," said her dad.

"How can he be related to me? You're human, aren't you? You're just a demon summoner, like me." Vara felt less certain the longer she stared at the twin fires that danced in the lenses of his thick glasses.

"No," he said quietly. "And you know it's true. I can see the demon power growing within you."

She had thought it was god power inherited from her mom. Demon power . . . ? It felt icky having it within her. Like some foreign cancer, ready to devour her from within and completely take her over. How had she not known she wasn't completely human? Her hand that clutched Austen's felt human, but apparently she wasn't. She never had been. Her life had been a lie. "No. It can't be."

"She'll never accept us," the mist creature whispered. "She was scared of me that day three years ago in this building and she still denies us now."

"Varandarath. . . . You were my first summoned imp!" Vara exclaimed. She could still see him sitting in front of her, his red eyes dancing with pure malice. He had trashed her dorm room, eaten all of her class notes, ripped apart her books, and terrorized poor Lulu. She had banished him within twenty minutes of having summoned him. She had thought she had done something wrong with the spell since he hadn't obeyed any of her commands. She felt her eyes narrow. "You burned down the school!"

"You didn't like me," he said. "I could feel your fear and hate. You're my sister!"

"I'm sorry."

"No, you're not." The mist shifted to form teeth. "You will never accept that you're one of us, and for that you will pay."

"Pay?" The fire had been deliberate. He had all but admitted it. "You mean this is why you turned Mom. . . ."

"And will turn all the others you are close to," he said.

"No!"

"Varandarath, she's not yours to play with," said her dad. His eyes glowed red and his skin grew hazy for a moment.

"But she's one of us," the mist creature argued.

"General, take the girl back to the demon dimension where she belongs and be done with it," said Ms. Clarke. "I don't have time for this. The demons are released as we agreed. And now you will give me proper payment. I want the wolf power."

The mist creature sniffed at Ms.Clarke hungrily. He didn't wait for the offer to be repeated and dove into her chest. Her eyes blazed like mini-suns. The power surrounding her shot up in temperature and sizzled everything around her.

She pointed a white gloved finger at Vara. "You should have joined us when you had the chance. Sister or no sister, I will destroy you for turning your back on me."

"No!" her dad shouted. His body shimmered and turned into smoke, his eyes sank until they were the hollow black eye sockets she knew so well. Fire burned deep within them. He reached a hand in Ms. Clarke's direction. The air turned to black electricity around them as it pushed against them like a dense sponge.

Ms. Clarke threw her head back and laughed. "I have obeyed my last order. I shall never bow to anyone ever again! But you, dear sister, shall die where you stand." She contracted her gloved hand.

Vara heard a snap and then pain rocketed through her, and another snap, as if her ribs were being crushed inward.

There was a sudden pain in her hand, and warmth raced up her arm. She looked down. Austen gripped her hand so hard his fingers were turning white. His white complexion had turned sallow, and his knees shook.

He was funneling all of his magic into her. She looked inward at the expanse of dark demon magic bubbling inside her. It looked endless, but she knew it wasn't strong enough.

She felt another rib snap and cried out in pain. She gripped Austen's hand tighter. She couldn't give up. She reached inside and pulled up everything she could find inside her—all the darkness, all the light, all the warm nature, and pushed.

Ms. Clarke screeched. It was an awful, pain-filled sound.

Vara should not have been able to do that. There was a hand on her other shoulder—a bright shining hand with magic that dripped down her arm and twisted, churning where she was funneling everything out. It amplified it to a magnitude that she had never seen before.

"Don't stop," her mom whispered. She smiled at Vara. Her other hand she raised into the air. Wind whipped at the hem of Vara's skirt and yanked at her hair and scoured her skin raw with a chill. Voices chattered around them and white wisps of hundreds of demons chased around them in a whirlwind.

Ms. Clarke howled and rose through the air. She shrieked and screamed as if she was being torn apart. Vara shoved her with all the power she had inside her into the mirror at the end of the hallway.

"Varandarath, be gone!" Vara commanded.

The wind surged with a biting force and her ears popped

and there was a loud crunch and a shattering that sounded like it could be heard for miles, if not continents. Millions of flakes of silver glass rained down on them.

Austen released her hand and collapsed. He sat down on the ground behind her. "What happened?"

"Did we do it?" she asked and looked at her mother next to her. Her mom looked completely back to normal, though her dress was torn and showed skin in several places. "Are they all back in the demon realm?"

"Yes." But it wasn't her mother who answered. A smoky white demon hovered in front of them. He shimmered and shifted and finally condensed into the solid shape of a man with glasses perched on the end of his nose. "I never meant for any of this to happen." There was human sadness in his hollow black eye sockets. "I know you don't like how it was asked, but the invitation is open. Will you join me and accept who you are?"

"Vara, no!" said her mom.

"I can't hide in Salvation City for the rest of my life, Mom."

"But, Vara, the demon realm—"

She looked behind her mom at Austen, Lulu, Laris, Derek, and Zavian who struggled to their feet. Laris checked her teeth with a finger and Zavian ran a hand through his hair, nonchalantly checking his ears for points, and Lulu smiled, just like the same carefree smiles she used to wear every day back when they roomed together.

"I still have a job to do here."

Her dad smiled. "Then there is still hope you might change your mind." He raised his hand and snapped his fingers together. And in a nose-curling stench, he vanished.

"Vara!"

She barely had a chance to look up before she felt a weight careen into her. It scooped her up in a bone-crunching hug that felt almost as powerful as when Varandarath had tried to crush the life out of her. "You did it!" Derek said as he whirled her around.

"Almost. I just have to do one more thing."

Vara drew the transit circle and ported them back to her dad's basement. She had conquered her fear of demons and commanded them, but there was still one more fear she needed to face.

She put her hand against the blood stain. Her dad's hardened blood stain was a light ring in the cement with her darker more recent stain above it. The portal still swirled and doused the room in a dark red glow.

"Are you sure about this?" asked Austen as he lit the candles. "I don't know if I have enough power to bring you back once you die."

"As your brother said, it's the only way to completely close the portal and save both of our worlds. And you did give him your word."

Austen grumbled. "I only made that promise so he would send me back here."

"You should still keep your promise," she said as she reminded herself of the promise to her mom that she broke. "Once you break it, it's not always a simple mend."

She scooped up the ritual knife from the floor and ran her thumb along the blade. It bit into her skin and a river of blood flowed from the shallow wound. She closed her eyes, lifted the blade, and rammed it into her chest.

Pain ripped through Vara's body and a sensation of pins and needles and then a numbing coldness. She couldn't feel her hands or feet or legs, and then they vanished underneath her and the floor rushed at her.

She felt sticky warmth on the floor next to her chest and breathing became a difficult chore. The sound of her heartbeat pounded in her ears like a thunderstorm. It crashed in the distance as it drifted farther and farther away. Her ears strained to hear anything, one last time. . . . And then she was alone in the darkness. And then she was no more. . . .

Chapter 37

"She's so cold," whispered Derek. He had tears in his gold eyes.

"I'm sorry." Austen had his hands pressed against the wound in her chest where she had plunged the knife.

"It was a stupid idea," Derek said. "I should never have let her go through with it."

"But it was the only way," said Austen. "If she hadn't, my brother would have killed her himself. And then she would have been beyond my help."

The flickering red glow from the portal had vanished precious moments after her head had hit the concrete of the basement floor with a sickening crack.

In a flash they had whisked her from the basement to the front lawn so Austen could properly call to nature for the mending spell. He still had one hand pressed to the bright green grass, in a silent plea, as he listened to everything growing, the pulse of the world itself.

But in the moments that had slipped away, she had lost a lot of blood and her body had turned a waxy white. Her chest had long since ceased to rise and fall. She had saved their world and put a stop to the flood of demons, but at what price?

Derek had one of her small hands clasped in his. He cradled it as if it was the most cherished object in the universe. His black shirt glistened with streaks of her wet blood.

"You two can get your filthy paws off her! She deserves better than to be cried over by a half-breed and a fur rug!"

Austen felt his eyes burn with hatred and strength surged in him. "How dare you!" Austen shouted. "As if the months of taunting while I was working for your uncle weren't enough, what's she to you?"

"She's my girlfriend, of course." Zavian looked at him smugly. "She saved the world, didn't she? I will see to it that she gets a proper burial and her name will not soon be forgotten."

Girlfriend? Austen felt something inside himself curl up and die. He looked at her from an entirely new perspective. What could she possibly see in a scum like Zavian? He owed her his life, but did he really want to throw away all his energy on someone who actually liked Zavian?

He heard the low growl before he saw the blur of red launch itself at Zavian. It knocked down the black robed teenager in a swirl of silk. Derek towered over Zavian. One of his massive muscular hands clutched Zavian's thin throat.

Zavian gave him a smug smile. "You don't really want to hurt me, do you? I could ruin your entire family. All of your brothers and sisters would be out on the street."

Anger flashed in Derek's gold eyes.

"Don't," Vara whispered. She didn't think it had been louder than a whisper of wind, but all of their heads whipped toward her.

Zavian smiled. "You're alive, my love!"

She could feel his luxurious voice wrap around her foggy head. It lulled her into a peaceful bliss and coaxed her to agree with everything he said.

"Tell these two clods you are mine," he commanded.

"Vara." Derek looked at her with tear-streaked eyes.

Her hand curled around the warm hand that still rested on her chest. It felt like a jolt of electricity raced through her.

The fog that wrapped itself around her brain was gone and she could think clearly. She sat up and immediately wished she hadn't as the world dizzyingly pitched. The world steadied itself and she felt strength flood into her the longer she clasped Austen's hand.

"Do you love Zavian?" Austen asked. There was something in his eyes that pleaded with her to say no.

Vara couldn't look at Derek. She didn't want to see the look on his face.

She glanced over at dark-haired Zavian. His black silk robes were rumpled and torn from his scuffle with Derek. He had a large black streak across his face, in addition to the cut that trailed down his cheek from earlier.

"Tell them that you love me," he whispered. She felt his voice wrap around her, as invisible fingers stroked her hair. His eyes fixed on her with a burning intensity. But through the intensity she could see pure desperation and loneliness. He needed her.

"I want to. . . ." She needed to. The loneliness was so much like her own. But was the need actually love?

"I'm not in love with you," she said. "I'm sorry."

Zavian rose elegantly from the ground and dusted off his robes. "So be it. I'm sorry for you." He turned and walked away in a swirl of silver stars and black silk.

What had she done?

Vara released Austen and no sooner than she had, then warm muscular arms wrapped around her, scooped her off the ground, and into a bear hug. She felt herself swirled around with her feet dancing in the air.

"I could kiss you," Derek whispered in her ear. And he did.

'Spiritualist Speaks From Beyond the Grave' read the newspaper headline. 'Famed millionaire exorcist named Lord Stadler as her killer' read the smaller line underneath it. It was by Harrison Carter. The reporter's picture gleefully grinned above it.

"You'll notice he made certain to say Laris was innocent of everything and just a victim of circumstance," Austen noted as he read over Vara's shoulder.

"Are you ready for this?" Laris asked. She tossed her blonde curls and gave Vara her film starlet smile. Vara wondered just how much of it was façade. With her father awaiting trial and everything else that had happened, she was surprised Laris wasn't an emotional wreck.

Vara folded up the newspaper and shoved it into her

purse. "No, but I doubt that would stop you," she answered. She glanced behind her at Laris's bodyguard and for once Derek wasn't scowling. A sly smile devilishly skirted his lips. He gave Vara a playful wink. She could do this.

The only one of them who wasn't smiling was Austen. He fidgeted and attempted to flatten his wild curls. "Are you sure you want me along? I could wait outside."

"You attempted to kill a wolf for me, yet you can't talk to your bosses?" Laris's laugh had a warm musical quality to it.

His face flushed a brilliant red, which made his skin look like some kind of weird reverse tattoo with the marks of his white circular scars.

She lifted his chin and gave him a light playful kiss on the lips.

His blue eyes widened in surprise and Vara tried not to laugh as he stumbled.

They rode the elevator all the way up to the Agency reception room. The place was in a state of panic. The front desk had several lines of people. Most of them didn't look happy, and others looked downright scared. Vara noticed belatedly that not a single one of them had a demon in tow. A crowd of people populated the cushioned chairs next to the windows and more people milled around anywhere they could.

The lady at the front desk with a pair of gold-rimmed glasses perched on the end of her nose waved frantically in their direction. She whispered something to one of the men who stood behind the desk next to her and then rushed over to them.

"We've been expecting you for a couple of days now. Where have you been? The company heads are refusing to do anything until they've spoken to you." She quickly turned on her heel. "Follow me."

She led them through the door behind the front desk and down the hallway past meeting rooms that were full of people all arguing at the top of their lungs. She opened the large door at the end of the hallway and stood impatiently as she waited for them to enter.

Laris strode forward as if she owned the place. Austen,

however, gawked at the spacious interior as Vara had the first time she had been there. He tripped over an edge of the tile. Laris tried to hide a snicker. He gave her a sheepish smile and continued on, though his attention still looked like it was riveted somewhere in the mile-high rafters of the room.

Vara tried to ignore the pounding of her heart. She reminded herself that this time Derek was with her. She didn't want him to see her be intimidated, even if these were the people who were responsible for her paycheck.

At the end of the room, perched on top of a ledge, forcing them to look up at it, was the desk of the bosses. Instead of four people though, this time there were only the three men in black business suits. Raw power radiated from them which made Vara's skin feel like it was on a sizzling grill.

Crane Kendrick stood in the center. His face was a muddle of shifting features as if he were trying to decide which characteristics might intimidate her more.

Vara took a deep breath. "I have come to ask you to release all of us from our blood contracts."

Mr. Kendrick looked down on her. At least she assumed he did since the features of his face were still shifting. "We are willing to agree to your request and release all of your friends from their contracts since they are all friends of the new company head."

"What new company head?" she asked as she glanced at Ms. Clarke's seat, just to confirm that it was still indeed empty.

"You will be taking over her chair, Miss Harper."

"That was not part of the deal," Vara protested.

"You were the one to force our colleague into early retirement, were you not?" he asked.

"Yes, sir."

"There is order to this office, Miss Harper. Whenever anyone removes one of us from our positions, that person has to take over our empty seat."

"I will not!"

"Come, Miss Harper, we know that you are between jobs and that you have been having difficulty for the better part of three years at finding a job in Salvation City," he reminded her.

"Was that because of the Agency?"

"No, of course not." Mr. Kendrick smiled at her. "Well, perhaps a little," he admitted. "I am sorry, but you have no choice in the matter. Congratulations are in order, I should think. How often does one inherit a position as a head of a vastly powerful corporation?"

He had a point and she was in need of a job.

About the Author

Gypsy Madden lives in Honolulu, Hawaii and loves fantasy, science fiction, and anything British. She adores making costumes, dressing up at conventions (You may have seen her dressed as Harry Potter, Legolas and Arwen from Lord of the Rings, as a Jedi, Wondergirl from Teen Titans, or many other outfits. She even claims to have knitted a 17-foot Doctor Who scarf), and can even be spotted in the Naruto fan movie Konaha vs Chaos and in LOST as a mental patient. Hired by a Demon is her first novel with more to come in the near future.

Connect with Gypsy online:

Twitter: http://twitter.com/GypsyMMadden
Facebook: http://www.facebook.com/Gypsy.Madden.Author/
Blog: http://timelady.livejournal.com/

http://www.smashwords.com/profile/view/gypsymmadden/
http://www.amazon.com/Gypsy-Madden/e/B007GP78TS/
https://www.goodreads.com/author/show/7170704.Gypsy_Madden

If you enjoyed
Hired by a DEMON
*Check out more titles by Myrddin
Publishing authors*

www.myrddinpublishing.com

Excerpt from

The Prophecy Thief

by Gypsy Madden

"Everyone knows if you don't have a prophecy to work toward, you don't have a future. Your loser brother's never going to make anything of himself. Even the Oracle knows that obviously."

His blood chilled in his veins. He must have heard it wrong. Emily liked him. She smiled at him every time he saw her.

"Take it back!" demanded Robin.

"You know it's true. I feel sorry for him that he's too dumb to know there's something wrong with him."

Too dumb? His heart pounded in his ears and his face grew hot. Who was *she* to call him dumb? She was just a stupid, ugly, phony-looking girl, who didn't know anything. He itched to pound something flat.

He twisted the knob of his door so hard he nearly wrenched it off and threw open his door, letting the creak echo through the house. *Let them all hear!* He slammed it behind him and threw himself on his bed.

Why couldn't everyone just let it go? So what if he didn't have a prophecy?

It had been bad enough enduring that first year of teasing and having all his classmates rub it in his face as each of them got their prophecies on their fourteenth birthday while he was the only one not to get one. And then came having to watch all of them leave on their quests. At least it meant an end to school for him. *The classes were all boring anyway.*

He had spent the rest of the year lurking around the local market every day, trying to engage just about everyone in conversation to find out if they had ever heard of anyone not getting one before, but no one, back as far as their father's father, had not been given a prophecy. He had gritted his teeth listening to gallant adventures of slaying monsters (some of which he was certain had been embellished), of miraculous love-at-first sight with the women regaling about to swoon (*ick!*), and the odd (and often gross) freak occurrences (he hunted a pig born with two heads!)

Jay had a future. The Oracle was just saving something extra-specially big for him. *And his sister was really a princess in disguise. Yeah, right.* He had been passed over, same as everything else in his life. He'd show Emily and the rest of them. He'd get a prophecy of his own—one that would be important.

He felt something cold and solid digging into his back through the thick material of his pocket. He pulled out the silver knife he had managed to palm from the store when he had backed up against the shelf and smiled—his first stolen treasure that hadn't been something just lying around the house. Maybe he could be successful at being a thief after all. And then he'd show Emily and all the others.

If he couldn't get a prophecy of his own, he'd have to take it.

His fingers curled around the handle of the knife liking the idea the more he thought about it. But who's prophecy should he take? After all this time of not having a prophecy, it needed to be something that would actually change his life. It needed to be something that everyone would notice and actually acknowledge that he had done something important— something that he could rub in everyone's faces. Logically, important people got important prophecies. But who was important enough in his town to rate an important prophecy?

"Jay?" a voice peeped from outside his door followed by a quiet knock.

He opened it a crack. One of Robin's brown eyes fixed on him through the opening. She turned her head back in the direction of her room for a moment, giving him an eyeful of her hair parted in the back and bound in two long brown braids. She turned back to face him, again.

"Did you . . . ?" She paused. There was a rustle of

clothes and she looked down for a moment. "It's not true."

If her friend thought he was dumb, he figured he might as well play the part. "What's not true?" he asked, trying not to let his voice crack.

Robin let a small breath out and smiled up at him through the doorway. "Never mind. We're almost ready to go."

"Pass. I don't want to walk with a group of *girls*," he said letting his voice drawl the last word as if it was a disease.

"But you said you would," her voice piped. "Mom said. . . ."

"I don't care what Mom said." Their mother had left strict instructions that she didn't want Robin on her own at the party. But she was thirteen, nearly fourteen, and could take care of herself. And he certainly didn't want to tag along with her group, not now.

"I'm telling *Mom*," whined Robin. *Make that thirteen with all the maturity of a ten-year-old when she wanted something her way.* She disappeared from his doorway and he could hear a patter of small feet disappear down the hallway and the front door slam.

He didn't want to go to the stupid party anyway. It was just a bunch of rich people showing off how rich they were by giving the town food and fireworks in celebration of golden-boy Lathan's fourteenth birthday. Everyone knew Lathan would eventually inherit his father's position as the king's knight-commander. Now *he* certainly had a famous future already planned for him. And he wouldn't need an additional prophecy.

The front door flew open, slamming against the inside wall with a crack.

"Jay!" his mother's voice bellowed through his closed door. He could hear the threat of punishment in her voice. She would probably have him dust and polish everything in the store with her watching over him every single minute. Or had she noticed the knife was missing? She couldn't punish him, if he couldn't be found.

He pushed the windowpane up and squeezed through the open window. It was a tight fit and he could feel the wooden sill pulling at his woolen jacket. He tumbled into the overgrown grass of their small backyard.

Hopefully she'd think he had escaped to the party. She just needed time to cool off and his sister and her group could do without him for the evening. Not like they really wanted him or needed him around anyway.

He scooted away from the window and edged around his house to the street. Shadows were already stretching along the grey cobblestones and the sky had grown a brilliant pinkish-orange with the beginning of sunset.

He needed to hurry if he actually wanted to put this plan into motion. He felt the weight of the knife in his pocket, reassuringly solid and cold against his thigh, even through the thick wool of his jacket. Yes, he did want to do this.

He set off at a run, through the winding street, skipping over uneven cobblestones, pushing aside slow pedestrians. Just as his legs started to ache and with his heart hammering in his chest, he finally passed the last of the small houses on the outskirts of town, and the road turned from cobbles into a small dirt path continuing on into a thick forest of lonely trees.

He used to play all the time in the forest with the other kids a lifetime ago before everyone turned their backs on him and turned him into a laughing stock just because he didn't get a prophecy. It seemed almost stupid that such a little thing could turn his life to a living hell.

He turned off the worn path and pushed on through the forest, well remembering the trees he used to hide behind, and the trees he used to pretend were his fellow soldiers as he laid siege with the other kids. His legs climbed a small bare hill. The ground grew rocky under his feet and then back to grass as he passed over the top and the incline began, his momentum carrying him forward toward the tree line at the bottom. And then the trees disappeared around him as they opened into a small grassy meadow with a lake at its center.

He stopped and dropped into a crouch as he caught sight of a thin teenage boy, dressed in an expensive green leather jerkin, standing at the center of the meadow with the last rays of the setting sun throwing him into silhouette. Lathan was the only one who dressed like that around town, proudly showing off his father's wealth.

Gypsy Madden

Jay watched as Lathan knelt down next to the edge of the lake and reached up under his matching green cap, pulling free a handful of golden hair. The tradition went that the person turning fourteen just needed to put a bit of something that would identify them into the lake at sunset and stare into it until they would be given their prophecy.

When Jay had tossed in the bit of his own scraggly mud brown hair into the lake on his fourteenth a year ago, nothing had happened. He had waited, watching the wind stir the surface, listening to the birds as they finished their evening songs, until it was completely dark and the crickets and frogs started their nightly symphony.

His mother had found him sleeping in the muddy bank the next morning. And then there was the disappointment plain in her eyes when he told her what had happened. Word that he hadn't gotten a prophecy spread like wind around their tiny town. And then came the constant humiliation as everyone in school teased him and everyone else whispered behind his back.

As Lathan dropped the bits into the pond, Jay made his move. He jumped out of his hiding spot and launched himself across the small clearing, tackling Lathan about the waist, bringing the both of them down into the mud.

Water saturated the wool of his jacket, dragging him down as they rolled from the bank into the reeds and right into the lake itself. Tears of sweat poured off him and blood dribbled from a cut in his cheek from where Lathan had scratched him. Jay put a hand to his cheek to stanch the pain and smiled. He had to have left enough of himself in the lake to turn the summoned prophecy into his.

Jay pushed the other boy away and stood. The water was only about a foot deep, but the mud at the bottom sucked and pulled at his boots. He stared at the surface and held his breath. There would finally be an end to the all the teasing. And he'd actually, finally have a destiny and not be forced to work in his mother's shop for the rest of his life in the same town he had been born in. He'd have a reason to leave and never look back.

A chilled musky evergreen breeze stirred the water and

the last ray of sunlight glinted through the reflected trees behind him. The prophecy should have come by now. Why hadn't anything happened? Could he have corrupted the lake too much?

The water stilled around him and his reflection rippled, though the breeze had ceased. The prophecy was coming! And it would be for him. After all these years, it had to be for him.

"You're ruining it!" Lathan shrieked, pulling Jay by the front of his tattered mud-covered jacket out of the water and shoved him hard, pushing him onto the grass. The surface of the lake crackled and frosted over like a pane of glass. Mist danced over its surface.

Lathan rushed back to the bank of the lake and stared down into it. As if it was a window, an old woman peered back at them. She had cobwebs in her matted grey hair and stared from one to the other of them with one eye glued shut as if she had gotten punched in a bar fight.

"A long journey lies ahead, for in four days time he will soon be dead," the old crone chanted. *"To the North you must go, and you will face both friend and foe. To find the man defeated by fate, and succeed in his stead before it is too late. But there is a chance when hope is lost, though a heart may be the hero's cost. When in doubt, search for the three, advice will be given despite appearances be. Change the world of their belief, and just rewards will come to the Prophecy Thief."*

The image of the crone faded with the last bits of sunlight and darkness descended on the forest like a velvet curtain.

Jay pulled his frozen, soaked jacket around him. "Guess I've got a journey ahead of me then," he said.

"What do you mean, *you've got*?" said Lathan. "It's *my* prophecy!" Lathan glared at Jay and stood with his hands on his hips. His green cap had been knocked off during the fight and long mud-caked blonde hair hung about his thin shoulders.

Lathan didn't have long hair.

"You're not Lathan!" Jay said, more surprised than anything else. Everything else about the boy looked like

Gypsy Madden

Lathan—from the imperious attitude, to the polished, though now muddied black leather boots, to the narrowed grey eyes roiling with fury.

Jay just had to know, "Who are you?"

www.ingramcontent.com/pod-product-compliance
Lightning Source LLC
Chambersburg PA
CBHW070553130626
46556CB00001B/143